# THE PIT GIRL

## LYNETTE REES

**Boldwood**

First published in Great Britain in 2025 by Boldwood Books Ltd.

Cover Design by Colin Thomas

Cover Images: Colin Thomas

A CIP catalogue record for this book is available from the British Library.

Paperback ISBN 978-1-83633-803-1

Large Print ISBN 978-1-83633-802-4

Hardback ISBN 978-1-83633-801-7

Trade Paperback ISBN 978-1-80635-290-6

Ebook ISBN 978-1-83633-804-8

Kindle ISBN 978-1-83633-805-5

Audio CD ISBN 978-1-83633-796-6

MP3 CD ISBN 978-1-83633-797-3

Digital audio download ISBN 978-1-83633-800-0

This book is printed on certified sustainable paper. Boldwood Books is dedicated to putting sustainability at the heart of our business. For more information please visit https://www.boldwoodbooks.com/about-us/sustainability/

Boldwood Books Ltd, 23 Bowerdean Street, London, SW6 3TN

www.boldwoodbooks.com

*For the villagers of Abercanaid, Merthyr Tydfil, who suffered two tragic pit disasters in 1862 and 1865, respectively.*

# 1

## ABERCANAID, MERTHYR TYDFIL 1866

Thirteen-year-old Mari Evans's head rebounded as she felt a sharp crack against her cheek when her father struck her yet again, her hand flying to her face in a desperate act of self-protection.

Her only crime had been in allowing the fire in the hearth to go out when he was due home from the pub that night, which was a bitterly cold one at that. He did not even give her the chance to explain the reason she'd not fed the ferocious beast that required constant attention – because Mam had sent her to fetch Doctor Pritchard to her poorly brother. The doctor had moved house recently and was now living in Troedyrhiw, a neighbouring village, which was a fair walk away. Mam had stayed by Tom's side as she'd wiped his fevered brow with a cold, wet cloth and tried to keep him awake.

It had all happened after Gwynfor Evans had set off for the pub when Tom had taken sick. The day before he'd been playing near the River Taff. Some claimed the new sickness sweeping through the valley was waterborne, so those living near the canal and rivers were more at risk. It had already claimed thirty or more lives in the town, so her mother was particularly concerned that her youngest son be seen by the doctor as soon as possible. But Doctor Pritchard hadn't been at his home when Mari arrived, as he'd been out tending to some other patients in the community. So, with bated breath and a silver shilling in her sweaty palm, she'd waited anxiously as the seconds ticked by.

Finally, she found her voice. 'B... but Dad!' she said as tears blurred her eyes. 'The reason the fire is out... is because I had to run to fetch the doctor to see our Tommy.'

Her father, who appeared contrite now, seemed to suddenly sober up, his eyes widening. 'T... Tommy? But what's the matter with him? Why didn't you come to the pub to fetch me?' There was no mistaking that Tommy was her father's favourite child, and the mere mention of his name was enough to soften her father's heart.

Mari shook her head. 'There was no time. Doctor Pritchard was out on house calls when I arrived, so I had to wait, and then finally, only an hour or so ago, he showed up and took me with him in his coach. He only left here about twenty minutes ago and Mam said it was dark and too late to go to the pub to fetch you, honestly, she did.' Her voice had a pleading tone to it now and she detested herself for it, hated showing her vulnerability to him.

Pushing her roughly out of the way, her father made for the stone staircase, which was hidden behind a small door, making his way to Tommy's bed. She listened through the open door as he chastised her mother for not sending her to fetch him. Then she heard her mother telling him to calm down and keep quiet as Tommy wasn't well at all.

And then all went silent.

Not knowing what to do next, Mari did what people often do when uncertain or in times of trouble: she boiled the kettle. First, she filled it with clean water from the pump in the yard outside and then, remembering the fire had almost gone out, realised in her haste that she needed to stoke it up with the poker to get some air into it and then build it up again with screwed-up balls of newspaper and lumps of coal, before drawing it up with the metal blower. Finally, with the fire rescued, she could place the kettle on top of it.

She recalled only last spring when her father had been softer towards her. On a day when the sky was clear blue and the sun high up in the sky, he'd taken her for a walk up the mountain, way past the pit where he worked as a coal miner. It was a blot on the landscape, that black grimy place with the constant cranking of the pit wheel. They had climbed for what seemed a long time through woodland and jumped over a babbling brook, where her father had given her his hand to help her to the other side for fear she should fall on the slippery embankment. He had been tender towards her then and in high spirits too as he sang songs he remembered from his youth. Then afterwards there'd been a small hillock to ascend, and just when Mari had felt she couldn't climb much higher as she was out of puff, there on top of it was a large concentration of the most glorious golden daffodils she'd ever seen, bowing their heads in the breeze. Her breath had hitched in her chest to see such a sight.

Beyond the daffodils was a pond, encircled by trees and teeming with wildlife: dragonflies, birds of various types and, under the water, tadpoles and small fish. It was a world away from the valley below. Her mother had once said that her father was scarred like the valley itself. Mari had seen those blue scars for herself where the black coal dust had mingled with the wounds of his hard labour. Those blue marks were battle scars that all miners succumbed to at some time or another, and they were with them for life ever after.

It was some time before Mam appeared downstairs, and when she did, it startled Mari from her reflection of times gone by. She studied her mother's weary-looking face for a moment. There was a sadness in her eyes that she'd not seen before.

'It's coming for us...' was all she managed to say.

Mari had no idea who or what she meant so, frowning for a moment, she asked, 'Who's coming for us, Mam?'

'The sickness...' her mother said as she stared at some point in the distance.

Mari had heard of the sickness that had been sweeping the valley of late and claiming many lives. It was as if her mother was afraid to even say the name 'cholera' for fear it should infect them.

Stepping forward, Mari laid her hand on her mother's fore-arm. 'Mam,' she said softly, 'the doctor told us he didn't think it was that particular sickness. Shall I make a cup of tea?'

'Well, if it's not that sickness, then what on earth is it? Tommy was out playing all day, and I've just found out from Mrs Griffiths in number six that he was with her Alfie and some other boys. They were playing on the banks of the River Taff. It must be the sickness.'

Mari shook her head. 'No, Doctor Pritchard said he thinks it's a mild stomach upset and not to feed him anything for now; to starve him for a full day and night and only to give him cool, previously boiled water.' She remembered the doctor stressing that, now cholera had hit the town, they all needed to keep their hands clean by washing them more often.

Her mother raised her head and, fixing her gaze on her, said, 'I suppose the doctor must know what he's talking about.'

'Yes, of course, Mam. Take a seat by the table and I'll brew that tea. What about Dad? Do you think he'll want any?'

Her mother shook her head. 'No, he's full of the ale and he said he'll sleep in the boys' room tonight.'

Ten-year-old Tommy shared his room with his older brother, Bryn. He was a collier at the nearby coal pit like their father. Bryn had gone underground at the age of twelve and was now sixteen years old. Mari herself shared a bedroom with her younger sister, Nerys. The third, larger bedroom was shared by her parents. There were times when it was late at night or maybe in the early hours of the morning, when she'd hear her father come in from the pub and hushed voices in her parents' bedroom. It sounded to her as if her mother was sometimes protesting about something, but she wasn't quite sure what. Dad's drinking maybe? Then after a few minutes there would be the inevitable sounds of the bed's mattress squeaking rhythmically against its springs. She was never quite sure what was going on there, but it never went on for too long and then she'd hear a loud groan coming from her father through the bedroom wall and the next thing she knew, he was snoring very loudly. Usually, in the morning, her mother came down to breakfast with a worried expression on her face.

Mari had once plucked up the courage to ask Bryn what was going on and why Mam sometimes looked so concerned in the mornings. Bryn had pursed his lips disapprovingly as though forcing himself not to say anything, but then as he had a good sense of humour, had just thrown back his head and, laughing, had said, 'It's grown-up stuff. Nothing for you to worry about, our Mari. It's probably because Mam doesn't want to have any more babies at her age and Dad, when he comes home from the pub, gets a bit fruity, shall we say.'

Mari had no idea what her brother meant by 'fruity' but, for the time being, she accepted his explanation. She could well understand why her mother might not want any more children.

Life was hard enough for them as it was. Even though Dad worked at the pit, he seemed to spend a lot of his time and wages on alcohol at the pub. If it wasn't for Bryn, then they might well have starved for what their father contributed towards the family coffers.

Tonight, her brother was working a night shift at the pit, and she was grateful her father was sleeping in Tommy's room, but she was understandably concerned he might drift off into a deep slumber after all that ale he'd supped and not hear if Tommy was ill during the night. Still, her mother would get more rest with her father not being in the marital bed – that was, if she could sleep.

* * *

The following morning there was no sign of Dad, but her mother looked a lot happier as she sliced a loaf of bread and began to butter the slices. Bryn was due home at any moment following his night shift.

Her mother smiled when she saw Mari approach.

'Seems the doctor was right – Tommy's feeling a lot better this morning,' she said, smiling. 'He's even asking for something to eat.'

Remembering what Doctor Pritchard had told them, Mari bit on her bottom lip. 'Best not to give him any food like the doctor said, Mam. Just cool boiled water. Food might make him ill again.'

Her mother's cheeks flushed. 'Oh, I clean forgot. I just took him up a plate of toast and a cup of tea.'

She made to go upstairs, but Mari, realising she'd be quicker, said, 'I'll go...' She ran as fast as her legs would carry her to her brother's room as he was about to tuck into a slice of hot, buttery toast. Snatching it from his grasp, she asked, 'How many slices did Mam give you?'

'Only this one!' He blinked.

'Well, I'm sorry, you can't have it. Have you touched your cup of tea yet?'

He shook his head. 'But why not?' His eyes looked large with sunken dark shadows beneath them.

'Because the doctor said you're not to eat or drink anything other than plain water for a full day. And the water must be boiled and all.'

His eyes were brimming with tears now. So she sat on the bed beside him and put a comforting arm around his shoulders. 'Look, you don't want to go chucking up again like you did yesterday, do you?'

He shook his head.

'Just have some patience,' she said kindly. 'I know you're thirsty, so I'll fetch you that water. I'll have to wait for it to cool though.'

He nodded and forced a smile. 'Why does it have to be boiled, our Mari?'

'Because of that new sickness that's going around. The doctor doesn't think you have it but they're warning people to keep clean and only drink boiled water.' She wished she didn't have to explain this to him and felt bad he wasn't able to eat normally, but realising the importance of the doctor's words, she wanted to stick to her guns. Mam seemed so half-soaked these days, unaware somehow of what was going on around her. Even when Dad struck Mari like he had last night, her mother seemed not to take in what was going on. She so wished she had the sort of mother who would stand up to her father. He was taking liberties in all manner of ways these days, staying out late at the pub, being handy with the odd slap or two in her direction, even taking liberties with their mother by the sound of it. Only once had he ever been challenged about striking Mari and that was when Bryn had come in from a night shift unexpectedly and caught him forcefully shaking her by the shoulders as she'd somehow managed to burn the toast. Mostly he was a clever bugger, doing things like that to her when no one else was around to see it. The strange thing was he never touched Tommy or Nerys. And he wouldn't have dared try it on with Bryn either, as these days he was as tall as him. So why did it have to be her? Why was she the scapegoat of the family?

Her life had become a misery of late, so she tended to try to stay out of his way. And to make matters worse, there was evidence that she was turning into a young woman. She had begun to develop breasts, and her mother had told her it wouldn't be too long until she received her monthly bleeds. That was something she wasn't looking forward to, as according to a girl she knew, Mattie Connor, it was then you could get pregnant. So she was going to have to stay away from boys at all costs. Not that she had much time for them as she was either busy helping Mam around the house or had her head in a book. Life, though, in general, was becoming miserable for her the way her parents were behaving lately.

It was while Mari was out walking in the village, with her wicker shopping basket over the crook of her arm, that she heard some women gossiping on the doorstep of one of the small huddle of houses. She was about to turn the corner and head towards the shop when she heard her father's name mentioned. The women hadn't noticed her approach, and she had her shawl wrapped around her head. They were so engrossed in conversation that they weren't aware who was around them.

'Course, Gwynfor Evans has been knocking that Blodwyn one off for a long time,' the woman with the hooked nose and dark hair was saying, arms folded and her lips pursed in a disapproving fashion. Her appearance reminded Mari of a witch she'd once seen in a storybook she'd read to her brother and sister. There was a brazen, hard look to the woman that Mari didn't much care for.

Blodwyn? Who on earth was she? And what did the term 'knocking off' mean? It was a new one on her. But then as the conversation continued, it became increasingly obvious what those women meant.

The lady with the red hair, who was shorter than her companion, had dark brown beady-looking eyes, reminding Mari of a little bird pecking on crumbs as her head nodded back and forth as she'd been listening. 'Yes,' she said. 'Blodwyn has got the brass neck to have him under her roof while he has a wife and family in upper Abercanaid, poor dabs those kids. Imagine them having a father like that!'

Mari's mouth gaped open in horror at what the women were saying, and she snapped it shut again. Surely Mam and Bryn knew nothing of this? And the two younger children most definitely didn't.

The conversation then switched to a different topic, something about the weather and was there any chance of rain today, as Mrs Bird had just pegged out a line full of washing.

Mari, feeling disconcerted now, dashed quickly around the corner, out of sight, as she did not want them to see or recognise her. Panting, she stood with her back against the stone wall of the end house, taking deep breaths to compose herself.

A few minutes ago life had seemed as it always had for her,

mundane and monotonous, yet, within a short space of time, those women's words had cut through her like a knife, making her question her very existence. It all seemed a lie. She already disliked her father. It was the way he'd changed lately, becoming aggressive in drink, but now, she hated him with a vengeance. She had the urge to rush home and blurt out everything to her mother, then wake her brother up who would be sleeping after his night shift and do the same thing, demanding to know if what those women had said was true. But her mother was relying on her to fetch some provisions from the shop. She'd sent Mari out to bring home a loaf of bread, a hunk of cheese and some eggs. She'd also thought to purchase a poke of boiled sweets for Tommy, which she'd give him when it was safe for him to eat again, to make up for snatching his breakfast away. Now she felt unable to concentrate, her mind racing a mile a minute to process what she'd just heard.

Her father was having a dalliance with a woman called Blodwyn! Is that why he was drinking so much lately, trying in some sense to blot out his sins from his mind?

She barely remembered entering the shop, even unaware of the tinkle of the small bell above the door as her thoughts drowned it out – it was almost as though the real Mari was someplace else and now she was an observer. It was busy as Mrs Jones was handing over several packages to a woman at the counter, who then placed them in her basket, while three other women waited patiently in the queue. Mari did not feel patient though; she wanted all the women out of there, so it was just her and kindly Mrs Jones who'd smile at her and utter some comforting words. But now she had the humiliation of waiting at the end of the queue, all the while wondering if any of those women knew about her father and this so-called Blodwyn he'd taken up with.

Finally, though, the queue dwindled, and she was left facing Mrs Jones.

Gladys Jones was an elderly woman with pure white hair and a welcoming smile. Her cornflower-blue eyes illuminated warmly as she addressed Mari.

'Well, hello there, stranger! I've not seen you for some time. How have you been keeping, *cariad*?' she said in her sing-song tone of voice.

Mari didn't know if she could bear anyone being so nice to her right now, as tears weren't far from the surface. She swallowed hard as she tried to fight them off, but there was no fooling the elderly woman.

'What is it, *bach*?'

'I... I...' To Mari's horror, huge, shuddering sobs engulfed her body. It was as if the upset of yesterday with rushing to fetch the doctor for her brother, her father slapping her across the face and now hearing gossip from those women had all come to a head.

When she was unable to reply, Mrs Jones lowered her voice and spoke softly. 'Now I'll tell you what we'll do. I'm having a quiet period and could do with a break, so I'll just turn the sign to "closed" on the shop door, and we'll retire to the back and have ourselves a cup of tea, or you can have some of my home-made lemonade if you prefer. How's that suit?'

Mari thought it suited very well and she managed a nod of appreciation, but the lump that had been growing in her throat was making it hard to speak. The elderly woman sprang into action as she came scurrying from behind the counter, crossed the shop floor, flipped the sign on the glass panel of the door and slid the bolt across it.

'There, we shan't be disturbed,' she said as she made her way back over to where Mari was standing. 'Come through to the back room with me.'

Mari didn't need asking twice and she followed the woman past the shop counter, through a small door into the back room. The room was more of a storage place. Several sacks of flour and potatoes were stacked up on the floor and a multitude of tins of food lined various shelves. Mari could see from the labels they were tinned fruit and meat and beside those were jars of preserves, pickles and jams.

Near the window was a small table with two wooden chairs. 'Now you sit yourself down, dearie, while I put the kettle on to boil.' She placed the old, blackened sooty kettle on top of the fire in the hearth. 'It won't take a tick as I'd previously boiled it ready to have a brew when that sudden flurry of customers arrived!' She chuckled. 'It's always the same thing around here, all or nothing!' Mari felt she'd have preferred the lemonade but was too proud to say so, yet as if reading her thoughts, the woman turned towards her and said, 'Oh, I did mention lemonade to you, didn't I?'

Mari smiled and nodded. 'Yes, please,' she answered, finding her voice for the first time.

'Then the lemonade you shall have.' She headed off to the pantry, where she drew out an earthenware jug and poured the cloudy mixture into a glass. 'Only made it yesterday, so it's quite fresh. Been in the pantry all this time to keep cool. Take a seat, dear.'

Mari did as told, and after placing her basket on the table, she drew out a chair and sat, then Mrs Jones handed her the glass and she went off to brew a cuppa for herself. The kettle on the fire was now puffing out clouds of steam. Mari closed her eyes after taking a sip of the cool, refreshing liquid. It did taste good and all. Mam had tried making lemonade once, but it wasn't as nice as Mrs Jones's. Mam's had tasted a bit sour but this version had the right amount of sweetness. You could still taste the lemonade but it didn't make you wince. Mrs Jones was a very clever woman, as she sometimes sold her lemonade and ginger beer in the summer months to folk. She also occasionally baked and sold slabs of *bara brith* and miniature sponge cakes, which went down a treat with customers.

'I asked if the lemonade is all right for you, Mari!' Mrs Jones was saying now as she tilted her head to one side with concern.

Oh dear. Mari hadn't realised the woman had been asking her a question. She'd been absorbed in her own thoughts and didn't wish to appear rude. 'Yes, it's lovely, Mrs Jones, thank you.'

'That's good to hear, *cariad*. You can have another glass when you finish that, if you like?'

Mari nodded gratefully.

Mrs Jones carried her cup of tea over to the table and, drawing out a chair, she sat opposite Mari. 'Now then, young lady, why are you looking so upset this morning?'

Mari explained all that had gone on since yesterday with her brother and the doctor being summoned and what she'd over-heard before calling to the shop, though she didn't mention that her father had slapped her hard across the face last night.

Mrs Jones frowned, her blue eyes clouding over so they now appeared almost grey. 'To be truthful,' she said, her fingers circling the rim of her teacup as though giving her something to concentrate on, 'there has been some gossip amongst folk in the village. I don't hold with gossip myself and quite often I'll straighten someone out if they say something I know is untrue or spiteful, just to spread things around. There are some in this village who are gleeful about putting others down, but not me.'

'I realise that,' said Mari. She'd known the woman a long time and Mrs Jones had only ever exhibited kindness towards her.

'But in the case of your father and that Blodwyn one, I have to say there is no smoke without fire. They've been spotted together on several occasions and there was one time when I was walking on the canal bank, I spotted them speaking with one another outside the pub. I mean, there's nothing wrong with that. A man and woman don't have to be in that sort of a relationship to make small talk with one another, enquire how the other is, that kind of thing. But...' She bit her bottom lip. 'In that case, your father put his arm around her and ushered her inside the pub. My guess is he didn't want folk to see them together. Oh, those men in company with one another supping ale would rather keep quiet than tell their wives what one of them is up to. It's an unspoken agreement amongst such men. But a pub is no place for a good God-fearing woman! It shows what women of her ilk are up to!'

Mari had no idea what the word 'ilk' meant but she could guess Mrs Jones meant 'her sort'. And just what sort was this Blodwyn, she wanted to know. Mari, herself, didn't know of any women who frequented pubs or hung around with married men.

'Now I know it's a lot for you to take in, Mari. And I wouldn't be telling you any of this, but since you've heard the gossip, it's better that you know. But I don't know whether you should tell your mother. It might upset her. Though, then again, she might hear from someone else anyhow. I'll leave it up to you.'

Oh dear, what a dilemma. Mari's first thought had been to tell her mother what she'd heard but she didn't know what to do. She thought by telling Mam she'd quash any rumours, but now after what Mrs Jones had just said it sounded as though the rumours were true.

'I just don't know what to do, Mrs Jones,' she said, then she took a few sips from her glass, draining it and setting it down on the table.

'Then perhaps do nothing for now?' suggested Mrs Jones. 'That's if you don't feel right about it.'

'I could mention it to my brother to see if he's heard anything.

But then again, he's so big and strong these days, he might thump our father.'

'Yes, that brother of yours has grown up a lot lately. Being a hewer at the pit has made him muscular and strong like that. I really don't know what to suggest to you, as anything you say might cause trouble one way or another. Though from what I can see, your father has brought trouble on himself recently.'

Mari had to agree the woman was right. It was all beginning to make sense now with her father being missing so much from the family home of late. He kept some very tardy hours and one night he'd not returned home at all, claiming when confronted by her mother the following morning that he'd slept in Geraint Harris's house. Geraint had a farm on the hill overlooking the village. Mari remembered thinking at the time, even if her father had supped a lot of ale, it would be easier for him to walk home to his own house than up the ruddy mountain in the dark! It had been raining that night too, so slipping was a possibility.

No, her father had been lying – she was sure of it.

'Now, let me fetch you another glass of that lemonade,' said Mrs Jones. 'I've got a tin of freshly baked Welsh cakes in the cupboard; we'll have a couple of those too.'

Mari didn't feel like eating but realised it might do her good, as she hadn't consumed much that morning.

In fact, it had been a strange twenty-four hours altogether and she'd be relieved when the day was finally over.

## 2

When Mari arrived home all was peaceful in the house. She laid down her wicker basket on the scullery table, wondering where Mam was. A loud snoring noise emanated from above. She often wondered if Bryn disturbed Tommy when he came home from a night shift, as they shared a room. Wondering where her younger brother was right now, she peeped into her bedroom to see him sitting up in the bed she shared with Nerys, reading a book. He must have crept in there after she'd left the house. A big smile broke out on his face as soon as he saw her. He'd probably escaped there to get away from the snoring in the room next door.

'Hello, Mari!' he yelled.

'Sssh!' she said, placing her index finger to her lips while she hid the other hand behind her back.

Tommy's eyes enlarged. 'What have you got there then?' he whispered.

'I decided not to fetch you any boiled sweets after all,' she said, shaking her head with a solemn expression on her face as she wagged a finger at him. His face crumpled. But then she said, 'But I have brought you these instead!'

That was enough to perk up his spirits as he leapt out of bed and tried to wrestle the paper bag of sweets out of her hands.

Smiling, she handed it over to him. 'Well, there's a difference to yesterday! You look as fit as a flea today!'

'What sweets did you fetch me, Mari?'

'Sherbet bonbons!'

He smiled. 'My favourite!'

'Yes, I know. Now if I were you, I'd make the most of reading a book in bed with a bag of sweets. As soon as Mam sees you're back to normal, she'll have you downstairs helping with the chores. Where is she, by the way?'

'Not sure, think she's gone somewhere with Nerys,' he said, and then he popped a bonbon into his mouth and closed his eyes to savour it. It was right enough; he wouldn't get to lie about in bed much longer. Though Dad, if he came home, would molly-coddle him for sure. It was strange how her father favoured Tommy over all the others in the family – she often wondered why that was.

Mari left her brother to his own devices and returned to the scullery to unpack the provisions from her basket. Her concern for him had been the reason she'd gone upstairs to see him immediately. Thankfully, his health appeared to have been restored, but there'd be no more messing around by the river for him while the sickness was on the rampage – it was far too risky. The doctor had explained that years ago it was thought cholera was an airborne disease but now it was known to be carried in the water. Apparently, there'd been some water pump in London that had originally caused the first outbreak. All of this made Mari concerned that the communal pump they used might spread the disease too, but the doctor had explained how something had got into that water system, and anyway, there was far more overcrowding in London. Doctor Pritchard had gone on to explain that although there were some cholera cases now cropping up in Merthyr – the population of Merthyr Tydfil had swelled over the years, as people came to work in its ironworks, travelling near and far and some even arrived from overseas – Abercanaid might be more fortunate as the area wasn't as overcrowded as some other parts of the town.

Mam had told her there'd been a particularly nasty outbreak of the disease some years ago, prompting the building of a special graveyard near the St Tydfil's Workhouse. She supposed some of the deaths would have arisen from the workhouse itself.

Where on earth were Mam and Nerys, though? It wasn't like her mother to have left the house for so long at this time of the day. Dad had departed early this morning too, which was odd as his shift didn't begin until the afternoon. It was highly unusual for him to act in such a manner, and she experienced an unsettling sensation in her stomach, suggesting that something was amiss.

Mari busied herself, tidying the small abode, picking up her brother's discarded heavy work boots. Steel-capped and with several segs in their soles, they made a heck of a noise when he crossed the cobbles with those on his feet. They were necessary wear for underground work, though, where falls of coal could sometimes happen or crush accidents from drams carrying coal. She sighed as she placed the boots in the cupboard under the stairs. She knew how exhausted her brother was. He could barely keep his eyes open after swilling off the coal dust in the old tin bath in the backyard with water filled from the pump, topped up with hot water from several boiled pans from the stove. The coal miners rarely washed their backs as it was thought to 'weaken the man', so it only got a good scrub if they had a couple of days off work or were going somewhere like on a date with a special sweetheart. Mam thought it a silly old wives' tale but, tale or not, the colliers in the area were so superstitious they felt it might cause some ill to befall them.

But Mari thought there might be something in that old wives' tale. Only last Christmas there'd been an explosion at the pit where thirty-four men and boys had lost their lives. The village hadn't fully recovered from that, and everyone knew someone involved in that accident. People had lost fathers, husbands, sons, grandsons and other relatives along with good friends. And some of those who hadn't lost their lives had bad injuries that prevented them from ever working again.

Mam always insisted on giving her brother a good breakfast before his head hit his pillow to sleep. Usually, it was a couple of rashers of thick bacon with fried eggs and bread and butter all washed down with a couple of cups of strong tea. She maintained that a working man needed more fuel than most, and Bryn was grateful for it too. Of course, she had been doing the same thing for their father for years.

Mari continued tidying up the place and dusting around. The coal fire created a lot of dirty grime that landed on surfaces, but it was easily solved with a quick wipe from a damp cloth. Then she swilled out some dirty laundry discarded in the corner of the scullery, pegging it out on the washing line to dry. She wasn't as thorough as Mam was when it came to the washing and her mother might chastise her later for leaving stains embedded in the clothing but, in any case, she hoped she'd be pleased with her efforts. Any work she could do for her mother would ease her burden later, she worked so hard for her family and deserved a rest.

A thud from above told her that her elder brother had awoken from his slumber. She could tell by the heavy sounds above that it was Bryn and not Tommy, who was much lighter on his feet. No wonder people worried about him – he was small for his age and light as a feather.

The scullery door opened, and Bryn stood there blinking, his hair dishevelled as he yawned. His eyes were black-lined from coal dust, despite washing earlier. When Mam was around, she usually insisted they each took a clean, wet flannel to wash thoroughly around their eyes after a shift, saying that eyes were precious things, and they didn't want to lose their sight like some of those pit ponies. But even the ponies were blinkered, and the men were not, so getting coal dust into their eyes wasn't a good thing at all.

'Hello, Mari. Where's our mam?' Bryn asked, his voice low and husky.

'I'm not sure. She sent me to the shop earlier on an errand and when I returned, she and Nerys weren't here. Tommy thinks they've gone somewhere together.'

'Maybe,' he said, smiling, and then he glanced at the brown earthenware teapot on the pine table.

'Would you like a cup of tea?' she offered.

'Aye, I would an' all. Funny how you can read my mind, Mari!' He chuckled. 'Hey, I heard about what happened with Tommy yesterday. That was a bit of a set-to, wasn't it?'

She nodded as she poured him a cup of tea from the pot, then refilled her own cup. 'He seems fine though now, bouncing around on the bed he was when I returned from the shop with some sweets for him! I had to tell him to pipe down in case he woke you.'

'Aye, well, that's good to hear when you realise what the alternative might have been!' Bryn drew out a chair and sat by the table. He propped his head on his hand, supported by his elbow, still clearly exhausted. He worked hard and any sleep he could get was precious to him. 'You're looking tired today?' he said as he studied her face.

She took a seat opposite him and explained what had happened with their father slapping her hard across the face.

'The bloody beast!' yelled Bryn. 'Someone needs to teach that brute a lesson. The way he treats you is atrocious!'

'It's worse than that, Bryn... I heard a rumour just this morning about him.'

Her brother's eyes were wide and unblinking now. Then they narrowed to almost slits as he asked, 'Rumour? What bloody rumour?'

Mari swallowed hard, realising things would never be the same again once she told him what she'd overheard. 'I was walking to the shop when I heard these two women talking about him on the doorstep. They reckoned he's seeing a woman by the name of Blodwyn.'

Bryn half laughed until he realised his sister was serious about the matter. His face now deadpan, he sat forward in his seat. 'Are you sure they were talking about our father though?'

'Oh, yes.' She nodded. 'One named him and said he has a wife and kids and is living in upper Abercanaid. It couldn't be anyone else as there's only one Gwynfor Evans living here.'

Bryn's face paled and Mari shovelled a couple of spoonfuls of sugar into her brother's cup, as wasn't it supposed to be good for shock? She well understood his rising emotion, as she'd felt the same way not a couple of hours since. Then she noticed how his lips became set in a grim line as he flexed and unflexed his fingers. It was as if he needed to do something with them, then he bunched both hands into fists so tight that his knuckles turned white. If their father came through the door right now, she had no doubts that Bryn would thump him – she could only hope he wouldn't.

\* \* \*

It was a couple of hours later before Mam returned to the house with Nerys in tow, both seeming weary and worn out. Meanwhile, after convincing Bryn to return to his bed as he needed his sleep before another night shift, Mari sighed a breath of relief. Tommy had risen from his bed now through boredom and was seated at the scullery table with a cup of cool, boiled water in front of him. Mari was determined to listen to the doctor's advice as she didn't want any setbacks for him.

'Mam,' Mari said gently as her mother approached, her face pale, features drawn. She undid the ribbons of her bonnet and placed it down on the table and then patted her hair with both hands. 'Where have you been all this time?'

Mari, catching a glimpse of her sister in her mother's shadow, could sense an expression of confusion on her sister's face.

'There was somewhere I needed to go to – that was all...'

'We went to see a lady,' piped up Nerys. 'She's living in Pond Row on the canal bank.'

Mam's shocked expression said it all. She obviously hadn't expected that from her youngest daughter, probably thinking that Nerys wouldn't mention it, as maybe she'd warned her not to.

Feeling brave now, Mari asked, 'Is that woman's name Blodwyn by any chance?'

Her mother nodded with a deep sadness in her sea-green eyes. 'But how do you know, Mari?' Her mother angled her head to one side in puzzlement.

Mari swallowed; this wasn't going to be easy. 'It was something I overheard this morning when I was shopping in the village. Two women were speaking about her and...'

'Your father's name cropped up?'

Mari nodded. 'How long have you known, Mam?'

'Oh, I've suspected something for a few months now but I didn't want to believe the rumours. Mrs Griffiths, Alfie's mother, called me in for a cup of tea a couple of days ago and told me all she's heard. She took no pleasure in telling me, mind you. Not like others would in these parts.' Her eyes widened for a moment. 'You've not said anything to your brother, I hope?'

Mari's face suffused with heat, and she bit her lower lip. 'Sorry, Mam. Bryn rose from bed earlier when you were out, so I told him. I had to, as I couldn't believe it myself.'

Mam nodded with understanding. 'I suppose he'd find out eventually anyhow. It's just I don't much fancy having any more strife beneath this roof.'

Mari thought back to her brother's earlier words and his manner as his hands had formed fists as though he was ready to punch the living daylights out of their father. It all made sense though why their mother had seemed in a world of her own yesterday. Poor Mam having to cope with all of that. What a dreadful shock that must have been for her.

'So, did you get to speak to her to see if the gossip is true? Blodwyn, I mean?'

'Who's Blodwyn?' Tommy appeared every bit as confused as Nerys.

'Never you mind,' said Mari. 'Nerys and Tommy, go outside to the yard to play for a few minutes – the fresh air will do you good, Tommy!'

When they'd left via the back door of the scullery, banging it behind them, Mam smiled appreciatively. 'Thank you, Mari. You're old enough to understand a little of what's going on here, but that pair aren't.'

She drew out a chair to sit at the table and then rested her head in her hands.

After a moment, she raised her head and looked at her daughter. 'No, Blodwyn wasn't at home when I called at the house, but I did speak to her mother. It's true, all right. All those times your father has been missing from home, he's been there with that floozy. Her mother's a widow woman, see. There's no father in the house, no head of the home. So, Blodwyn's taken my husband, your father, into her bed – against her mother's wishes, I might add. The woman doesn't like what's going on under her roof. It's giving her only daughter a bad name, and her too for condoning it. She said if her husband was alive, their daughter wouldn't have dared to move her "fancy man" in!'

Mari didn't quite understand what her mother meant by Blodwyn 'taking her father into her bed'. Didn't her father always sleep in his own bed with Mam? She thought she'd ask Bryn about that later; he'd know what their mam meant.

* * *

Subdued, Mam barely spoke for the rest of the day, and by teatime when Bryn was due to be fed before his night shift at the pit, as the family sat around the table preparing to tuck into the meal she'd just made, everyone's eyes fell upon the empty chair at the head of the table, aware that Dad wasn't where he usually sat. Although often missing from the family home, dinner was one meal he never missed. This meal of the day was sacrosanct, and everyone sat there as the mantel clock ticked away, but when the hands of the clock reached five minutes past the hour, Mam – with some determination – said, 'Well, your father's not coming now, is he? Please make a start, everyone!'

Nerys and Tommy exchanged nervous glances with one another. This was unknown territory. Mam never defied Dad. This meal of the day was always on the table at precisely the same time on the hour in the evening, like clockwork, and if it wasn't, woe betide. Mam would dish up the most food on Dad's plate and then everyone at the table would wait patiently for him to take his first mouthful before beginning themselves. Now everyone seemed reluctant to make a start, until Bryn, lifting his knife and fork, said, 'You heard Mam. Come on, I'm starving! Get it down you!' And his knife speared a piece of beef in gravy as their mother smiled nervously at them all.

It wasn't long before everyone had picked up their knife and fork and begun digging in themselves. There was a clinking of cutlery against their plates as they ate. This evening it was boiled beef with potatoes, carrots and cabbage, followed by apple pie. The family didn't eat like this every evening – often Mam would prepare a bowl of lamb cawl or stew – but one evening midweek, she always made a larger meal for the family. But the best meal of all was on a Sunday. Following chapel, they'd get to tuck into roast chicken or pork. Dad had fallen away from the chapel services lately and now Mari wondered if that was because he'd realised that, in the eyes of God, what he was doing was sinful. But surely, he needed to give an account of himself first before being condemned by them all? Although she disliked her father intensely of late, she did think it was best for them all to see what he had to say about the situation himself.

By the time Bryn had got himself ready for his shift, Dad still hadn't returned home. Before leaving with his metal snap tin containing a cheese sandwich, an apple, and a Welsh cake, her brother draped a reassuring arm around their mother.

'Look, I'll see what I can find out about his whereabouts when I get to the pit. He should have worked a day shift today and we don't know why he left the house so early this morning either. Try not to fret too much. He's like a bad penny that one – he always turns up in the end!' He stooped to peck a kiss on their mother's cheek and then he turned and left through the back door. Mari watched Mam's drawn face as, just at that moment, a solitary tear coursed down her cheek.

Poor Mam, she'd been battling to hold things together and now her eldest son had left the house, she seemed about to crumble.

'Why don't you go to bed and get an early night, Mam? I can see to Tommy and Nerys,' Mari suggested.

Her mother sniffed and shook her head vigorously. 'No, I want to be here when your father gets in from the pub, as there are things I am of a mind to say to him!' Her eyes glinted with anger.

Mari had never seen her mother so determined. She'd gone from being in a world of her own these past couple of days to being very focused and forthright.

That night in bed, Mari found it difficult to get to sleep. Every creak and groan in the house seemed magnified and she realised the reason she was feeling so frightened was because there was no man about the house. If only Bryn hadn't had to work this very night. It seemed an age until she drifted off and then she thought she heard footsteps on the landing, accompanied by mumbling, but she dismissed it as a dream or maybe pure imagination.

She was awoken by the sound of Bryn and her mother speaking downstairs. What on earth was the time? She was usually washed and dressed well before he returned home in the morning. The amount of light filtering in through a chink in the curtains confirmed it was later than she usually rose. Her father would be so angry with her; he didn't encourage any of his children to lie around in their beds. If they weren't up and at it by eight o'clock at the latest, he'd raise the mattress and tip them out of their bed onto the floor. Why hadn't Mam awakened her though? She always helped her to light the fire and prepare breakfast.

Mari quickly swilled her face and hands in the porcelain bowl on the washstand and dried herself using the towel draped over a chair. She removed her nightgown and replaced it with her dress, which she slipped over her head, and then barefoot, she descended the cold stone steps to go downstairs.

As she approached the scullery, the door was ajar and, unseen, she paused to listen a while.

'Aye, our father's the talk of the pit; seems the swine has absconded with that Blodwyn one! The foreman told me he called there early this morning before I'd set off for home to insist upon his wages a day early. He'd given Mr Roberts some cock-and-bull story about needing the money to pay the doctor as our Tommy is so ill he'll require several home visits! I ask you, using his own son like that in some lie to get his hands on his wages. So, I'm afraid he's not going to be tipping up those flamin' wages to you today! Oh no! They're going to be spent on his fancy piece, no doubt! It was too early for Mr Thomas, the wages clerk, to be at his desk, so Mr Roberts took the key to the safe and signed in the book for them himself! Most unprecedented, I'd say!'

There was no response from their mother as Bryn carried on.

'I don't think my wages are going to be enough to provide for us all. It'll be a struggle. Feeding five mouths will take some doing on what I earn. We had two wages feeding six of us before this and he was on better money than me.'

Still there was no sign of a response from Mam.

All went quiet for a spell, the silence finally broken by Bryn saying softly, 'Please don't cry, Mam. We'll work something out. You're better off without that brute – the way he treats you.'

Mari swallowed the lump that had formed in her throat. The

way her father was behaving was an abomination towards them. How could he hurt their mother like that? And come to that, all his children too? Mam would have given her last crust of bread to anyone, even a total stranger, in need of it. There had been times in the past when she'd even gone without herself, so her family could have what they needed. Mari recalled an occasion where she and Nerys had needed new frocks for the Sunday school Christmas party that year, and Mam, who didn't have enough money, took apart one of her favourite day gowns and had worked all night long to transform it into two pretty dresses, with lace collars. Then there was the time following a bad pit explosion where there was no work for the men for weeks on end, so to support the family she'd taken in other people's washing and ironing. All this along with the work she had to do in the home. Up at the crack of dawn lighting the coal fires, chopping sticks for firewood in the back-yard, scrubbing the floors on her hands and knees as well as shopping and cooking for them all. Her poor hands were red raw, so ruined by all the household chores that had to be done. Poor Mam would never have hands like a lady, all soft and white.

Bitter tears stung the backs of Mari's eyes as she thought of what her mother was going through right now. She had intended leaving it a while after what she'd heard Bryn say but now, on impulse, she found herself bursting through the scullery door where her brother and mother were seated at the table opposite one another, Mam still openly weeping.

Mari threw her arms around her mother's neck.

'You heard all that?' Mam looked at her through glistening eyes.

'Yes, Mam. We'll cope though somehow; you'll see we will. I love you so very much!'

Hearing those words of comfort from her eldest daughter had Mam in tears again. 'I love you too, Mari.' She sniffed. Fixing her gaze on Bryn, she said, 'In fact, I love all of you.' Which prompted Bryn to stretch his hand across the table and take his mother's free hand, the one that wasn't hugging his sister.

'Mari's right, Mam. We'll survive this. If Dad doesn't come back, I've been thinking I might ask the foreman if he'll give me some extra hours to work next week.'

Their mother's forehead creased into a soft frown. 'Oh, I don't know if that's a good idea with all the hours you already work and in dangerous conditions too. If you get overly tired, it might cause an accident if you're not with it.'

Bryn nodded but, after looking thoughtful for a moment, and as if to make a joke of things said, 'Pity they no longer take young girls underground. Our Mari could pass for a boy if she cut her hair and wore a flat cap!' He threw back his head and chuckled.

The thought amused Mari, and she began to laugh until it was difficult to stop, but when the laughter abated, she realised her brother's thought might not be such a bad idea. If things got to the stage where the family needed more money, it was always an option.

Bryn, by now, had moved on to another topic: he was speaking about the foreman again and Mam, who had ceased crying, was nodding at him in agreement. But Mari had no idea what they were saying, as she couldn't get the idea out of her head. Dressing up as a boy to work at the pit? She knew for a fact there were boys of her age and younger who worked under-ground with Bryn. She was as fit and strong as any of those. What she did know was that she was a hard worker. She remembered her brother mentioning that there were 'breaker boys' whose job was to break the lumps of freshly hewn coal into pieces and then sort them into size. He also mentioned 'tipper boys' who tipped the coal down the chute. As much as sixteen to seventeen tonnes could be loaded in one day. She could do either of those jobs. The only jobs for girls were working on top of the pit, not beneath ground. They called those 'tip girls', but the wages weren't as good for the girls as they were for the lads. Maybe she could ask at the pit about one of those jobs?

Mari was shaken out of her reverie when Mam said, 'Can you please do me a favour, *cariad*?'

She nodded enthusiastically, anything to help her mother right now. 'Yes, Mam.'

Her mother drew a composing breath and released it. 'Go to Mrs Jones's shop and ask her if she'll allow us some provisions on tick for a few days...'

Mari wrinkled her freckled nose. 'What's tick?'

'It means,' said Bryn, 'that goods will be supplied to us without having to pay the supplier there and then, but we promise to settle the account by a certain date or when we have the means to do so.'

It never ceased to amaze Mari how clever her brother was; despite only having a few years of schooling, he seemed to know a lot and was clever with sums and handling money too. Whenever he had the chance, his head was buried in a book or he was leafing through the newspaper.

'Oh,' said Mari. An image flooded her mind of a woman called Mrs Hennessy who had a lot of children. Mari had been standing behind her in the queue one day last month and the woman had asked Mrs Jones to put all her purchases 'on the slate'. She guessed that must be the same thing as 'tick'.

'But,' continued Bryn, 'there'll be no need for any of that. I was going to wait until after tonight's shift and pick up my wages in the morning, but as it was evident Dad's not going to be tipping up his wages this week, Mr Roberts has arranged for me to collect mine from the office this afternoon. I don't think the wages clerk minded too much as everyone at the pit seems aware that bugger has done a runner by now!'

Mam's face softened. 'Oh, there's good you are, Bryn. I don't know what I'd do without you, either of you.' Her eyes were shining now. 'The other two are too young to understand what's going on.'

'It's all right, Mam. We must all pull together. Please don't ask for tick right now, not until it's necessary. I don't want folk feeling sorry for us – any of us,' said Bryn, stoically.

Mam nodded and Mari had to agree. They were about to be the subject of further gossip; that much was for sure.

## 3

Realising their mother was a very proud woman, Mari knew how much all the gossip and speculation in the village regarding her father's whereabouts and behaviour would affect her. Mam wasn't the sort to stand gossiping on the doorstep.

'Tittle-tattle' was what Bryn called gossip, referring to such people as 'curtain twitchers'. Mari thought it amusing that none of the men in the village were ever referred to in such a manner. There was no 'nosy parker' reference to any of those men, oh no! Yet, they might just as easily be caught shooting off their mouths in the pub at night too. In fact, a lot of the gossip in the village seemed to stem either from something overheard at the pub or from one of several small shops in the local community.

Mari realised that Mrs Jones wasn't one to spread gossip herself, but of course, the woman had no say in how her customers conducted themselves, especially outside the shop. So, for the following few weeks, if there was any shopping that needed doing, Mari was despatched to fetch it to prevent Mam from being humiliated by those who wished to inject their poison and revel in her situation.

Thank goodness for Bryn still bringing in a weekly wage to the home. They could just about manage on his wages, though Mari had noticed her mother had begun to make several cutbacks with regards to the family finances. There was now no longer a proper midweek meal; instead they made do with something that might last several days and even be added to, such as a stew or a saucepan of cawl. On a Sunday there was no longer a fancy roast after chapel. Instead, Mam did wonders with meat offcuts from the butcher and the bones saved to boil up a broth afterwards.

Mam hadn't stopped going to chapel, as she felt able to face folk when she was surrounded by her family and her faith fortified her. Bryn would rise especially to escort Mam there, even following a night shift, fiercely proud as he took their mother by the arm. The pew the family usually sat in was towards the back of the chapel, so Mam didn't feel all eyes on her. But there had been one service where Reverend Isaiah Bevan had mentioned the evils of adultery and fornication. Mari had noticed her mother's colour rise as the minister spoke. Mam had shifted about uncomfortably in the pew as heads turned and several gazes were directed towards them. But then the organist had struck up a jubilant hymn that was sung by all, which placated Mari as it seemed to defuse the tension.

Mari had noticed Bryn had begun to make eyes at a pretty young woman called Glenda Harper. Glenda attended chapel with her parents twice a day on Sunday and had recently started attending a midweek Bible study group, which Bryn himself had been quick to sign up for. Mari had never seen her brother become so fired up about attending chapel, but it wasn't just that – there was something different about him since their father had abandoned the family. It was as though he'd realised he now had to become 'head of the home', growing more steadfast and taking care of them all. Bryn was shaping up into a fine young man and he took his family beneath his wing.

There was still no word though from Dad. Even Blodwyn's mother, Mrs Parry, hadn't heard anything from her daughter for a month, until one day she called to the house to let them know she'd received a letter. There were tears in her eyes as she spoke.

'Just as you've lost your husband, Mrs Evans, I've also lost my daughter! My only child. The pair have gone to London of all places! They might as well have gone to the flipping moon! Perhaps she'll never return to Merthyr Tydfil ever again! I tell you, she's had her head turned by that man of yours! She was such a good girl before she encountered him!'

'He's no man of mine!' shouted Mam, her eyes glittering now and her tone of voice savage. 'And your daughter is old enough to make her own decision, isn't she? And in fact, while you're at it, please don't deliver any more news to this door about your daughter and my husband, as he's now dead to me – as if he were buried six feet under in the cemetery!'

Mari, who had been eavesdropping behind the scullery door, gasped loudly. As much as she disliked her father's behaviour, she didn't want to be cut off from him altogether, though Bryn had said he didn't know what he'd do if he ever laid eyes on him again. Reverend Bevan had said there was only one who could mete out justice in this case and that was the Almighty himself. God would deal with the sinner in his own time and his own way, and the best scenario the family could hope for was if Gwynfor Evans finally came to his senses and returned home to his family, promising never to take up with that harlot, or indeed any harlot, ever again.

All fire and brimstone was Reverend Bevan as he reminded his congregation of the wrath of God.

\* \* \*

Days settled down very much into a pattern since Dad's departure – the family was coping after a fashion. Bryn's wages just about covered the rent and food bills. Though there were a couple of occasions when tick was needed from the corner shop, but it was while Mari was pegging out the washing on the line one morning that matters took a turn. She'd been feeling mighty pleased with herself as she stood back to admire her handiwork: several shirts and pinafores were merrily flapping around in the breeze. Mam would be satisfied with how she'd attended to the laundry, as instead of giving the clothes a quick swill in the old tin tub, she'd soaked all the light-coloured items in cold salted water overnight. It made it much easier to shift the food stains made by Tommy and Nerys the following day. Tommy's shirt had greasy gravy stains on the cuff of its sleeve, as he'd accidentally dipped it in his dinner plate trying to reach out for the salt cellar. Nerys's white pinafore had several grass stains from playing roly-poly down the hill with neighbouring children. And Bryn had requested a clean white shirt, as he was meeting Glenda at the Bible study class that evening.

*Yes*, Mari reminded herself, *I've done a good morning's work here!*

Mam was over at Mrs Griffiths's house, her only real confidante these days. Mari often wondered what the women spoke about, but she understood that her mother might have things she didn't want to share with her children. Being more of a family woman, she had few friends, though the friends she did have were solid gold. Mam wouldn't dream of telling everyone her business, but one person she did trust was Rhoswen Griffiths.

Bryn was now working a day shift and Tommy and Nerys were out playing somewhere, when there was a furious hammering at the front door. She hoped it wasn't that Blodwyn's mother come to cause trouble with further news of the pair's shenanigans. Wiping her damp hands on her pinafore, she made for the front door, to be met with the sombre face of Elwyn Roberts, foreman at the coal pit. His face was slaked with coal dust so that only the whites of his eyes and his ivory-coloured teeth were on show.

'Hello, Mr Roberts.' She angled her head to one side with curiosity, but she couldn't make out whether he was frowning beneath his sooty-looking face.

'Is your mother at home, *bach*?'

What did he want Mam for? 'No, Mr Roberts. She's gone to visit Mrs—'

'You must fetch her immediately. There's been another accident at the pit.' He fingered his shirt collar as though it were too tight for him.

Mari's heart began to pound profusely. 'Another explosion?' She blinked several times.

He shook his head. 'No, thankfully this accident is not as serious as that last one, but a few of the men have been buried in a roof collapse caused by a coal slip. At this point, there are no fatalities, but the men are working hard to rescue them, and someone's gone to fetch the doctor.'

'Bryn? Is he all right?' was all Mari managed to say.

'Aye, he's one of them what's buried. Be a good girl and run and tell your mother, will you, *bach*?'

She nodded, open-mouthed. Somehow, she was finding the man's words hard to take in. Was this a dream and she'd wake up at any moment? But no, it couldn't be; all that washing she'd done and hung out on the line this morning was real enough.

The foreman sighed. 'But impress on her the men are conscious for the moment and still alive, as we've spoken to them, and please stress the doctor is on his way,' the man said. 'Try not to worry her too much.'

Mari closed her mouth as she watched the man hobble away. Maybe he'd hurt himself too? Or was it just old age and maybe his legs were bad anyhow? He had a very peculiar gait.

An overwhelming urge to vomit hit Mari and she took a deep, composing breath to calm herself, steadying her countenance by gripping the wooden door. There was no use her becoming ill when she needed to tell her mother what had occurred as a matter of urgency.

Slamming the front door behind her and then lifting her skirts, she ran towards Mrs Griffiths's house. The woman only lived a couple of minutes away. She might have given Mr Roberts the address but maybe he had other wives and mothers to inform about the accident.

Almost out of breath, she tried to compose herself on the doorstep of the house, which was one of the ironworkers' cottages with one bedroom upstairs and one living room and a scullery down below. Despite the house being small, Mrs Griffiths always kept it immaculate, sweeping and washing her front doorstep every day, taking immense pride in her home.

Mari lifted her hand to rap the door knocker several times.

'Hang on, where's the fire?' she heard the woman call out on the way to open the door. Then it swung open.

'Is my mam still here with you, Mrs Griffiths?' Mari's mouth felt dry with apprehension, her tongue almost sticking to the roof of her mouth.

'Yes, come in, dear.' The woman opened the door wider to allow Mari access, but she was under the impression Mrs Griffiths was going to offer her some sort of hospitality in the form of a drink and maybe a piece of cake, which given the circumstances, she didn't want or need right now, though a drink would have been welcome.

'Mr Roberts, the foreman at the pit, just called saying there's been an accident. Our Bryn is buried beneath a coal slip...' She bit her lip.

Mrs Griffiths's eyes enlarged as she yelled out for Mam to come quickly. Her poor mother had probably been enjoying a natter and a cup of tea as she managed to relax for once, but now Mari was aware everything would change for her, for them all really.

* * *

Mam rose from the armchair she'd been seated in as Mari entered the cosy little living room. A fire was dancing merrily in the grate and what should have been a form of respite for her was now turned into a moment of horror as Mari related what the foreman had said to her. Mari could tell by the look on her mother's face how shocked she was by the news. She opened her mouth to say something and snapped it shut again.

'Now you've had a nasty shock, Mavis,' said Mrs Griffiths, 'but you need to get to the pit to find out what's happening.'

Mam nodded with a blank expression on her face. Mari laid her hand on her mother's arm. 'Mr Roberts said at the moment all the men are still alive as far as he knows, as they've been answering, so that's good, eh, Mam?'

Mam grabbed her daughter by the forearm. 'But where are Nerys and Tommy?' she asked, her eyes searching her daughter's for answers.

'They're out playing.'

'Then you go and find them and take them home with you. I'll head to the pit right away.'

'And I'll come with you, Mavis,' Mrs Griffiths said firmly as she whipped her shawl from a peg behind the living room door, wrapping it around her shoulders.

Mari would have preferred to accompany her mother to the pit but realised that Nerys and Tommy needed someone to stay with them. They'd have to be fed and taken care of, as who knew how long Mam would be gone for. And what about Dad? There was no way of letting him know what had happened to her brother. But there was no use wasting time thinking about him when it would be her younger brother and sister who needed her most. If she didn't get them home right away, there was always the chance that someone else might tell them what had happened and she didn't want that; she wanted to explain to them herself.

Shadowing her mother and Mrs Griffiths on her way back to the house, she could feel her heart in her mouth. A sense of urgency pursued them as they walked briskly along. Mari noticed a woman who had a young baby wrapped in a shawl, staring in the direction of the pit from her doorstep. Was she one of the wives whose husband was caught up in the accident too? There was a feeling of uncertainty in the air. Her mother kissed her forehead before she left, telling her she'd be back when she had some news.

Mari watched until both women became specks in the distance, all the while wondering how much more the family would have to endure.

* * *

Mam returned home four hours later, and during that time her mother had been away, Mari's mind had been in turmoil wondering what had happened to Bryn. She'd managed to placate her younger brother and sister by playing the situation down. When Mam explained that Bryn had been rescued but was in good spirits, she felt a sense of relief wash over her. Her mother said he'd been examined by the doctor who'd informed them he'd experienced a crush injury to one of his feet and had injured several ribs. Other than that, though, he was fully conscious and able to make conversation with the doctor. But that meant there'd be no work for him for some time. He'd be laid off work for months. But at least he still had his life intact. Five other men had also been rescued with similar injuries but one, unfortunately, who was older than the rest, hadn't been so lucky. It made Mari realise how fortunate Bryn had been to survive that pit fall.

Mam had come home to prepare things ready for Bryn's arrival. Once the men had been examined by the doctor, provisions were made to transport them to their houses. A couple of local men who owned horse and carts had offered their services.

Darkness had fallen by the time Dai Brewster brought Bryn home, helping him into the house with the aid of his son, Bobby. Bobby was only a year or so older than Mari and he smiled with recognition when he saw her.

'Oh, thank you so much, Mr Brewster!' Mam enthused as she went to move a wooden stool out of their path, directing them over to the armchair closest to the fireplace, the one that had been their father's favourite.

Mari could tell, by the way Bryn was wincing, that he was in a lot of pain.

'Sit down now, Bryn,' said Mam softly as she watched him partly hop over to the armchair after being released by Dai and Bobby. Once he'd heaved himself down, Bryn closed his eyes and gasped.

'Are you all right?' asked Mari.

Bryn's eyes flicked open, the whites seeming whiter than usual as his face was still slicked with coal dust. 'I'll live, I suppose!' He gave a wry chuckle. 'My ribs hurt like merry hell though!'

Dai Brewster passed a brown bottle with a cork stopper in the top over to Mam. 'Give him some of this,' he instructed.

Mam frowned. 'What is it?'

'Something medicinal, of course!' he said, winking at Bryn.

'Oh?' Mam's eyes rounded like two saucers as Dai chuckled.

'It's all right, it's only a drop of whisky. Jack from the pub used to be a miner and he got some bottles filled for the injured.'

'That was good of him.' Mam smiled.

'Aye, well, he knows what it's like as he was buried under a fall of coal himself after that first pit explosion.'

'He'd know full well then,' said Mam. 'But if the pain gets too much, I can always ask the doctor for some laudanum for you, Bryn?'

Bryn shook his head as he held up a palm. 'No, Mam. Medicine like that costs a lot of money that we don't have. I'll make do with this for the time being.'

'Very well, you know best. Now I expect you're starving after all of that?'

'I am a bit peckish, aye.'

Then looking at Dai and his son, she added, 'You two, too?'

Bobby nodded enthusiastically, but then his father waved a hand. 'Thank you very much for the offer, Mrs Evans, but the wife will have something waiting for us back home. Speaking of which, we'd better get back. Your Bryn was the last trip of the day for us.'

'Let me show you out then,' said Mam.

Mari wondered if Dai Brewster was only saying that because he realised they were on their uppers and didn't want to take any food from their mouths.

Mam escorted them to the door and Mari heard her thanking

them both, then she closed it behind them and returned to the hearth.

'That was nice of them, don't you think?' Mam said, fixing her gaze on Bryn, but he was busy staring into the flames of the fire.

Mari wondered what her brother was thinking.

* * *

When Mam had given Bryn a bowl of stew to eat with a crust of buttered bread, she handed him a cup of tea. 'I've put some sugar in it for the shock,' she said.

Bryn grimaced. 'You know I don't like sugar in my tea, Mam,' he moaned.

'Just drink it on this occasion. You've had a bad outing today. Then you can tell us what happened.'

He nodded soberly, taking a sip from his cup, then set it down in the fire grate as he let out a long sigh. Blinking, he began, 'Me and the lads, we'd started working on a new coal seam. Hacking away at it with our pickaxes. It had been quite a good shift, and most of us were happy enough singing along, "Calon Lan" and songs like that. Some good voices the men have...'

For a moment, Mari thought her brother would go off-track and wander from what happened that afternoon, but then he seemed to jolt back to the present moment.

'Then, for a while, it went silent, totally silent. And maybe that was just as well as Emrys Morris from down the village, suddenly said, "Hey, what's that?" Well, I couldn't hear much to begin with but then I heard a creaking sound and then something splitting. Turned out it was coming from above. The timber was giving way. One or two men managed to escape it, but most of us felt the rock and coal come crashing on top of us. I tell you I thought I was going to die...'

Mari closed her eyes as if to block out the image. She didn't like to think of that happening to Bryn and the other men. The most recent explosion wasn't all that far away in everyone's minds and what a horror that had been, but lessons had been learned, supposedly, as it had transpired that the explosion was caused by neglecting to follow safety precautions.

Bryn lifted his head to look at his mother and sister, then he shook it. 'I'll never forget that sickening sound. There was this sort of low rumble that got louder and louder, then we were buried beneath a mountain of rock and coal... It all happened so fast; I didn't even have time to panic. All was deathly silent for a while, just like before Emrys heard the timber split above us.' He swallowed hard.

'What happened to the other men?' Mam asked.

'Most were rescued like me,' said Bryn, 'but when I got taken up from underground and onto the surface, I heard word that Emrys, his brother Jim, and a young lad who had just started work at the pit, not more than a week ago, were still buried. And just before I got taken home, I heard someone say that old fella, Albert Barker, hadn't made it; they'd just recovered his body, poor dab.'

Mari gasped. She hadn't been expecting her brother to say that. Things were even worse than she realised.

'Well,' said Mam stoically after a while, 'we'll pray they all get out alive. That poor young lad's parents, I can't imagine what they're going through.' Then quite spontaneously she stooped to plant a kiss on Bryn's cheek.

'Aye, I'm one of the lucky ones I suppose, and Dad.'

'What on earth do you mean?' Mam was frowning now.

'If you think about it, Mam, if he hadn't run off with that hussy, he'd have been working alongside me this week.'

A shiver coursed down Mari's spine; she hadn't even considered that. Maybe her father would have been buried too and who knew if he'd have got out of there alive.

Mam shook her head and sniffed. 'If stood stiff in a blind man's pocket!' she said tersely.

And when she had left the room, Bryn turned to his sister and said, 'I think she means how can we possibly know whether something would have happened to him or not. She's still very angry with him for leaving us.'

Mari nodded, knowing her brother was right.

## 4

Mari knew it wasn't going to be easy with Bryn being laid off from work, but it was even harder than anyone imagined. It turned out that her brother needed more than a drop of whisky to take away the pain. The following day, he endured the most excruciating agony he said he'd ever felt in his life. Mari was sent to fetch the doctor who sold Mam a bottle of laudanum with instructions for it to be used sparingly as, the doctor explained, sometimes people became too accustomed to it. The main source of pain was in Bryn's foot, but from time to time if he sat awkwardly or rolled over in bed, his fractured ribs gave him hell too.

Mam, even with all she had to do caring for Bryn and the rest of the family, had taken in washing for folk, which made Mari feel extremely guilty and helpless. It seemed, as a young girl, there was not a lot she could offer other than to help Mam around the house and to assist with the washing work when she could. And that was only washing and scrubbing, drying and ironing – all for a few pennies a week. No, what she needed to do was look for some work herself. She decided that she'd call to see Mrs Jones at the shop to ask if she needed any assistance.

Mrs Jones shook her head as she bit her lower lip. 'I'm sorry, Mari. I can't afford to pay anyone to help me here at the moment, though I could do with the help, I suppose,' said the woman as she stroked her chin.

'Oh, very well then.' Mari shrugged, then something occurred to her. 'How about I help you now and then for a loaf of bread or a few eggs?' she asked hopefully.

'Now, that I could manage.' Mrs Jones smiled. 'I tell you what, my busiest times are in the afternoons, when I'm feeling worn out. It's then they all seem to crowd in here. How about you come in at two o'clock every afternoon for an hour or two, so then I can put my feet up in the back room with a cuppa knowing I won't be disturbed by anyone. And maybe the odd morning where necessary?'

Mari smiled. 'I think I can manage that,' she said, pleased with herself. It would be something at least.

* * *

The following afternoon, Mari turned up at the shop just before two o'clock.

'I've been rushed off my feet,' Mrs Jones said, smiling, pleased to see her, as she sprang from behind the counter. She pointed at a group of women gossiping in front of them. 'Mrs Williams can't make up her mind what to buy her husband for his tea today and Mrs Price keeps putting her off everything she finally chooses!' She chuckled. 'Now, I've already shown you what to do and where everything is, so go into the back room and put on a pinny, then you can relieve me.'

Mari nodded, her stomach flipping over as she looked at the group of five women whom, if she was telling the truth, she wouldn't like to cross swords with. In the event, by the time Mrs Jones was sipping her well-earned cuppa in the back room, Mari had sorted the women out by making several suggestions – going by what her mother might have chosen when they had more money to live off. She had worried in case any of the women asked about her father, but during those two hours, only one had enquired and, even then, the woman had been most sympathetic, not gossipy at all.

Maybe the lack of venom was because her brother had been injured, and most would have realised this, knowing not to add further fuel to the fire. How lucky he'd been though, as now they'd learned the fate of the remaining men in the pit. A young lad had been found dead beneath the fall of coal with barely a mark on him, suffocated, and the person who had alerted everyone to the incident, Emrys, was also found dead. Fortunately, Emrys's brother Jim, who had worked on the seam just a few feet away, had been found alive but his leg bone was shattered in a few places, a far worse injury than Bryn's by all accounts.

Mari ended up working at the shop for two and a half hours in total. After her tea break, Mrs Jones had been able to restock the shelves and sort out the stockroom. A job she'd been meaning to get around to for ages.

'Why, you are such a godsend, Mari!' said the woman as she handed over a loaf of bread, two eggs and a jar of home-made jam she'd made herself. 'I don't think you'd better come here every day though, as I can't keep giving you my stock.'

Mari felt her heart sink to her boots. The woman was probably right, as this shop was her livelihood. She'd been widowed a few years ago and, probably while still living fairly comfortably in her old age, had to work long hours to see the benefit.

Then as if to ease things, she added, 'But you could do this for me once a week, maybe? With the same terms and conditions applying!'

Mari frowned. What did Mrs Jones mean by that?

'I'll give you a few provisions but only once a week, otherwise I'll go bankrupt!'

Mari chuckled. 'Thank you, Mrs Jones.'

'No problem, *cariad*. I'll just fetch my wicker basket for you to take those home in.'

\* \* \*

When Mari arrived home, feeling accomplished with her work for the day, her mother was not best pleased. 'The shop?' she said with her hands on her hips. 'Why humiliate me further with handouts from that hive of gossip! Now everyone in the village will know how hard up we are since your father left!'

Painful tears pricked the backs of Mari's eyes. 'I was only trying to help,' she said as she swallowed down a sob and placed the basket on the table. 'I didn't get these for nothing; they're not on tick. Mrs Jones gave them to me for helping her. There's a loaf of bread here, some eggs and a pot of strawberry jam she made herself.'

Mam's eyes softened. 'I'm sorry,' she said, placing a hand on her daughter's shoulder. 'I shouldn't have snapped at you like that. It's just all I'm doing here is getting me down. If I ever see your father again, I swear I'll swing for him after what he's put me through.' Then, watching as a tear slipped down her daughter's cheek, she added, 'In fact what he's put us *all* through.'

\* \* \*

Despite her mother's initial upset about her being at the shop, Mari continued to assist there, being a great help to Mrs Jones who wasn't getting any younger, but she realised the family needed more money to sustain them all. A loaf of bread and other things from the shop were welcome, of course, but they didn't last longer than a day or so.

It was while she pondered the situation that what her brother had said came to mind, *'Pity they no longer take young girls underground. Our Mari could pass for a boy if she cut her hair and wore a flat cap!'*

The more she considered it, the more she realised it might work. There was an old flat cap belonging to her father in the drawer upstairs; she could use that. He'd left a lot of his stuff behind when he went off with his fancy piece. But where could she get some boys' clothing from? Tommy's clothing wouldn't fit her, and neither would Bryn's. Then she had a thought: that boy of Dai Brewster's, Bobby, he wasn't far off her age and around the same height as her. She might ask him. Yes, that's what she'd do.

She set off for the village with extreme purpose with every step she took. What was the worst thing that might happen? There was no harm in asking. Bobby might always say 'no'. And even if he didn't want to help her, she'd find a way to get that clothing.

When she arrived on the long street that mirrored the houses opposite, all was quiet except for a couple of children playing with a kitten at one end and a man with a horse and cart at the other, who appeared to be loading the cart up with several wooden crates. She was relieved that he wasn't paying her any attention, so absorbed in the task at hand was he. And the children seemed besotted with their playmate.

Now which number was the house? Was it number 15 or 16? She couldn't quite remember. Her father had brought her here once to visit Dai Brewster when he was off sick from the pit. She couldn't recall what had happened to him exactly but what she did remember was his leg had been elevated on a wooden stool and there'd been talk of a possible amputation. She hadn't understood at the time what the word meant, but now being that much older she did and had been relieved that word hadn't been mentioned in Bryn's case. In the event, someone up above must have been watching over Dai, as the man's foot had healed very well with no need for the doctor to amputate at all. Her mother had put it down to the prayers from the congregation at chapel as, that very same morning, he said he'd felt a warmth in his leg and there was no further pain afterwards. A miracle, her mother had described it as. No wonder the man had been so keen to loan his services recently to those injured in that fall at the pit. Apparently, he'd been one of the first on the scene.

She was still unsure whether it was the house with the pristine-looking white lace curtains or the house next door with the shabby scuffed door. She decided to knock on the posh door first but there was no answer, so she tried rapping the knocker of the other and it opened wide. A small woman stood before her, short in stature, who was around her mother's age.

'Are you Mari Evans?' asked the woman, and Mari nodded. '*Duw, duw*, but you've grown so tall since I last set eyes on you, my lovely!'

There was something familiar about the woman, but Mari wasn't sure if she was Dai's wife or not, so she smiled and asked, 'Is your Bobby in, please?'

Then she felt a sense of relief wash over her as the woman smiled and nodded, she had chosen the right house after all. 'No, he's not arrived back home yet. He's gone out on the cart with his father to Merthyr market. We've got an allotment now, you see. So they've taken some vegetables with a view to selling them on the outdoor market today. How's your brother since the accident?'

Mari huffed out a breath. 'Oh, he's doing well, thank you, Mrs Brewster. Gets a bit impatient from the pain sometimes and frustrated from not being able to work.'

The woman chewed her bottom lip. 'Must be hard though with your, er, father not being around?'

Mari nodded and, to her horror, she felt tears sting her eyes. Usually, she managed to keep her emotions in check, but Mrs Brewster was being so nice to her that the floodgates were starting to open.

Noticing her distress, the woman said, 'Come inside, dear. Bobby won't be long; we can have a cup of tea together and you can tell me all about it.'

Mari nodded gratefully, stepping over the threshold inside the house, which didn't look as shabby inside as it did outside. The interior was warm and cosy with a fire blazing in the grate. In the middle of the room was a table set out for three people, knives and forks, empty plates and cups and saucers, as though expecting the arrival of the menfolk at any moment.

'I've not long brewed up, so I'll fetch you a cup of tea. Sugar?'

Mari nodded. Usually, she went without it – they had to these days as it was expensive and since Dad had gone it was one cutback they could all cope with – but a cup of sugared tea would be a comfort for her right now.

'Have a sit-down by the fireside and I'll fetch you one. It's bitterly cold out there today. You look like you need warming up.'

When the woman had left the room, Mari flexed her blue fingers in front of the golden glow of the fire, and then she gazed around the room. On the windowsill was an oil lamp, on the mantelpiece were a couple of candles in holders, and on the walls several paintings of religious scenes. One was of Jesus holding a shepherd's crook in one arm and a baby lamb in the other. Mari decided she liked that painting as it looked like Jesus took care of even the smallest and most vulnerable in this world. Then she remembered the story she'd once been told at Sunday school where there was a shepherd who went to look for his missing sheep and he didn't give up looking until he found it. She recalled the Bible verse that said: *What man of you, having an hundred sheep, if he lose one of them, doth not leave the ninety and nine in the wilderness, and go after that which is lost, until he find it?*

For some reason that biblical parable had stuck in her mind. Miss Sampson, who had been her Sunday school teacher at that time, had asked her class to learn a Bible verse to read out during the full chapel service the following Sunday. Some of the children had forgotten all about it while some others had difficulty remembering theirs. But Mari had taken that verse, and as well as remembering it had meditated on it in her mind. What she'd loved most about it was how afterwards Jesus had said that once the lost sheep was found there would be rejoicing. Maybe that's what her father was at the moment: a lost sheep.

Mrs Brewster returned with a welcome cup of tea with a biscuit in the saucer and handed it to her. 'I won't have one myself as it's so near to our teatime now.' She smiled. 'I expect the menfolk will be ravenous.'

Mari nodded and smiled tentatively as she accepted the cup from the woman's outstretched hand. 'I'd better leave then after I've drunk this,' she said, fearing she was holding the woman up.

'Oh, don't be so silly now, you.' Mrs Brewster chuckled softly. 'You can stay and have a word with Bobby. It won't harm us to eat a few minutes later. It's only a beef stew I've prepared, so it won't spoil. Now then, tell me what's been upsetting you...' She took a seat near the hearth opposite Mari and settled herself down to listen.

Mari told her all that had happened with her father leaving home for *that woman*, Blodwyn. Mrs Brewster nodded sympathetically in all the right places and then Mari realised that the woman would have known all of this anyhow, as Dai had worked with her father and known he'd left his job to go off with her. Feeling silly now, she added, 'We just didn't see it coming at all.' Her eyes began to blur with unshed tears.

'But maybe your mam did though, lovely? Us women have a kind of intuition about these sorts of things when our menfolk aren't behaving themselves. It's happened to several around here, let me tell you. They're not always upfront about it either – some don't tell anyone at all but it's more commonplace than you think. Not necessarily running off with the woman in question like your dad has, mind you. But often they'll have someone else's arms to comfort them, spinning that fancy woman the age-old yarn of "My missus doesn't understand me!" The trouble is their missus usually understands them all too well and doesn't want to put up with their shenanigans any longer!' She chuckled and then sighed deeply. 'Sorry, Mari, you don't want to be hearing any of my ramblings, it's not helping you.'

'Oh, it is, Mrs Brewster, believe me, it really is. I didn't think this kind of thing happened to anyone else's family. It makes me feel heaps better that it's happening to others too, though of course I wouldn't wish it on anyone.'

'I know you wouldn't, dear. Now eat up your biscuit and drink your tea before it gets cold.'

Mari did as told, and after a little more conversation, both their heads turned towards the front door as it clicked open and Dai Brewster emerged with Bobby in tow.

'What have you two been up to then?' The woman laughed. 'You're later than usual.'

Dai beamed. 'Had a bit of good fortune.' He winked at his

wife, then seeing Mari by the fire he nodded at her. 'And to what do we owe the honour of this visit, young lady?'

Mari set her cup and saucer down on a low table beside her. 'I've come to see Bobby,' she said, smiling tentatively, all the while wondering now if it was such a good idea as all that.

'Well, don't keep the lady waiting,' boomed Dai to his son. 'Go and have a word with her in the scullery if you like, while I put my feet up by the fire!'

Mrs Brewster laughed again, offering her husband her seat, and Bobby approached Mari. If he was surprised she'd paid him a visit, he wasn't showing it. She watched as he removed his flat cap and jacket and hung them on a peg behind the front door. 'This way,' he said, leading her towards the scullery.

When they got there, he closed the door behind them, while in the distance Mari heard Dai relating some sort of tale to his wife, sounding well pleased with himself.

'What's happened?' She fixed her gaze on Bobby.

'It's Dad. He's happy 'cause he's struck a deal with a stall-holder who wishes to trade with us on a regular basis. He's got a vegetable stall on the market, and we can supply him with what he needs. His old supplier is no longer trading with him, so Dad asked at the right time.'

'That's good news.' Mari smiled, feeling really pleased for the family.

'So, what made you call to see me?' asked Bobby as though it were the last thing on earth he was expecting.

Mari explained about the idea of her dressing as a boy to try to get a job working underground.

There was a long silence, then Bobby said, 'It's tough, back-breaking work, but I suppose you already know that. It's illegal for girls and women to work underground. Now they can only work on the surface since that law was passed.'

'I know all that,' said Mari eagerly. 'I only want to do it to tide us over until Bryn gets back on his feet.'

'What does he think of your plan?'

'It was his idea!'

Bobby's eyes widened and he blinked in disbelief. 'Really?' he said in a scornful manner.

'Well, not exactly, he said it more in jest one day – about how he thought I could cut my hair and wear a flat cap and pass as a boy underground. He doesn't know that's what I'm planning to do though.'

Bobby sucked in a breath as he shook his head. 'I don't know, Mari. I wouldn't want to think of you getting hurt nor breathing in all that coal dust. That's why I'm glad Dad is thinking of leaving the pit to make a go of this market garden thing, to supply the marketplace with vegetables. It'll be my turn to go underground soon, but he said he doesn't want that for me; he wants me to be a scholar. Mr Inman, my teacher, thinks I might do well and go to college someday. Right now, that's only a dream though.'

Mari nodded. 'Well, I hope your dream comes true for you. Meanwhile, do you have any old clothing to spare? To make me look like a boy?'

'I daresay I do, but you'd better not tell Mam and Dad, as they'll try to stop you. I'm not happy with helping you myself, but I can tell what a determined young lady you are!' He chuckled. Mari caught his eye and laughed too. She'd always liked Bobby, ever since that time she'd fallen in the playground at school and he'd helped her to her feet. They'd been very young back then, but he'd always had a caring nature and that's what she liked most about him.

Bobby gesticulated with his hand. 'Come through to the backyard for a moment, will you?'

Mari followed him through the door and outside to the back-yard where an old metal bathtub was hanging on a hook from a brick wall. Most of the floor was flagstoned apart from one part of the yard that was surrounded by a circle of stones – and inside that circle was a pile of earth. As if realising that Mari might be curious about this, Bobby explained it was a small area his father had set up for his mother as she planned to grow roses there.

He headed towards a wooden shed and, opening the door, said, 'There are some old work clothes in here you can have. I've outgrown them. Mam was going to tear them up and use them as rags but I'm sure she won't mind you having them if she asks where they've disappeared to.' He gave a wry chuckle. 'Don't worry, I won't tell her what they're for, at least not for the time being.'

Mari smiled surreptitiously at him. 'Yes, best not say anything to anyone for now.'

'How are you going to explain to your mother, though, where you're disappearing to, Mari?'

'I've thought of that,' she said, feeling quite pleased with herself. 'I've been helping out Mrs Jones at the shop this past couple of weeks. I'll tell Mam she's unwell and needs more help – that's if my plan works, of course. Fortunately, the shop is open all hours, so it won't look odd even if I must go to work very early in the morning or late at night. Won't be able to manage a night shift though.'

'Something that's just occurred to me...' Bobby rubbed his chin. 'You can't leave home wearing that clobber, can you? You'll have to find somewhere to change before and after your shift.'

That was true. She honestly hadn't even considered that. 'Oh, what can I do? I'll need to find somewhere to keep the clothes dry.'

Bobby's eyes lit up and he held up his index finger. 'I have it! This shed is always unlocked anyhow as there's nothing of value in it. You can change in here. I'll just make sure the back gate is unbolted for you at the beginning and end of your shift. That's if you get a job that is. Here.' He handed the clothing to her. 'Get changed in there and I'll let you know how convincing you are.'

She nodded and did as told, ensuring the shed door was closed so he might not glimpse her partially clothed. There was a rough twill shirt, a pair of thick breeches, a flat cap and a well-patched jacket.

She giggled to herself as she put them on. The jacket was a little large for her frame, but she figured she could roll up the sleeves, and the rest of it fitted well enough.

'Ready?' prompted Bobby.

Mari emerged from the shed and did a little twirl.

'Well, I'd never have recognised you! I do reckon you might pass for a boy after all, but you'll have to do something about that hair, as it's tumbling down onto your shoulders. You'll have to get it cut!' Mari nodded. 'Hmmm,' said Bobby, 'and if you did that, your mother would ask questions, I'm sure. Maybe if you got some hair grips and clipped it up underneath your cap – you'd have to always keep it on during the shift though.'

That was something she hadn't considered. 'That might be a problem...'

'Or you could pretend to have nits and ask your mother to cut it short for you! That happened to my cousin once. She was lousy with them, picked them up from school. Her mother tried all ways to get rid of them: vinegar, using a fine-tooth comb, the lot! In the end, the only way she got rid of them was to cut Maisie's hair real short like a boy's.'

'Don't know if I'd fancy that much!'

'But it will grow back and, like you said, it's only until Bryn gets back on his feet.'

'I suppose.' The thought of all of this was making her insides churn up.

'Another thing, you'll need a stout pair of working boots if you don't want your feet to get injured.'

'I hadn't thought about that.' She looked at him hopefully.

'That I can't help you with, but you could try the pawn shop in town or there's a stall that sells second-hand ones on the outdoor market. You could save your wages from the shop to buy a pair.'

Mari recalled that stall. It was loaded with a jumble of old shoes and boots that folk had sold to the stallholder and people were often seen trying on the shoes beside the stall. Her own mother had even bought a pair of leather ankle boots for herself there once, which seemed good quality and hardly worn. Mam reckoned they were after some toff lady from one of the big houses in the town who had more money than sense.

'Mrs Jones can't afford to pay me with wages. She just gives me stuff like eggs or a loaf of bread,' said Mari sadly, shaking her head.

'Don't lose heart. What size do you take?'

'I'm not really sure. My ankle boots are getting a bit tight though. I suppose at a push I could wear these?' She held up one of the leather boots she'd been wearing.

'Oh no!' Bobby yelled. 'Those would give away you're a girl for sure; besides, they've got a small heel, you might trip in those underground. They'd be a safety hazard for you.'

Her plan to help the family now seemed to be drifting away from her.

Then Bobby's eyes lit up. 'I'll ask my friends if they've got any old boots knocking around that have gone too small for them.'

Mari forced a smile, but she couldn't imagine that any of their mothers could afford to give anything away for free. In these parts, old footwear was either passed on in the form of hand-me-downs to younger siblings or to other family members or sold on somewhere. An odd penny here or there might be the difference between the family eating a meal that day or going without. Many a woman in Merthyr Tydfil would sell the clothes off her back rather than see her kids go hungry.

* * *

It was a full five days later before Bobby turned up at Mari's house with a bulky newspaper package beneath his arm.

'What have you got there, Bobby?' Mrs Evans asked.

Mari noticed Bobby's face flush pink. 'A little gift for a neighbour Dad asked me to pass on.'

'Oh?' said Mam as though expecting some sort of clarification.

'Something what horses drop in the middle of the road!' He chuckled. 'Our horse, Glyn, produces enough of the stuff and Mr Smith said it will help his roses!'

The penny still hadn't dropped for Mari, and she thought it quite disgusting that Bobby would call for her while he was holding on to something like that.

Mam bade them farewell as she closed the door behind the pair. Mari was just about to give Bobby a ticking-off when he burst out laughing. 'You really think it's horse manure, don't you?'

Slowly, she nodded.

He laid down the newspaper package on the cobbles and, when he unwrapped it, she saw to her delight that it was a pair of work boots.

'Oh, my goodness!' She giggled. 'But how did you come by those? You didn't steal them, did you?'

Bobby retrieved the newspaper and the boots and then standing, looking quite affronted, said, 'No. I most certainly did not. I actually paid for them!'

Mari's hand flew to her face. 'Oh, Bobby, I'm so sorry. It's just I thought we had no chance of getting a pair, so I assumed maybe you'd have whipped them from that market stall you mentioned.'

'As if I'd do something like that!' he said, vehemently shaking his head. 'I'd never steal anyhow, but particularly not from market traders. After all, we're now one of them.'

'So, how did you come by the boots, then?' she asked, raising her brows.

'Like I said, I paid for them. I was helping Dad at the stall and noticed them. I didn't have quite enough money on me at the time, but the stallholder, knowing my father, said I can pay half now and half next week.'

Mari pursed her lips. 'But won't the man tell your father?'

'I doubt it. The stall's nowhere near ours in any case and I told him I was buying it for...' – he changed his voice to an affected tone – '...me poor younger brother Albie, who has to go down the pit soon...'

Mari grinned and, knowing full well that Bobby didn't have any brothers or sisters, said, 'Thank you, Bobby.' And quite spontaneously, she planted a kiss on his cheek. 'I won't be able to pay you back for some time though, not until I get paid – that's if I get a job in the first place.'

'No need for that. These are a gift from me to you!' She noticed his face flush again. Then it took on a solemn expression. 'But let's see if these fit you first. We'd better get away from here in case your mother comes out on the step and catches us. We'll go and find a rock you can sit on down by the river so you can try them on.'

Mam had told her to keep away from the river because of the cholera outbreak, but she thought it wouldn't matter on this occasion as she had no desire to go and paddle in it as she usually did; it was far too cold. So, quite happily, she followed her benefactor to the riverbank and, selecting a large rock, perched on it, removing her ankle boots. She slipped on the work boots. 'They're a bit loose,' she said, grimacing.

'That's all right. Look, you need to tighten the laces.' He knelt and deftly tightened them for her, drawing the laces closely together and then firmly tying a knot on each one. 'Now step down on the bank there and try walking in them.'

She did as instructed. 'That's a lot better.' She smiled. 'They're still a bit big though.'

'Well, never mind too much about that,' said Bobby, standing. 'We can always stuff them with bits of this newspaper I brought them in.'

Mari nodded enthusiastically, relieved that Bobby seemed to think of everything.

'I'll take them home with me and hide them in the shed,' Bobby said. 'I'd better find you a pair of thick socks too from somewhere. I have a few pairs Mam knitted for me.'

'Won't she notice if any go missing though?'

'Oh, I hadn't thought of that.'

'There are a few pairs Dad left behind I can put in your shed. No doubt they'll need changing if I'm underground.'

'Yes, my father said it can get very wet and damp along some underground coal seams, as the ground gets a bit waterlogged and even flooded at times. I'm so glad he's out of that place though after his accident.' Bobby's face clouded over for a moment, then he bit his lip. 'I hope you take care of yourself; wouldn't want you getting in no accidents, *cariad*.'

Mari gasped. He'd called her 'cariad', the Welsh word for darling or sweetheart. He'd never called her that before. Is that how he really saw her? As his sweetheart? It made her feel all warm and cosy inside.

# 5

Mari was in the middle of balancing on an old wooden stepladder, replacing a jar of mixed boiled sweets on the shelf behind the counter, when Mrs Thomas summoned her. Marguerite Thomas seemed to think herself above most in the village apart from Mrs Hazel Davenport, who lived in the large house on the canal bank, which overshadowed and looked down on all the mineworkers' cottages.

Becoming aware of being watched, Mari turned red-faced to fix her gaze on the woman, who was standing at the head of the queue with her wicker basket hooked over the crook of her arm, her ruby lips pursed. There was no threadbare, well-worn woollen shawl draped around her shoulders like the rest of the women – oh no, she wore a velvet cape. Mari guessed it was a cast-off from Mrs Davenport's own wardrobe as Mrs Thomas was a housekeeper at the residence. It was probably one of the perks of her job that she wanted to show off to folk. The problem was that didn't exactly ingratiate her towards her friends and neighbours – if anything it set her apart from them.

Mari descended the ladder and then forced a smile. In truth, she wasn't all that keen on the woman; she disliked the fact she thought she was better than anyone else in Abercanaid, barring Mr and Mrs Davenport, of course. Mrs Jones had told her once that her real name wasn't Marguerite anyhow, it was simply Margaret, but she'd tarted it up to appear exotic. That story had made her smile. She'd even gone home and related the tale to Mam, who had laughed uproariously at the woman's pomposity.

Mrs Jones had chosen this time of all times to leave the shop and now Mari was left alone to deal with the woman and a host of impatient customers. This wasn't going to be easy.

'Where's Mrs Jones this morning?' Marguerite demanded.

'She's nipped out somewhere for a few minutes, Mrs Thomas.'

The woman snorted and made a sound that was akin to a *harrumph!* Then she rolled her eyes. 'Well, how long will she be?'

'I'm sorry, I can't exactly say.'

'Don't you know when she'll be back or where she's gone?'

Mari shook her head.

'A right state of affairs.' She turned towards the women behind her, who were all now listening with avid interest. 'I tell you, leaving a chit of a young girl here to run the shop! And from that Evans family too; why, she's no more than an imbecile!'

Mari felt her hackles begin to rise. The woman could have a go at her but to have a pop at her family just wasn't right. She lifted her head to make eye contact. 'And what does my family have to do with my work here, Mrs Thomas?' She realised her voice sounded shaky, but it needed to be said.

'That father of yours for a start, he's a no-good womaniser!' she said as she crossed her hands and sniffed loudly as though there was the whiff of something unpleasant beneath her nostrils.

Mari became aware of the gasps of the other women in the shop as they realised Mrs Thomas was overstepping the mark.

'Come along now, Marguerite,' said one of them, 'it's hardly the girl's fault, is it?'

'He's a heathen...' she carried on. 'Not fit to raise his head in this community ever again! Taking up with a trollop like that!'

A lump formed in Mari's throat as tears sprang to her eyes, but she didn't want to give the woman the satisfaction of seeing her cry.

Gritting her teeth, Mari emerged from behind the counter, not quite as tall as the woman but not that far off her height. Poking her in the chest with her index finger, she said, 'I don't know what my family has to do with you, you old trout!'

There was a loud gasp from one of the women and Mari watched as Mrs Thomas's eyes enlarged, not quite believing how Mari was behaving towards her.

'Go on! What do you have to say about the rest of my family then?' she said, invading the woman's space even further, forcing Marguerite to take a step back. 'That my mother's a poor washer-woman? Or that my brother Bryn has a gammy foot? Or what about Nerys and Tommy? My younger sister and brother. What do you have to say about them? And for that matter, what about me? That I look like a street urchin? You. Stuck. Up. Snotty. Nosed. Old. Cow!'

Mrs Thomas opened her mouth as though about to say something and then snapped it shut again. A deadly hush descended on the small congregation and Mari, realising she might have gone too far, watched as the woman suddenly turned her back on her and marched quickly through the crowd that parted like the Red Sea to allow her to get to the door. All was silent until there was a little tinkle as the door slammed shut behind her.

Oh no, she was for it now! Those women would probably lynch her, but to her surprise she heard someone clap their hands, then another and another, until one of them yelled, 'Well done, Mari! That stuck-up mare has had it coming for some time! She picked on the wrong one when she chose to have a go at you!'

Mari didn't quite know whether to laugh or cry but then the door tinkled again and, fearing the woman had returned, she held her breath in anticipation. But seeing who it was, she breathed out a sigh of relief.

'What's been going on here?' Mrs Jones asked, her eyes glittering with amusement as she noticed that some of the women were patting Mari on the back.

'You've missed all the drama, Gladys!' Mrs O'Flaherty laughed. 'This girl of yours here is real feisty and not to be messed with! She's just put old snotty drawers, Marguerite, in her place!'

Mrs Jones chuckled. 'Not a moment too soon if you ask me. Well done, Mari! But better ensure it doesn't happen again, as the old saying goes, "The customer is always right."'

Mari noticed that the woman had a twinkle in her eyes and was only half serious about the situation.

She realised full well that it had been the emotion of the confrontation and the mention of her family that had put her back up like that. She was going to have to keep her temper in check though and bite her tongue in future, if she possibly could, that was.

* * *

It was a good half an hour or so before things calmed down after that and when the final customer had been served, Mrs Jones locked the door.

'I don't usually do this,' she said, 'but it's been a temperamental time for you – the way that woman spoke to you this morning, insulting your family like that. She thinks she's a cut above, that one. Just because Mrs Davenport's husband's the manager at the coal mine and he's rumoured to have shares in it. She acts like the Davenports are royalty! Always boasting about that large monkey puzzle tree they have in front of the house!' Mrs Jones shook her head.

Mari frowned. 'Huh?'

'Monkey puzzle trees are a sign of wealth. Several well-off people in the town have them in their gardens.'

'Oh, I see,' said Mari.

'Let's have a cuppa for ten minutes in the back room,' Mrs Jones said, shooting Mari a surreptitious grin as though the pair were about to do something naughty, and in a way they were. Mrs Jones never shut the shop unless she had to. Before Mari had arrived, she'd been at the beck and call of her customers all day long from morning until night.

As Mrs Jones went off to brew up, Mari noticed a large pair of scissors discarded on the counter. The woman had probably used that to cut open a couple of flour sacks that had been tightly tied with twine. Now if she could sneak that out and cut her hair, that would make life easier for her when she went to ask for a job at the coal pit.

## 6

'What on earth have you done to your beautiful long hair?' Mam had her by the shoulders and was forcibly shaking her, while tears streamed down Mari's face. It felt as though a lump was blocking her throat, preventing her from speaking or even breathing properly.

The door burst open and Bryn limped his way into the scullery.

'What's going on by here, you two?' he growled. Mari realised her brother must have been surprised to see their mother's reaction, as she was usually soft-spoken and gentle.

Mam stopped shaking Mari for a moment and then turned towards her son. 'I should think that's obvious! Your sister has only gone and ruined her lovely hair.'

As Bryn drew closer, his eyes widened, seeing that their mother was right. 'There must be some reason for it, for our Mari to have hacked away at her hair like that.' Then he narrowed his gaze. 'Or did someone do it purposely?'

Mari shook her head, finally finding her voice now that Mam

had stopped shaking her so much that her teeth rattled in her head. 'No, it was me. I cut my own hair.'

'But why, Mari?' Bryn's voice was full of sympathy as he supported himself, laying one hand on the table. He'd been told by the doctor not to bear weight on his injured foot if he might possibly help it.

'Because...' She sobbed loudly.

There was a scraping noise on the flagstone floor as Bryn drew out a chair from the table and sat. 'Sorry, I must sit a moment. You sit too, Mari, and you, Mam.'

Both of them followed Bryn's lead.

'Now, you were saying, Mari?' Bryn leaned forward to listen intently.

'She was just saying how she'd hacked her hair off herself!' Mam scowled.

'I get that,' said Bryn, 'but I want to know *why* she did it!'

Mari nodded. 'I did it as I've got head lice!'

Mam gasped and then her hands flew to her face as though Mari had just said she had the cholera that was sweeping the town.

'Oh, I see.' Bryn smiled. 'Well, if you'd have asked me, I'd have cut your hair for you and made a better job of it!'

'I'm sorry, Mam,' said Mari, looking at her mother with regret now to have upset her so much. 'I didn't want to trouble anyone and I thought it best to cut my long hair, especially as I'm working at the shop. The customers won't want to see me scratching my head.'

'But there's been no sign of you having any head lice of late!' Mam tilted her head with a puzzled expression on her face. 'Every couple of weeks I go through your hair with a fine-tooth comb and apply vinegar if there are any nits present.'

'It can happen overnight though, Mam,' said Bryn with a sympathetic tone to his voice. 'And although Mari looks more like a lad with her hair like that, it'll soon grow again.'

'Oh!' said their mother, suddenly rising from the table as she made to leave the room. 'I'd better go and check Nerys's and Tommy's hair too, and yours as well, Bryn. Then someone can check mine.'

Bryn chuckled. 'I don't think I've got any, mind you.'

When their mother had gone off to check her younger children's heads, Bryn fixed his gaze on his sister. 'Look, if I were you, I'd get Mam to tidy that haystack of a hairdo for you. It's sprouting out from all angles. You look like a ruddy scarecrow trying to ward off predators in a field of crops!'

Mari nodded and then smiled at her brother's description. 'I didn't mean to make Mam angry though.'

'I know you didn't.' He sighed and then stretched out across the table towards her, patting her hand in reassurance. 'It's not what you've done at all. I reckon it's the anger since Dad left. At first, she seemed just sad but, in a way, I'm glad she's feeling angry these days and rightly so. He's abandoned her, after all she's done for him. In fact, he's abandoned us all.'

Mari nodded with understanding. 'I'll make a cup of tea for us, shall I?'

Bryn shot her a wry smile. 'Aye, that'll be most welcome. Though I feel I'm swimming in the stuff these days since being laid off from the pit.'

Thinking for a moment, Mari hesitated before speaking. 'When you first applied for a job at the pit, who did you speak to?'

Bryn blinked. 'Why do you ask?'

'Bobby just mentioned he's thinking about working underground, that's all.'

Bryn narrowed his eyes. 'Well, that's strange as his father told me he doesn't want him to go down the pit like he did after suffering that accident.' He blew out a hard breath. 'But maybe the lad has other ideas.'

Mari shrugged, all the while feeling bad at having to lie to her brother. 'So, who was it? So I can let him know.'

'It was the foreman I spoke to, Elwyn Roberts.'

'Oh, I see.' Mari smiled. 'I've spoken to him already.'

'What do you mean, already?' Bryn raised a curious brow.

'Er, what I meant was he was the person who called here looking for Mam when you were in that pit accident.'

She realised she'd almost got caught out there so needed to think on her feet; no way did she want her brother to know of her plan to work underground, at least not for the time being. She knew he'd try to stop her doing such a thing, even though it was he who had sparked the idea in the first place.

Deciding to say no more on the subject so as not to arouse suspicion, she said, 'Thanks. I'll pass the name on to Bobby, and he can decide for himself. I suppose he didn't ask his father for the name as he'd have tried to put him off going for a job there.'

'I would think so. Now where's the cup of tea you promised me?'

* * *

Later, when Mam had checked the kids' heads and Bryn's, and she'd had hers checked too, she inspected Mari's.

'Well, there's no sign of any lice now. I'll tidy up that mess for you,' she said, though this time there was no edge of anger to her voice.

Her mother then proceeded to neaten up her hair with a pair

of sharp scissors, snipping here and there with so much skill that she might be a hairdresser or a gentleman's barber. Mari had to admit afterwards that it looked so much neater. Now it gave her face an almost elfin look, though it had gladdened her heart when Bryn had mentioned she looked like a boy. Early tomorrow morning she decided she'd call to the pit to see the foreman. Would he recognise her though? She'd make sure that flat cap of her father's was pulled down low over her forehead and disguise her voice too. She'd only met the man the once when he'd called to the house regarding Bryn's pit accident; her hair had been long and loose on her shoulders then, with a pretty yellow ribbon tied in a bow on top of her head, so hopefully he wouldn't recognise her now.

* * *

It was still dark when Mari rose from her bed the following morning. All she could make out were the dark and cumbersome shapes of the furniture in her bedroom. Her intention was to creep out of the house before Mam and Bryn awoke. She'd have to be careful not to disturb Nerys, who was still asleep in the bed they shared. Mari watched the soft rise and fall of her sister's chest beneath the bedclothes and the gentle snores she emitted from time to time. Oh, she wouldn't want for her sister or Tommy to go underground, even though she understood that many a young girl and boy had gone down the pit and worked lengthy shifts before that law forbidding it came to pass.

Her idea was to get to Bobby's shed and changed into her working garb before his folks woke up too. If she were discovered, then it might put paid to her plans before the very first day.

Bobby's house was only a few minutes' walk away, so she was up and dressed, with a cheese sandwich wrapped up in a piece of muslin stuffed into the pocket of her jacket, just in case she was lucky to secure a position at the pit that day.

To her surprise, Bobby was waiting for her behind the tall wooden back gate, having already unbolted it for her that morning. She smiled tentatively at him and he gasped when he saw her hair.

'I know you said you were thinking of cutting your mane, Mari, but I had no idea you'd go through with it,' he said in a hushed whisper.

'What do you think?'

He nodded. 'Well, it does make you look more like a boy now, I have to admit.'

That thought pleased her. She watched him unlock the shed door and she nipped in there to get changed into her 'work clothes'. Something she'd realised was that she needed to bind down her breasts as she was beginning to transform into a young lady. She'd managed to find an old cotton bandage that Mam left over from the time that Dad had injured his hand, so she'd wrapped that tightly around her bust before leaving the house.

After a couple of minutes, Bobby knocked quietly on the shed door. 'You'd better hurry as my parents will be awake soon. Are you ready?'

'Yes, as ready as I'll ever be!' she hissed back. As she emerged from the shed, a strange flutter like the wings of a small butterfly came from the pit of her stomach. She could barely see with the peak of her father's cap lodged over her eyes, so she adjusted it. 'How do I look?'

Bobby stood speechless for a moment with the palms of his hands on the back of his head, his eyes widening so the whites were on show. 'Like a boy!' he gasped. He dropped his hands to his sides as he approached her. 'Is that really you in there, Mari? What are you going to call yourself?'

'Oh, I hadn't considered that.' She thought for a moment as the name of a place in upper Abercanaid called Lewis Square popped into her mind. It was where Mam's friend Rhoswen Griffiths lived. 'How about Lewis? Lewis Lloyd?'

'Yes, that sounds a good name to me!' He nodded his approval. 'Just one thing though, I reckon you need to deepen your voice a little bit. Try it now with me.'

'I don't know what you mean,' she said in a tone that sounded almost as low as her brother Bryn's voice.

'That's too much,' Bobby scolded her. 'Try again.'

'Does this sound better?' she said in a low tone, but not at the bass level she'd previously used.

'Much better,' he said. 'Now remember when you arrive at the pit to tilt that cap over your eyes in case the foreman recognises you.'

'I will do.'

'Now go quickly before Mam and Dad come out here to see what I'm up to. I'll lock the shed with your clothes in and I'm going to hide the key under that large stone over there!' He pointed to a corner of the garden that appeared to be a bit of a rockery.

She sauntered off through the back gate, turning to wink at him before he closed it firmly shut behind her.

* * *

As she neared the pit, Mari's stomach somersaulted as she watched the pit wheel turn with a cranking sound. She noticed several women and girls scurrying around. Some were known as tip girls, whose job it was to sort and screen the coal and to load up the wooden props. They wore aprons and headscarves, and their clothing was filthy. Some wore hats with artificial flowers or feathers sprouting from them and some even wore earrings. Mari guessed that maybe it was their way to stamp their mark upon their drab outfits, to stand out from the rest. Those were the only duties these days for women at the pit since that law had been enforced. The only other women who were allowed to work at the pit were those who worked in the lamp room and one or two others who did other menial work above ground. Below ground these days was the reserve of the men and boys over ten years of age. As much as she'd love to work as a tip girl, she'd been told by her brother that they weren't paid as much as the men at the pit. Her goal was to get as much money as she possibly could for her family and the only way to do that was to work as a boy not a girl.

She noticed a woman called Aggie whom she recognised from living in the village. Aggie called into the shop occasionally, sometimes on her way home from work with the coal dust ingrained on her face and a shawl wrapped around her head, her apron greyed and her hands rough and calloused. Mari had guessed maybe those who worked at the pit rarely washed their clothing as it was only going to get dirty again. Though Mam insisted on washing her brother's at least once a month.

Forgetting where she was for a moment, she was about to approach her and say 'Hello' when she remembered, for her time at the pit, she was a boy. Today she was Lewis Lloyd from the Rhydycar area of the town. She had chosen that place as she knew one or two folk living there and could mention their names if people asked her about the place. One was an old relative of hers called Eira Phillips, otherwise known as 'Bopa'. She was an aunt of her mother's so in reality was Mari's great-aunt.

One of the women turned her head in her direction, away from the dram she'd been sorting. Mari just lowered the peak of her cap and nodded at the woman, who smiled at her as she scurried past.

Now where was the office? She'd been here once with her father when he'd popped in to collect his wages. She hadn't been allowed inside though; he'd told her to wait outside while he had business to discuss with the foreman. The door had been ajar as she'd stood patiently waiting for him and she'd been taken by surprise to hear him ask for an advance on his wages, claiming the family was on its uppers that particular week, when she knew full well they weren't. Of course, in retrospect, she wondered if her father had asked for his pay early as he had other things to spend it on, namely one Blodwyn Parry!

Pushing that thought away, she took a deep breath, rapping her knuckles on the door of the foreman's office. She could hear voices from inside.

Finally, the door swung open. A large collier stood there, his broad shoulders almost filling the doorway. He chuckled. 'What do we have here then?'

'I'm Lewis Lloyd,' said Mari, remembering to lower her voice, though not too much as Bobby had advised. 'I need to see the foreman about a job, please, sir.'

'I'll just give him a shout for you, lad,' said the man as he turned, and his voice boomed inside the small room. 'Elwyn, there's someone here to see you. A Mister Lewis Lloyd!' He turned and then, grinning at Mari, brushed past her as Elwyn Roberts arrived in the doorway.

This would be the test: whether the foreman recognised her or not. 'Yes, sonny. I heard your name. So, you're seeking a job here, are you?'

'Yes, sir.'

Mr Roberts drummed his fingertips thoughtfully on his chin. 'Well, I can't give you anything full-time. But I could give you three shifts a week. They won't always be the same days each week, mind you. It'll be at my request. You know, if we're short and that. You'd be told when you're needed.'

'Oh, that would be good,' said Mari, nodding at him.

'Are you fit and strong?'

'Yes, I'm as strong as an ox, sir.'

'Well, you'll need to be, as I'll have several different duties for you – helping to hew away at the coal and fill the drams, tipping the coal down the chute, that kind of thing. Some days we load sixteen to seventeen tonnes of the stuff into the drams. It's back-breaking work, mind.'

'I can do all of that,' said Mari, with a confidence she didn't really feel inside. She didn't know for sure just how strong she was.

'Very well then,' said Mr Roberts. 'Come back early light at six o'clock tomorrow morning. Your shift will last for twelve hours.'

Mari gulped. She realised of course how long the shifts were, as her brother and father had worked at the pit, but in her naivety, she had thought that maybe young people would work fewer hours. 'Can't I start work here today?'

'No,' said Mr Roberts firmly. 'All the workforce has already gone down in the cage, and we don't need the help today, but we'll need it tomorrow.'

Mari sighed. Now what was she to do? She was already togged up and ready to go. She'd need to change back out of her clothing and return home.

* * *

Gingerly, she popped her head around the back gate that led into Bobby's backyard, but there was no sign of the lad. She couldn't risk knocking the back door, so instead she located the key beneath the stone and nipped into the shed and quickly changed out of her clobber, slipping back into her everyday clothing. What could she tell her mother now though? Mam thought she was working for Mrs Jones today.

Hurriedly, she shut the shed door behind herself, ensuring it was locked, returning the key beneath the stone, and then she slipped out of the back gate for fear someone might see her and questions might be asked. If Bobby's parents caught her dressed as a boy, they'd surely begin to question what was going on. If they didn't recognise her, then they'd think some lad had broken into their shed to thieve something from them. She'd carefully stashed her work clothing beneath an old tarpaulin. Stealthily, she made her way back home.

* * *

Mari's heart exploded with fear as the clanking and whirring mechanism of the metal cage sounded. It began to descend into the bowels of the earth, forcing her to tightly shut her eyes. She was closely packed into it with all the other colliers, just like sardines in a tin can. Most of them were towering over her. The only others of her sort of stature and below were the young boys who worked here. It was quite claustrophobic so, thankfully, the journey down didn't last all that long.

As the cage door opened, one of the miners, who was a large bear of a man, stepped out with her. 'Sonny, you're new here?'

'Yes,' she answered in a gruff voice, which she realised was far too low. The man didn't seem to notice anything amiss though.

'I'm Alwyn Probert. Big Al to most around here. I need a butty to help me this morning. I can show you the ropes at the same time. All right?'

She smiled at him beneath her flat cap. He was holding one of those safety lamps her father and brothers spoke of. Davy lamps, they called them. Dad had once told her that before the men had used naked flames to light their path, which had been extremely dangerous as if there was a build-up of gas, the candles would cause it to ignite and could, hence, cause an explosion.

Al located the foreman who seemed to be in a deep conversation with a collier, interrupting him while Mari kept her distance. She noticed Mr Roberts glance in her direction. He'd only met her yesterday so was aware she was about to start today.

Her stomach flipped as he walked towards her and, patting her on the shoulder, said, 'You'll do all right for your first day if you work with Mr Probert. He's good with the new boys. Now you'll have to walk a couple of miles or so to get to the seam he's working on, and when you get there, don't be alarmed but it's very low. He'll need your help to pass him the tools he needs and to help fill the dram.'

Mari swallowed and gulped. She hoped neither man would notice how petrified she was. She hadn't realised she'd have to walk for quite some time to get to the seam itself.

Al's strong arm patted her shoulder. 'Come on, sonny. You'll be all right with me. What's your name anyhow?'

'Lewis Lloyd.'

'Oh. I know some of the Lloyds from the village. Related to them, are you?'

'Er no, sir.' Mari felt herself grow hot. 'We're a different family of Lloyds.'

'Lewis Lloyd is a bit of a mouthful if you ask me, so I'll just call you Lew, if that's all right? You don't mind, do you?'

Mari shook her head with relief. Al obviously believed she really was a lad and she'd managed to get herself out of a tricky situation there. 'I don't mind at all, Mr Probert.'

"Course most of the men and boys who work here have nicknames. There's Dic Canal, as he lives near the canal bank, John

Chewbacca as he chews tobacco, and then there's Wyn Gander, referred to as such as he keeps geese.'

'Er?' Mari wrinkled her nose.

'He's called Gander – from the nursery rhyme, "Goosey Goosey Gander"!' Al began to roar with laughter. 'Come on,' he chided. 'We best get going as the shift'll be over if we stand here chatting.' He lifted his pick and rested it on his shoulder to prepare for the long journey ahead.

The foreman nodded at Al as he led Mari away. It was cold and dark beneath the ground and Mari wondered how her brother and father had stuck it out here for so many years. In some ways she wished they were with her right now. But then she had to remind herself that the reason she was doing this in the first place was because her father had left them all in a pickle and her brother was now no longer able to work.

On the walk there, Mari noticed a small boy pass them, who looked no older than Tommy. 'Who's he, Mr Probert?'

'He's a trapper lad.'

'What's that?' She'd heard the term in passing from her brother and father, but neither had gone into detail about it.

'He's headed for the door that allows ventilation in here to stop the build-up of dangerous gases. Every so often he must open it to allow fresh air in. He'll be relieving the other lad who's been there overnight.'

'That's all he does?'

'Aye, yes. Not the best job in the world, granted, as he has to sit for hours in the darkness sometimes. The foreman only chooses the smallest lads for that particular task. Although he looks young, he is ten years old as the law requires. But I remember a time in my youth when a boy of around five years of age was used for that job.'

Mari gasped. 'I had no idea.'

'Well, why would you? There were also women underground and young girls back then. This is no place for them in my opinion.' He shook his head.

Mari felt the hairs stiffen on the back of her neck. *If only you knew, Mr Probert!*

As they advanced further along the tunnel, there was a rumbling noise and a clinking and, to Mari's surprise, she saw a lad almost on all fours with a chain linked to him around his waist, to which was attached a dram behind him.

'What is that boy doing?' she asked, even though it was obvious.

'He's what's known as a drammer – those lads work in low tunnels and the carts can carry about a hundredweight or more of coal. You'll get to see the ponies in a moment, we use those for the heavier tasks around here.'

'Oh, I've heard about those!' Mari said with excitement, forgetting herself for a moment. 'My dad told me about them...'

'So, your father works underground too, does he, Lew? Maybe I know him.'

Oh no. She'd almost slipped up there. 'Er, no, Mr Probert. He just knows all about them, that's all.'

Al said no more about it and Mari didn't need any introduction to the pit ponies as they were about to pass one of them. The large horse had blinkers over its eyes, led by a lad of around her age.

'This is William,' said Al. 'He's been working here for a couple of years and takes care of our pit ponies in this section of the pit. We have an underground stable, see.' Al held up his lamp in front of the lad's face for Mari to take a good look. She was relieved to see he was no one she recognised from the village, otherwise that might have been awkward for her.

William smiled. 'Hello. I haven't seen you here before. You're new?'

'Yes,' said Mari. 'I'm starting work here today.'

'Well, Al will take care of you,' William reassured her. 'He took care of me on my first day too, didn't you, Al?'

'Oi! Mr Probert to you!' Al laughed, good-naturedly. 'I'm forgetting my manners. This is Lew. Lewis Lloyd.'

So now another one at the pit knew her 'name'.

After leaving William and the pit pony in their wake, the trudge forward seemed endless. And to think she'd need to do this every time she worked here! Not just once either as she'd have to return in the opposite direction too when it was time to leave for home.

It seemed an age until they reached the section that Al wanted to work on; all the while, the tunnel they followed became narrower and Al needed to stoop now to walk through it. The coal dust in the air seemed to clog Mari's lungs, forcing her to cough, but Al seemed used to it, though he also had to expectorate occasionally. Her mother had always said the air in the pit was full of coal dust and bad for her father's and brother's lungs. It was her hope that someday soon Bryn would find himself another job elsewhere, enabling him to breathe clean air instead.

Finally, they reached a narrow, low seam where an empty dram lay close by. 'Now then,' said Al. 'We're going to have to crawl on our hands and knees by here, as this seam is only two and a half feet high! I must warn you to be careful as some colliers end up skinning their backs as the coal is so jagged. Don't want you to hurt yourself that badly on your first day!' He chuckled. 'Your mam would pulverise me!'

*Mam!* Mari wondered for a moment what she was doing. She'd told her mother she would be working in the shop today and tomorrow, when in truth, she'd be working at the pit instead.

Crawling along the seam made her feel hemmed in. Mari hadn't been expecting this. She realised of course that it was dark and dangerous at the pit, but she didn't realise she'd have to work in such a confined space and at this section there was only Al's safety lamp to lead the way.

'Now, I've got to hew out the coal as they say,' explained Al. 'What you must do is pass me any tools I need from my bag and then collect the lumps of coal I extract, and take them over to that dram we passed on the way in. Do you think you can manage that?'

'Yes, Mr Probert.'

'And there's no need to address me so formally in here, Lew. You can call me Al. We are colleagues now,' he said with good humour.

Mari thanked her lucky stars she was spending her first day with someone who was treating her so well.

Al had given her some sort of deep metal tray to place the lumps in. It was hard work crawling with the coal back to the dram each time, but she was physically fit and she managed it, being careful at the same time not to skin her back as she dragged it along. Unfortunately, it felt even harder to breathe in such a confined space, but she didn't know if it was her imagination running away with her. Maybe it was the feeling of entombment that placed her on the edge of panic.

They'd been working for some time, when Al said, 'Well, I think we deserve a break now, don't you?'

Mari nodded.

'You've brought your snap tin with you, I hope?'

'Er no, but I brought some bread and cheese with me wrapped in a cloth.'

'That's not a suitable way to bring your tuck down here. There is so much dust and, not only that, the rats might get at it!'

'Rats?' Mari felt her teeth on edge at the mention of the word. The only rats she'd seen had been near the river or canal bank and her mother warned her to stay well away from those as she said they carried disease.

Al held his lamp aloft to get a good look at her face. 'Don't be alarmed, Lew. They won't usually harm you unless you threaten them. A few rats together are better than one cornered, in my experience – the single rat is more likely to bite you as it will feel threatened. Mostly they leave us alone and we leave them be. We exist together – they have as much right to be here as we do. Now don't worry, I have some food in my snap tin if yours is ruined.'

Mari dipped her hand into her jacket pocket but, to her dismay, it was empty! The cheese sandwich she'd prepared that morning wasn't there. Then she remembered she must have left it in Bobby's shed when she'd got changed. 'Oh, I must have left it at home,' she said solemnly.

'Not to worry. I've got a jam sandwich you can have here. My missus usually packs one of each, one cheese and one jam. Unless you prefer the cheese?'

She would have preferred the cheese indeed, but Al was a large bloke who needed his sustenance, so she accepted the jam one with gratitude, feeling a little guilty she was robbing him of his fair portion of sustenance that day.

'I've got a billy can of cold tea we can share to wash it down with.'

Mari had never tasted cold tea as it was always hot or at least warm in the pot at home. She didn't much like the sound of it, but her mouth felt dry and dusty, so it was a welcome respite.

When they'd both eaten and drunk their fill, Mari realised she needed to pass water. 'Where's the privy, Al?' she asked.

Suddenly he laughed loudly, his laugh echoing off the coal seam. 'There aren't any privies down here!' he bellowed. 'You have to do it somewhere away from where you're working. Go back along the seam until you can stand upright near that dram you're filling and pee there. Don't splash any on the dram itself, mind, as it can leave a pungent smell behind. Where's the privy?' he said in a teasing fashion. 'Oh, my. You are a one, Lew!'

It was something that hadn't occurred to her before now. Neither her father nor her brother had ever mentioned anything about doing their business underground but, then again, why would they?

She was mindful though that at least she'd get a chance to squat down and urinate without Al or any of the other miners seeing her do so, and for that she was extremely grateful.

\* \* \*

Apart from having to crawl along the low seam, another difficult thing for Mari was that her eyes began to feel sore and irritated from the dust. At one point Al told her to stop rubbing them as it would make them far worse. 'Blink several times instead to make them water a bit,' he'd advised. 'Then when you get home bathe them in some boiled but cool water with a clean cloth.'

Mari honestly hadn't realised just how taxing a day working underground could be and it gave her a whole new respect for the men and boys like her father and brother who toiled here from dawn till dusk and even during the night-time too.

She breathed a sigh of relief when Al drew his old, battered watch on a chain from his pocket and peered at the time with his lamp. 'Home time at last, young Lew! It's time to go!'

Mari didn't know whether to laugh or cry, because now, of course, they had to face the long, gruelling journey to get back to the cage. Though her arms, legs and back ached all over, optimism spurred her on as she crawled out of that seam and soon both were standing near a full dram of coal. Al handed her his bag containing some tools, his snap tin and the billy can. She proudly carried it for him as she walked behind him, his pickaxe hoisted over his right shoulder. One thing was for sure, she wouldn't have trouble sleeping tonight.

But first she was going to have to face the music, because going by the state of her, Mam and Bryn would see for themselves that she hadn't been working at Mrs Jones's shop after all.

## 7

How Mari managed to walk home after working that long, gruelling twelve-hour shift, she just didn't know. Somehow, she staggered down the hill and across the canal bank in the direction of home and, in her tiredness, forgot to return her clothing to Bobby's shed.

The house was unusually quiet when she arrived, but then she saw Bryn seated at the scullery table. He looked at her and frowned. 'So, the wanderer returns, eh? Well, you've caused a right set-to for our mam today, young lady!'

'How's that?'

'She sent Nerys with a message for you to the shop, but you weren't there. But going by your appearance, you look like you've spent all day down a ruddy coal mine! Did Mrs Jones get you to clean out her coal cwtch or something like that?'

'That's 'cause I have spent all day down a ruddy coal mine!' she yelled, surprising herself with the tone of her voice.

Bryn blinked and then, forgetting himself, rose from the chair, standing on his injured foot. He winced and then flopped back down in his seat. 'Ouch!' he yelled. 'You bloody little fool! What made you do that?'

She released a breath, realising she was going to have to tell him the truth. 'You gave me the idea. You said yourself if I cut my hair I could pass for a boy and work underground!'

Bryn groaned. Then, looking thoughtful for a moment, uttered in a quiet voice, 'You're right, I did say that.' Shaking his head and with a regretful look, he added, 'I'm sorry I gave you that idea, but I wouldn't want you to go down inside that hell on earth for all the tea in China, our Mari. I was only joking with you.'

'It's all right,' she said, drawing out a chair from the table and seating herself opposite him. 'I worked hard today, grant you. But a man called Big Al took me on as his butty and looked after me. I know you seem disappointed with me but just think, Bryn, by the end of the week when I get paid, I'll have money to help us all!'

Bryn nodded and then let out a little sigh. 'You're right of course, Mari. The money would be a big help now I'm laid off for a bit, but we can't expect you to do that for us. Good grief! I'm not expecting you to return to the pit!' Bryn looked away for a moment, suddenly thoughtful. 'He's a good 'un, though, is Al. He would have watched your back for you. So, he had no idea you're a girl?'

She shook her head.

'Well, I must admit you've done a good job then of fooling the foreman. But you must promise me you'll not return to the pit tomorrow. It would break Mam's heart and it's breaking enough already as it is.'

'I can't promise you that, Bryn. We need the money. But I promise I'll stop doing this when you return to work or find a job elsewhere.'

'It's not worth it though, Mari. You might be putting your life at risk. Stay at home or carry on helping Mrs Jones at the shop if you must. I know she doesn't pay you, but at least she gives you some free food for us all every so often.'

'It's not enough though, is it? Money's getting tight. I've noticed Mam is cutting back on the food rations and trying to eke things out more than usual. I can see how tired she's becoming of late too, because all of this with Dad is making her so worried. I just want to help, that's all.'

'I know, *cariad*,' Bryn said, speaking softly to her now. 'But I can't imagine Mam will let you carry on doing this anyhow. Just look at you! You're filthy and I bet you're sore all over?'

'Yes, I am, to tell you the truth. We had to work in a seam that was just two and a half feet high today, so I'm aching from head to foot. Speaking of Mam, where is she? And what message did she send to the shop for me?'

He shook his head. 'It's Alfie's mother, Mrs Griffiths. She's taken ill and she's gone around there to help out.'

'Oh, what's the matter with her? Not the sickness?'

He shook his head. 'No, she's having another baby by all accounts.'

'Not at her age?' Mrs Griffiths seemed quite middle-aged to Mari, not of the age she'd expect someone to be nursing a young infant at all, but then again, some people seemed so worn down by life that it was hard to be a good judge of how old they really were.

He nodded. 'Yes, and Mam said it's not going to do Mrs Griffiths the slightest bit of good, as the doctor warned her not to have any more babies, but apparently, nature had other ideas.'

It was some time before Mam returned home. By then Mari had managed to boil some water to have a good scrub in the old tin bath, but no matter how hard she tried, she wasn't able to completely remove the coal dust from her skin or embedded beneath her fingernails. Would her mother notice? She had considered going to bed before her mother's return, and as she'd need to be awake at the crack of dawn for her next shift at the pit, her mother might not see her anyhow. But according to Bryn, Mam had been frantic with worry all day at her daughter's disappearance, so in his book, honesty was the best policy. In any case, her mam might find the discarded work clothing she ought to have left in Bobby's shed.

When Mam emerged through the scullery door ten minutes later, looking weary, worn and troubled, Mari ran into her arms and wept. The sweat and toil she'd endured that day had made her overly tired and she'd not eaten since that jam sandwich she'd devoured from Big Al.

'Shush now, child,' soothed Mam. 'I haven't even come through the door properly yet. I've not seen anyone this relieved to see me in a long time.' She stroked her daughter's shorn locks as Mari clung on to her as though her very life depended upon it.

'Mari,' said Bryn, from his chair at the scullery table. 'Go and make Mam a nice cup of tea. That will allow her to take off her shawl and bonnet and settle herself, as you've something to tell her, haven't you?'

Mari nodded as she gazed up into her mother's face, which now seemed hazy and a blur in amongst her tears. She sniffed loudly before saying, 'Yes, Mam. I'll make that tea right now.' She left her mother's side to remove the kettle, which had previously boiled, from the hearth, using a thick piece of towelling not to burn her hand.

'Oh dear, I don't much like the sound of this...' said their mother as she untied the ribbons of her bonnet and placed it on the table. Then she removed her shawl and draped it over the back of her chair, which she drew out to seat herself upon. 'And why on earth are you looking so filthy? What have you been up to?' She narrowed her gaze.

Mari exchanged nervous glances with Bryn and then set about pouring the steaming water into the teapot while Bryn remained silent. It wasn't that often that her brother had nothing to say, as he'd become quite vocal lately, especially since their father had left the home. It was as though he had now taken his place.

When the tea was poured and all three settled at the table, Mari explained to her mother where she'd been all day.

'But I can't quite believe this!' Mam shook her head. 'I won't have a daughter of mine doing such a dirty and dangerous job! It's bad enough that your brother and father have had to endure it, but they're men, not young girls...'

'I'm sorry, Mam,' said Mari, now openly sobbing again.

'It's my fault in a way,' said Bryn in a soft voice.

'Your fault? How so?' Mam's eyes were flashing with fury now.

'Well, I suggested she cut her hair and pose as a boy to work underground to help the family finances, didn't I?'

Their mother took a deep, composing breath and let it go. Then she shook her head. 'Oh, I remember you saying that now. It was only a silly comment. Not to be taken seriously. It was your sense of humour, that was all.' She fixed her gaze on her daughter.

'But our Mari took it seriously. I should not have said it at all.' Bryn had a regretful tone to his voice.

'I only wanted to help out...' Mari sniffed.

'I know you did,' said Mam, having more understanding of the situation now. 'But you're not to return to the pit again tomorrow, do you hear me?'

'I have to though,' pleaded Mari. 'Otherwise, I won't get paid. I was promised three shifts this week. I think I might be able to do this for a few weeks until Bryn gets back on his feet. It will help us over a tight time.'

Bryn nodded. 'She's right, Mam. We're on our uppers as it is. And she's working with Big Al.'

Mam wrinkled her nose. 'Who's that?'

'You know him – Alwyn Probert from down the village.'

'Oh, I know. Your father spoke highly of him. His wife is a good sort too. I didn't know he was called Big Al.'

'Yes, it's his nickname to us colliers.'

'Please, Mam, I did well today,' said Mari. 'Mr Probert was very pleased with my work.'

'But what if you get caught out?' Mam stared at her. 'It's illegal these days. You could have asked to work on top as a tip girl or something instead, if you felt that strongly about it.'

'But those jobs are hard to come by,' Bryn said, siding with his sister. 'The foreman is only looking for people to work underground at the moment, to fill in as it were. He needs the young lads as they can get in confined spaces and such. Most of those tip girls are quite a bit older than Mari. You wouldn't want her mixing with some of them; they're like a bunch of fishwives when they get started. You want to hear the bad language on them. There are a few what like a nip on the bottle too!'

Mam nodded and sighed. 'Well, you learn something new every day.'

'Please, Mam. Allow me to work a few shifts and then I'll stop. I'm being paid on Friday for my shifts this week.' Mari looked at her mother expectantly.

Bryn studied his sister. 'Look, now we know about it, I can advise you how to take care of yourself underground. You shouldn't come to too much harm if you stick close to Al. Also watch the pit ponies and the drams, as you can get crush injuries from either. But once you're out working in the coal seam all you'll be doing is handing tools to Al and filling the dram as his butty. Those casual lads the foreman takes on don't even pull any of the drams,' said Bryn, now looking at their mother as he waited for a response. 'Then when I'm walking properly again, I'll try to get a job elsewhere. What do you say, Mam?'

'Go on then,' their mother said, forcing a smile. 'But it's only to be for a few weeks, mind.' Mam glanced at her daughter. 'I appreciate you trying to help, Mari. But next time when you return home after work, let me give you a good scrub instead!' Mari chuckled, glad that her mother wasn't as angry with her as she initially thought she might be. 'Now, let's get you fed, my girl!'

## 8

It was Friday evening and now Mari had worked three shifts at the pit. She was waiting in line outside the pit office with the men and boys. Some of the men were grumbling as they claimed they hadn't been offered any extra shifts that week and, the way a couple of them were glaring at her, she reckoned they thought she – and a couple of the other casual workers – were to blame.

'Pay no heed to them moaners and groaners by there,' bellowed Al, loud enough for them to hear. 'They're only sore as they haven't got enough drinking money to last the week! The foreman didn't need their services anyhow, as how many of them could have the stamina to work like a horse and get into confined spaces like you do?' Then he turned to face them. 'I've had enough of you lot having a go at the new lads! You do it every time they're taken on here!'

There were some further mumblings from a small group of the men, but none of them dared to tackle Al as he had a temper on him when he got started. Plus, he was as strong as an ox, so no one would wish to inflame his fiery nature. The truth was that most of the men agreed with him: it was just that bunch of slackers who blamed the new boys for not being offered more work. But that group of five men weren't up to it. They lacked the drive and stamina. More than once, Mari had sniffed the strong smell of ale on them in the pit cage. It was so bad she'd almost thrown up one morning. Al had explained to her then that some put their thirst for ale before any thought of their families.

'Just ignore them,' he advised now, in a low tone of voice so as not to be overheard. 'Just come to work, do your job, go home again and pick up your wages at the end of the week. In a few weeks' time, when another set of lads are employed, they'll turn their anger on those instead, as you won't be the new boy any longer. This has been going on since I started working here. It's human nature for some to wallow in self-pity.'

Mari nodded, but nevertheless, it gave her an uncomfortable feeling that some of the men felt spiteful towards her and the other new lads.

'Oi! Mind yer Ps and Qs, lads!' one of the colliers at the end of the queue shouted at them all.

Mari's head whipped around to see a familiar face heading towards her, wrapped up warmly in her velvet cape with matching bonnet and a wicker basket over the crook of her arm. It was Marguerite Thomas, she who thought so highly of herself! Mari hadn't seen her since the time she'd stood up to her at the shop. She quickly tugged the peak of her cap down over her eyes and raised the collar of her jacket for fear of being recognised by the woman, who would surely tear a strip off her and tell everyone who she really was if she caught sight of her.

'That's Mrs Hoity-Toity herself!' Al chuckled. 'Off to see her husband in the office.'

'Oh?' said Mari, puzzled now.

'Yes, he's the wages clerk. Course, she's gone above herself now she's working at the Davenport house as a housekeeper.

That's the only way she's got such fancy clothes to wear: they're all Mrs Davenport's cast-offs.'

Of course, Mari already realised this but couldn't tell Al, else questions might be asked of her.

The queue was beginning to move along to the window hatch where the wages were being paid and Mari heaved a sigh of relief that Mrs Thomas passed her by without paying any heed, though she realised she'd need to be careful when she drew up at the window if the woman was still in the office. She wondered what was inside her basket.

As if reading her mind, Al said, 'She brings food for her husband every day, no doubt leftovers from the grand food dished up at the big house. Fair play to Margaret though, for thinking of him, as she walks all the way up the hill to the pit come rain, come shine.'

Mari smirked at the fact Al had called the woman by her real name: Margaret. There were no airs and graces with anyone as far as he was concerned and Mari guessed he would treat folk the same whether they were baronets or beggars.

Mari watched as Al's earnings were handed over to him through the window hatch by someone who she assumed was Mr Thomas. The middle-aged man wore a pristine white shirt and navy waistcoat adorned with silver buttons. On the arms of his shirt sleeves were a pair of sleeve garters, to prevent them from slipping over his hands – a good thing as the man needed to constantly dip the nib of his pen into a black inkpot to record the men's wages in a large ledger. She'd noticed people who worked in offices tended to wear that sort of thing to keep themselves clean and tidy. Mr Thomas, who was balding on top of his head, attempted to disguise the fact with his hairstyle – he had what her brother referred to as 'a comb-over'. This involved growing one side of the hair longer than the other and then brushing it over his bald patch. The hair appeared gelled into place with pomade too, which Mari guessed was so the long part remained in place. She'd once seen a man in the village speaking with her father outside the pub on a windy day. The poor fella's face had glowed bright red when he realised his combed-over hair had blown out of place and one side of his hair was now touching his shoulder while the other side remained short as his shiny bald head made a sudden appearance. She stifled a giggle at the memory of it.

Mr Thomas was telling Al that he was being paid eighteen shillings that week and Al seeming content with that, took the coins placed into his palm and dropped them in his trouser pocket.

As Al moved from the window, he stepped to one side to wait for her. 'Go on, Lew,' he urged. 'Just say your name at the hatch.'

'Lewis Lloyd,' said Mari, then she gulped. What if she got found out? It was easier to disguise her appearance in the semi-darkness of underground, but now it was broad daylight, she didn't feel as confident. Mrs Thomas was now standing behind her husband, still with wicker basket in hand as though waiting for an appropriate time to interrupt him and hand his meal over.

'Speak up, lad,' said Mr Thomas.

Oh no! Her cover might be blown if the man's wife were to fix her gaze on her. 'Lewis Lloyd, sir,' Mari said to the man, now in a louder voice.

'That's better, sonny,' said Mr Thomas with a smile on his face. 'You're going to need to speak up for yourself, especially working here with some of the men. Don't take any nonsense off them. That's three shillings and sixpence you're owed for three shifts,' said Mr Thomas. 'Hold out your hand.'

It appeared that Mrs Thomas was about to raise her head from her basket where she'd been in the process of removing the tray cloth as though about to hand something to her husband, when they were interrupted by someone entering the office. Both their heads turned just in time; Mari grabbed hold of the coins, dropping them quickly into her jacket pocket, muttered her thanks, and then she followed Al out of the line and towards the pit gates in the direction of home.

Phew, that had been a close call.

'What's the matter with you, Lew?' asked Al as they left the pit behind and headed down the meandering hillside path.

'Oh, I was hoping for a bit more pay, to be honest,' said Mari.

'Well, you wouldn't get paid as much as me as I work the full week and I'm classed as skilled, you see. How much did he pay you?'

'Three shillings and sixpence for three days' work.'

Al shrugged. 'Sounds about right. The boys don't get paid as much as the men.'

She could hardly tell Al she'd been basing the pay she'd receive on the sum of wages her father and brother earned. It hadn't occurred to her she'd be paid less per day. In her mind, she assumed all colliers were paid the same amount. It wasn't going to be enough to put good food on the table at home. Was working underground worth her time and trouble? But then she reminded herself that she got no pay at all from working at Mrs Jones's shop; she just got paid the odd provision there for her trouble. So it was better than nothing and every little amount earned would help the family.

'Don't worry too much, Lew. If they decide to keep you on here permanently, the pay will increase a bit. It's just you're considered a casual worker here for the time being. You're being trialled, if you like – to see how well you work. And unfortunately...' – he huffed out a laboured breath – '...that's what men like that lot there...' – he hiked a thumb at the five complainers who had now reached the payment window – '...object to – you young 'uns who show them up! Pay no heed to them. Like I said, it will be someone else's turn next.'

Mari nodded with understanding as she jingled the coins in her jacket pocket. At least they could buy some more food now. Maybe a chicken for Sunday dinner? Her mother would be pleased at any rate.

* * *

The following day, as Mari didn't need to show up to the pit again for a shift for another four days, she thought she'd best go and see Mrs Jones and explain what had happened with a view to her still helping occasionally at the shop.

'I had wondered what had happened to you, *cariad*,' said her employer. 'I was expecting you here yesterday...'

'I'm sorry, Mrs Jones,' said Mari as her eyes welled with tears. 'I had to find a way to earn some money to help the family.'

'So, where have you gone to work then? At another shop in Merthyr? Somewhere they can afford to pay you a decent wage?'

Mari, who had a shawl over her head with just her fringe on show, shook her head. 'No, Mrs Jones. I've been working at the pit.'

Mrs Jones's eyes enlarged, then she held the palm of her hand to her chest. '*Duw, duw,* my hearing must be going. I could have sworn then you said you've been working at the pit, but I know that young girls aren't allowed to work underground there any longer, so I can't have heard you correctly.'

'You did hear right, Mrs Jones.' Mari nodded.

'But how? Why?'

Mari removed her shawl from around her head, where it had

been covering her shorn locks. 'I cut my hair and pretended to be a boy,' she said soberly.

'Oh, goodness gracious me! I didn't realise things were so bad for you that you had to resort to such tactics!'

'Please don't be angry with me, Mrs Jones. I'm still prepared to help out here when I'm not at the pit. I'm only working there three days a week.'

'Aye, and I bet you're working long hours too!' Mrs Jones folded her arms as if in protest. 'It's not you I'm angry with, Mari. It's the situation. Well, the situation your father has put you all in by his actions and the bad luck you've had since with your brother being injured an' all.' She laid a hand of reassurance on Mari's shoulders. 'Of course, you're welcome to still work here if you feel up to it?'

Mari nodded gratefully. 'I work twelve-hour shifts at the pit, but it won't feel like work here; it will feel more like rest after working there!' She chuckled.

'One thing though, you'll need to cover that short hair of yours with some sort of covering.' She glanced at the ceiling in thought. 'Oh, I have the very thing; just wait a mo, but cover your head with your shawl again in case a customer comes in, won't you?'

Mari smiled tentatively. Then watched as Mrs Jones left the counter to head towards the back room, returning in minutes with a white frilly cap.

'You can wear this mob cap! It'll do the trick, and folk will assume your hair is pinned up beneath it.'

Mari nodded eagerly. 'Thank you, Mrs Jones. So shall I return here to work tomorrow?'

'Aye, I'd like that.'

'Thank you. Have you seen Mrs Thomas lately?'

'Marguerite or Enid?' There was another customer with the surname who often frequented the shop.

'Marguerite.'

Mrs Jones shook her head. 'No, she hasn't been in the shop since you had a go at her. Why do you ask?'

Mari explained how she'd been queuing up at the hatch for her wages when she'd walked close by.

'Hmmm. If I were you, I'd keep a low profile, because if she discovers what you're doing, she'll make trouble for you. In fact, I wouldn't be surprised, and I don't know if I should tell you this...'

'Please go on,' urged Mari.

'I think it's from her that all the gossip about your father and that Blodwyn one started. It's working with the other staff at that house, see. The staff like a little gossip in the kitchen from time to time. Their lives are that mundane! So consequently, Mrs Thomas isn't out to do you and your family any favours, is she? Especially since you showed her up in the shop.'

Mari realised that was probably true. 'Well, I'll try to be careful from now on, especially if she comes in here.'

Mrs Jones smiled and nodded. 'That's the spirit. Now, let's have a cuppa out in the back room before it gets busy again.'

## 9

The aroma of a chicken roasting in the oven made Mari's stomach growl as she sat huddled up by the fireplace. Bryn was seated in the most comfortable armchair in the corner, the one that had been Dad's but now in his absence had been taken over by her brother at her mother's strong request. Mam had insisted on it, as now Bryn was laid up and required to rest his leg on a wooden stool, he needed to be as comfortable as possible, and Mari quite understood that.

Nerys and Tom were sitting in the opposite corner of the room, all spruced up, wearing their Sunday best.

Mam rushed into the room and, looking at Bryn said, 'Why aren't you dressed for chapel then?'

Bryn's face flushed pink as he shook his head. 'I don't feel up to it today, Mam.'

'Nonsense. Go and get ready. I feel better when you're with me. No one dares mutter any snide comments then about your father abandoning us all.'

Bryn forced a smile. It was then Mari realised there was something more serious about her brother not attending chapel that particular Sunday. She looked at her mother. 'Maybe it won't be a bad idea for Bryn to rest up just this once...'

Mam's eyes flashed. 'Rest up? That's all he's been doing this past couple of weeks. If he rests up any more, he'll turn into a marble statue!'

What on earth was the matter with their mother? She wasn't usually so obstreperous. She glanced at her brother, who was now looking as baffled as she felt.

'Now where's my best shawl? It's not on the back of the door where I left it.'

'I think I saw it on the chair in your bedroom, Mam.'

Their mother looked heavenward before shaking her head and muttering something unintelligible, then she left the room in search of her precious shawl, her old, everyday one definitely not fit to grace the Lord's House.

Mari fixed her gaze on her brother. 'What's up with Mam?'

Bryn shook his head. 'I've honestly no idea, but she seemed a little cross when she returned from Mrs Griffiths's house last night.'

'Maybe they've had words?'

'Possibly. I honestly thought she'd be in a good mood today though, especially as you've worked hard, Mari, to provide our very fine feast.'

'Me too. There's something troubling her though...' She paused before adding, 'And what's wrong with you? Why aren't you accompanying us to chapel today?'

Bryn let out a low groan. 'I thought I'd have felt up to it, as I can manage to walk as far as Mr Jenkins's cart and then I could rest up once inside...' Mr Jenkins was a kindly neighbour who often helped friends and neighbours get to chapel by aid of his horse and cart, especially the elderly or those unable to walk the distance. 'It's not that – it's just I'm embarrassed for Glenda to see me like this. After all, why would she want a sweetheart with a gammy leg when she's so pretty she can have her pick of young men in Abercanaid?'

Mari could well understand her brother's embarrassment, but what she couldn't comprehend was why the young woman hadn't even been to visit him since his accident. She must have known about it, as the whole village was discussing it. So why hadn't she come to check on him? Or had she, as her brother suggested, had her pick and chosen someone else instead?

The living room door creaked open, and Mam stood there with her best shawl around her shoulders. Tightening the ribbons of her bonnet, she said, 'Well, if you can't grace the Lord's House today, then maybe you can keep a check on the chicken for me, Bryn? Take it out of the oven in about an hour or so, in case we're late back. There's a visiting minister at chapel today.'

Bryn nodded and smiled at her. Mam returned the smile as she made her way over to him to peck a kiss on his cheek.

Then with tears in her eyes, she looked at her younger children and said, 'Come on, you two, we don't want to be late today of all days. It would be a bad impression to set in front of the new minister.' She glanced in her eldest daughter's direction. 'Come on, Mari. Hurry them up for me, please! Let's all get going, shall we?'

Mari ushered Tommy and Nerys towards the front door, and when they'd gone through it with their mother, she turned to wave to Bryn. It really was a mystery why Mam had flown off the handle like that. Still, attending chapel would be good to take her mind off whatever was troubling her.

The Reverend Isaiah Bevan's message that morning was about keeping strife out of everyday life. He introduced them to the new young minister, Huw Weatherfield, who he said would be stepping into his shoes over the next few weeks while he was attending to some important business at the Cardiff Bible College. What that important business was, no one had any idea, nor would anyone have had the mettle to ask. Isaiah Bevan was a formidable character.

During the service, Mari noticed several people glance in their direction, so much so that it was beginning to make her feel quite uncomfortable. She shot a sideways glance at her mother who appeared to be staring ahead at the minister as he spoke, as though wearing blinkers. But Mari did realise her mother was aware of those stares as, from time to time, she noticed her hands tremble, particularly when she held the hymn book to sing. Mam had a good strong voice, but this morning, it didn't sound as strong and on a couple of occasions she appeared to just mouth the words. What on earth was wrong with her and why were those people staring? Mari glared back at one woman whose gaze was particularly penetrating, who – shamefacedly – finally turned her head away.

Some of the people who had been watching them whispered behind the palms of their hands, which made Mari guess it must be something to do with her father. Maybe that accounted for her mother's earlier annoyance. She decided to ask her when they were on their way home.

But as the time came to leave, Mam made her and the other two children remain in their seats at the back of the chapel while the congregation filed out, some turning to glance in their direction.

Reverend Bevan summoned their mother. 'Might I have a word with you, Mrs Evans?' he asked, as he approached with a solemn expression on his face.

Was it Mari's imagination that, when her mother nodded, she appeared almost relieved?

Before ushering their mother away, the reverend introduced the children to the visiting minister, who stayed and chatted with them for a while until their mother returned.

Sniffing, Mam said, 'Thank you for keeping them occupied, Mr Weatherfield.'

He nodded and smiled, then glancing at the children said, 'I hope to see you next Sunday when I'm in the pulpit.'

All three smiled at him.

On the walk home, Mam was quiet, which prompted Mari to ask, 'What's happened, Mam?' The two children had run ahead so they couldn't hear their conversation. 'Why were all those people looking in our direction? And why did the Reverend Bevan ask to see you?'

Their mother let out a little groan. 'All right, you're old enough to know, but your father has returned to Abercanaid with that woman, right under everyone's noses. And to make matters worse, he's set up house with her an' all!'

Mari frowned. 'I don't understand, Mam. Do you mean Dad has moved into that woman's house with her mother living there too?'

Mam shook her head. 'No, by all accounts they're renting a room together from a woman who must have absolutely no morals whatsoever. She's just in it for the rent money she can get from that brazen pair! They're now living in the village in Nightingale Street.'

Now Mari understood why so many had been shooting such furtive glances at them. But they, evidently, were the last to know.

The walk back home seemed long and laborious. What should have been a pleasant Sunday afternoon following chapel with a nice Sunday dinner to look forward to now seemed steeped in misery.

Just before they reached the front door, Mam hesitated for a moment and then, looking at Mari, she laid her gloved hand on her shoulder. 'I'm glad now that Bryn didn't come to chapel, though I didn't think I'd ever say that, as he's such a support to me.' She bit her lower lip. 'But if he'd been there and seen all those people glancing our way and then the minister asking to speak to me, he might have lost his temper and that would have made things worse. We've been shown up enough as it is.'

Mari nodded in agreement. 'You'll have to tell him now though, Mam.'

'Aye, I will,' said her mother brusquely, 'but let's eat this dinner first so he can enjoy it without any worry on his mind, then I'll tell him afterwards. All right?' She looked deep into her daughter's eyes to ensure they were on the same page about that.

Mari drew a breath and, releasing it, said, 'Yes, you're right. Goodness knows we won't have much appetite now, but at least Tommy and Nerys seem unaware of what's been said this morning.'

Her mother forced a smile as they watched the children running up the street along the cobbles, playing tag with one another.

* * *

Once informed of the situation following Sunday dinner, it was a good few hours later before Bryn had calmed down. It seemed to upset him more than anyone, even their mother.

'To think he's brought that lady... well, I can hardly call her that... trollop more like, back to the village to flaunt her off beneath our noses.'

'Well, one good thing,' said Mam, 'Blodwyn's mother must have turned against the union as she's not taken them under her roof.'

Bryn nodded. Then narrowing his eyes said, 'Or is it more likely she doesn't want folk gossiping any more than they already are?'

Mam's eyes flashed. 'Whatever the reason, I don't know if that makes it even worse or better.'

'Worse, I suppose, Mam,' said Bryn.

'How'd you make that out?' Mari tilted her head to one side in puzzlement.

'He's showing folk he's serious about this Blodwyn, isn't he? A lot of men, if they take to a bit on the side, don't want to leave their families, or if they do, after they've had their fun, they return home. But not our bloody father!' He thumped his fist on the table, causing the crockery and cutlery to vibrate loudly and Mari's hair to stand on end.

Mam stood suddenly and rushed from the table.

'Aw, Mam,' said Bryn, rising from his chair, but he was unable to rush after her. 'I didn't mean to...'

'It doesn't matter,' said Mari in a gentle tone of voice. 'I'll follow after her to see if she's all right.'

He nodded at his sister, glum now. 'Tell our mam I'm sorry.'

Mari could see the remorse in her brother's hazel-brown eyes. He wouldn't hurt their mother for all the world. She smiled at him and rose from the table to find Mam.

Before leaving the scullery, she turned as she was about to open the door. 'This isn't your fault. I think Mam has been near to tears since attending chapel this morning, especially after all the stares we got from people and then Reverend Bevan asking to speak to her in private.'

\* \* \*

Mari trembled as she stacked the muslin-wrapped freshly baked loaves on the wooden counter. The bread was always the first thing to sell out of a morning as people wanted it fresh and it was supplied to the shop by the local bakehouse. It was Monday morning and her first day back helping at the shop. She'd be helping Mrs Jones out today and tomorrow and then back at the pit on Wednesday, Thursday and Friday for her three shifts underground.

But the reason for Mari's trepidation wasn't so much about her being discovered working at the coal pit, it was more to do with what folk might say about her father and her family, especially since the recent revelation he'd returned to the village. She'd already gone through this once when he first abandoned them all, but this felt ten times worse.

She watched as Mrs Jones unbolted the door to allow access to the first customers of the day.

'Brrr, it's parky out there!' said Mrs Inkerman, who walked over daily from the nearby village of Pentrebach for her bread. It didn't make much sense to Mari as there were a few shops over there that sold bread, but Mrs Inkerman obviously liked to make a trek of it, thinking the best bread of all was sold by Mrs Jones. Mrs Jones had confided in Mari one time that the same bakehouse supplied the shops in Pentrebach too, so Mrs Inkerman really was buying the same bread and her journey to do so was entirely unnecessary!

'She wouldn't thank us for telling her, mind!' Mrs Jones had chuckled at the time, and Mari guessed her employer was right about that. As long as the woman thought she had the best loaf of bread for miles around the Merthyr area, then she was satisfied.

'Yes,' replied Mrs Jones to Mrs Inkerman's remarks about the weather. 'It has got cold of late, next thing we'll know Christmas will be upon us!'

*Christmas!* Mari hadn't given a thought to the upcoming season so far. There had been far too many things on her mind of late, she'd realised. The previous Christmas had been a bad one for the villagers in general as the recent pit explosion had taken so many lives. It had spread a cloud of doom over the village, which was only now, slowly, beginning to lift. But her family's depressive state persisted while her father, Gwynfor Evans, was up to his shenanigans and flaunting everything he was up to beneath their noses.

If Mrs Inkerman was pondering about the man and wondering whether to ask Mari about her father, then she wasn't saying so, and for that, she was extremely grateful. But then again, the woman didn't live in Abercanaid itself, so maybe she hadn't even heard any of the gossip yet.

But Mari realised that if anyone spoke out of turn, particularly as she now helped out here, then Mrs Jones would put a stop to it.

'I was saying, a quarter of boiled ham, please?'

Mari jolted back to reality as she realised she'd been in a daydream. She smiled at the woman. 'Yes, Mrs Inkerman.'

Mari went off to slice and weigh the ham while Mrs Jones carried on a conversation with the woman. When Mari returned with the ham neatly wrapped in a sheet of paper, she placed the package in Mrs Inkerman's basket, alongside a loaf of bread and a pat of Welsh butter, which the woman had also requested.

The morning ticked along nicely and although one or two of the women seemed to fix their gazes more on Mari than usual, Mrs Jones's beady-eyed stare was enough to make them turn away shamefacedly. It was almost as though the woman was saying silently to them, *'You dare, you just ruddy well dare!'*

So, it was with some surprise that, later that afternoon, the shop bell tinkled as Mrs Marguerite Thomas breezed inside with two large baskets over each arm and a long list of provisions for Mrs Davenport. She didn't even glance in Mari's direction, preferring instead to pass on the list to Mrs Jones, who took it from her and then gave it to Mari. It was laughable really that the woman was speaking to her via Mrs Jones with requests such as: 'It's got to be your best bacon, mind. Nothing else will do!' and 'Make sure none of those apples are rotten!'

In return, Mari spoke back to the woman via Mrs Jones. 'Please tell Mrs Thomas that the bacon I've weighed and wrapped is the very best we have. I checked all the apples over and none are rotten...' Then under her breath she muttered, 'Except for one or two people around here I know...'

The woman could hardly respond even if she'd heard what Mari had said, as she wasn't speaking to her – that was clear enough – and the thought of confronting her in the future, if Mrs Jones wasn't around, put a smile on Mari's face.

'You did very well there with that woman,' said Mrs Jones when she'd finally left the shop. 'You don't want to go making an enemy of that one.'

'No, especially as her husband is working at the pit office and the management might discover they've employed a girl instead of a boy if she were to tell them.'

Mrs Jones nodded. 'Yes, very wise. Don't let anyone goad you today, you hear!' She wagged a finger of fun at her, a big grin on her face. Then the smile vanished as she sighed. 'I've heard all that gossip about your father and Blodwyn being back in the village, *cariad*. It can't be easy for any of you.'

'No, it's not, Mrs Jones, but we'll cope. We must.'

Mrs Jones grimaced in a concerned fashion. 'By the way, I've heard that a family living in Lewis Square has cholera.'

Mari gulped. 'But that's where Mrs Griffiths, my mother's friend, lives. I hope she's all right.'

Mrs Jones shook her head. 'I don't think it involves her house, fortunately. Whoever it is has been taking in lodgers lately. There's a lot of people crowded in there inside a small house!'

'Oh dear!' Mari frowned, realising she was going to have to inform her mother as soon as possible. She didn't want her to step foot in that area for fear she should fall ill herself. The community was so close-knit that they often popped inside one another's homes. If Mrs Griffiths had been inside that house or came into contact with someone, who knew what might happen to her and the unborn child she was carrying. Mari shuddered to think of it.

'By all accounts, Doctor Pritchard was summoned there along with some gentleman from the board of health. Do you know the house was found in an absolute filthy state! Apparently, there were piles of ashes in the bedroom and human excrement in the backyard!' A look of disgust washed over Mrs Jones's face as she grimaced and poked out her tongue, as though she'd just sucked on a lemon.

By the time Mari had returned home, with a view to relating the tale to her mother, Mam already knew.

'But how did you find out?'

'Gwennie next door told me all about it. That cholera is sweeping down the valley and taking everything in its path!'

'Don't exaggerate, Mam!' Bryn had put down the book he was reading to cast his mother a warning glance. 'You'll have our Mari a bundle of nerves like yourself.'

Bryn was becoming so short-tempered of late and Mari wondered if it was because he hadn't seen hide nor hair of his sweetheart, Glenda, since his accident. He'd got through a phenomenal number of books lately and Mari thought it was to divert his mind from his concern that maybe he'd lost his new love. There was a small lending library in the chapel hall where books could be borrowed freely if they were returned afterwards. He seemed to devour them, and she often thought that, for a simple, hard-working young man, her brother appeared educated and an open thinker.

Mam forced a smile and then made eye contact with Mari. 'Sorry. I didn't mean to worry you...'

But Mari was already concerned. She feared that lives in the village might be lost.

* * *

On her way to the shop the following day, Mari bumped into Bobby, who had loaded up the cart and was ready to get on it with his father. Dai had returned to the house as he'd forgotten something, so they were able to speak in confidence with one another.

'At least now you won't need to hide your pit clobber in our shed,' Bobby was saying, 'as your family know what you're up to!'

She nodded. 'But just because they know it doesn't mean I want anyone else to or it might get back to someone working at the pit and I'll be dismissed, as it's breaking the law.'

Bobby nodded slowly as he knocked back the peak of his cap as though to get a better view of her. 'Well, that goes without saying! So, you're wearing that frilly white thing on your head now, are you?' He chuckled.

Mari felt her face grow hot. 'I have to so that none of the customers can tell I've lopped my hair off. Does it look silly then?'

'It's quite becoming!' He grinned.

Mari didn't know whether he was poking fun at her or if he meant it, so to change the subject she said, 'I have to get on, as I

don't want to keep Mrs Jones waiting. That bread delivery is due
soon.'

'Have a good day.' He stooped slightly to peck a kiss on her
cheek, and it was then she realised that he'd seemed to get a little
taller lately and his voice was growing husky. There was no doubt
about it, Bobby was turning into a young man, and a handsome
one at that!

## 10

When Mari turned up for work at the pit, there was no sign of Big Al waiting for her. Where on earth was he? And what was she supposed to do now? She was soon to find out when Mr Roberts called her to one side. He explained that Alwyn had taken ill and word had been sent from his newly married daughter that he'd likely be off from work for a few days.

'Now, I know that's not the best thing for you, Lewis,' said Mr Roberts, 'as you've got used to working with Al and his ways, but I must assign you now to work with someone else.' He introduced her to a man known as Dan Sharpe. Mari gulped. Dan was one of the troublemakers that Al had got annoyed with as they'd queued for their wages last week. He was one of the men who was most put out by the casual young miners as they thought they were doing them out of work and pay.

Dan, though, was all smiles when the foreman approached to explain that 'Lewis Lloyd' would be his butty for the next three days.

'Watch me and you won't go far wrong!' he said, nodding at Mari, which made her think maybe things would be all right, but as soon as the foreman left her side to return to the cage to go back on top, Dan jabbed her in the arm and said sneeringly, 'If you think I'm going to make it nice and easy to work with me, laddie, then you've got another think coming!' Then he threw back his head and laughed. Two of his friends, who were stood nearby, clapped their hands gleefully.

'You give it to him, Dan! We'll soon get rid of these little tykes if we treat 'em mean!'

Mari wondered if the men had been drinking alcohol. Al reckoned they had, and that they did as little work as possible.

'Come on then!' yelled Dan. 'Follow me and keep up.' Then he handed Mari his heavy tool bag and pickaxe to carry.

Now she was dreading this shift. Never mind the next three days, would she get through this one?

\* \* \*

It became quite evident that Dan Sharpe hardly intended lifting a finger during his shift underground. Instead, he instructed Mari, who was already worn out from lugging the heavy tool bag, to hew away at the coal with the pickaxe she'd also hefted all that way. It was strange as Dan's tool bag seemed much heavier and bulkier than Al's to do the same job. Unused to such manual work, she found it most difficult, fearing that if she hacked away too hard, something might fall on her, causing her an injury.

Finally, Dan said, 'You're a little softie you are, lad! Gerrout of my way!' He removed his shirt, revealing his glistening bare chest, and she inhaled a faint whiff of perspiration mingled with tobacco. For a while, he hacked away at the coal, seeming to be quite good at it, but then appeared to get a bit bored. He threw down his pickaxe and then fixed his gaze on Mari. 'Fetch my tea can out of my work bag!'

She scrabbled around in the canvas bag and located the metal billy can and handed it to him, not expecting him to share his tea like Big Al had done. He slumped down on the ground and then began swigging from the can, gasping and groaning every so often. Then he wiped his mouth with the back of his hand and hiccupped loudly. It was then Mari realised there might not be any tea in his can at all; it probably contained some sort of alcohol. He could easily go to the pub to get it filled up.

'Whatcha looking at, son?' he growled.

'Nothing,' she said, shaking her head, deciding she'd do her level best to get through this shift in the hope the foreman might pair her with someone else tomorrow. Or maybe she could work with the horses. Even operating the door of the air shaft would be better than this, even if it meant sitting alone in the dark most of the time.

When he'd drunk his fill, Dan's head lolled to one side and, to her horror, by the sounds of the heavy snores emanating from him, it became evident he was fast asleep. What should she do now? She decided to find another collier for advice, preferably one who wasn't one of the five moaners and groaners who complained about the new lads taking their jobs. She had no idea where she was walking to as there were so many tunnels underground. She feared she might get lost in one of them and not find her way out again. But presently, upon hearing voices and a chiselling sound, she came towards a narrow seam where a collier was working with a young lad, side by side. They appeared to be working well together, the lad handing the man tools whenever asked, just as she'd done for Big Al.

'Excuse me, sir,' she said as she approached.

The man stopped what he was doing and, holding up his lamp, studied her carefully, the light causing her to blink.

'Hello, son. What can I do for you?'

She explained the situation to him, hoping he wouldn't side with the man she'd been working with, but she needn't have worried.

'Dan Sharpe, you say?'

'Yes, I've been working with him this morning.'

The man shook his head. 'He's not the best person for a new boy to work with. It's a right shame that Big Al took sick like that. You can stay with us if you like or return and wait for the end of the shift. I bet knowing him he'll be out for the count for ages.'

'But I'd rather keep busy, sir. That way the shift will go quicker for me...'

'Good lad. I like your spirit. Well, you can help the lad here to load up the dram. His name's Wally and I'm Duggie Mason.'

Wally was a very small lad, so she guessed he'd be an asset to get into difficult places underground.

Smiling, she blew out a breath of relief to be well away from Mr Sharpe. 'And my name's Lewis Lloyd.'

It was around two hours later when Mr Roberts arrived and by the look on his face he was fuming. No wonder too, thought Mari. He'd probably found Dan Sharpe fast asleep with no work completed in that seam whatsoever.

'Is that new lad with you?' Mr Roberts addressed Duggie as Mari and Wally were stood in his shadow.

'Yes, he's here helping me as...'

'Well, he's no right to be. He's left his post. Dan Sharpe's just made an official complaint about him to me. Said he's a lousy good-for-nothing who refused to help him.'

Pushing past Duggie, Mari confronted the foreman. 'That's just not true, Mr Roberts. He had me lugging that heavy bag of tools and the pickaxe for miles before we even started work, then he tried to get me to do all the hard work for him, hewing the coal. I later discovered he'd purposely weighed his bag down with lumps of coal to make it more difficult for me to carry! Then he told me he was going to drink his tea, but I don't even think it is tea in his can, I think it's alcohol! He was reeking of spirits and tobacco! And then to top it all, after drinking from his can, he fell fast asleep! So don't blame me; it's not my fault. I'm not even supposed to be hewing the coal, am I? Just helping with the tools and such.'

There was a long silence as the foreman mulled over what Mari had just told him.

'You'd better not be lying to me!' said Mr Roberts, wagging a warning finger.

'On my life, sir. He was fast asleep, so I didn't know what to do. I wanted to work so I came here to see if I could help.'

'That's true.' Duggie nodded. 'The lad's been a good help to me and Wally. Works like a Trojan, he does.'

'Very well, then. Carry on as you were,' said Mr Roberts. 'I'm going to have to take Dan Sharpe up to the surface and question him in my office...'

Then he turned his back on them and was gone as quickly as he'd arrived.

'Well done for speaking up, young Lewis.' Duggie smiled as he patted her shoulder.

Although Mari should have felt happy, for some reason she wasn't. She feared repercussions from telling tales on Dan Sharpe. At that moment, a feeling of great unease washed over her.

* * *

The following morning, Mari was relieved to be placed to work with Duggie again. Wally, due to his small stature, had been sent to work the trapdoor, a job he wasn't too pleased about according to Duggie.

Mari worked well with the man that morning but was relieved when they were finally able to take a break. Rivulets of perspiration had been running down her body and she was fearful of removing her jacket as Duggie had done himself, in case the new curves of her body would show and give her identity away. Even though she tried to bind her chest firmly every day, somehow the bandage managed to work its way down to her waist; at least the jacket covered her form.

The bread and cheese her mother had put into her brother's snap tin along with the billy can of water was enough to sustain her. Her mouth got so dry and dusty underground. Duggie was devouring a corned beef sandwich his wife, Edna, had prepared and he offered Mari one of the Welsh cakes the woman had baked. Mari gladly accepted, savouring the sugary treat.

She paused for a moment, realising they'd return to working together soon, so she wanted to get something out of the way, something that had been playing on her mind overnight and well into the morning.

'Mr Mason...' she began.

'Yes, Lew,' he said, looking up from his simple meal.

'That Dan Sharpe, what will have happened to him since I made that complaint about him to the foreman?'

Duggie scratched his chin. 'I daresay he'll be reprimanded if found guilty of what you accused him of.'

'And do you think he will?'

'Oh yes.' Duggie nodded. 'No doubt about it. He's been suspected of drinking on the job for a while now and smoking on occasion too. You see, we're not allowed to smoke down here, and we've been warned plenty of times about it, especially since the last two explosions where so many lost their lives. Can't afford to have a naked flame around as there are pockets of a natural type of gas and it can ignite and cause a terrific explosion! So, you did the right thing, as he's endangering lives.'

Mari blew out a breath. 'I remember my father said a man who worked here had been locked up in the Swansea House of Correction for ten days for smoking underground.'

Duggie narrowed his gaze. 'How'd you know that? Unless your father works here?'

Oh dear, she'd gone and done it again, almost given herself away. Now she was going to have to dig herself out of a tricky situation. 'I er... I think he overheard some colliers talking in the pub.'

'Oh, I see,' he said, smiling now. 'I know the fella it was. He ignited his cigarette from the light of his safety lamp. It had been locked at six o'clock that morning but was open when the manager saw him. Not worth taking any chances down here and he learned his lesson after that.'

'Does he still work here?'

'Oh, aye, he does.' He nodded and then paused for a moment and smiled. 'It was me, you see, Lew. I was the guilty party. I've not done anything like it since and don't intend to ever again. I've learned my lesson and in a way it did me good, as if I catch anyone being as foolish as I was, I can warn them what happened to me. It wasn't nice in that place in Swansea. Oh no, it wasn't...' He shook his head and then, lifting his pickaxe, began to hew away at the coal seam with great purpose.

* * *

It wasn't until later in the shift that word had got around that Dan Sharpe had been dismissed by the foreman. Mari's intention hadn't been for the man to lose his job, but how could she work with someone like that?

'You did right, Lew,' reassured Duggie, 'but if I were you don't tell anyone that you informed on him.'

'Won't people realise it was me though?'

'Well, did anyone see you go off to work with him?'

She bit her lip, remembering two of the man's friends had been there at the time. 'Actually, two men who seem to be Dan's friends saw me. They weren't very nice to me either.'

'Then keep quiet about it to the rest of the men. Deny it if you must. Of course, Dan might well tell them it was you; that's if he remembers your name. But it might have been any of the casual workers in reality. Stay away from Dan's mates if you can. This place will be a lot safer without the likes of him. Five down four to go...'

Mari frowned, puzzled for a moment at what Duggie meant by that remark, then she realised he was talking about the five men who stuck together, and all seemed as bad as one another.

'Yes, I'll keep quiet about it if I can. What about Mr Roberts? Might he tell some of the men though?'

'Oh no. I very much doubt it. He has more sense than that. He realises you're a good worker and they're hard to find. Also, it took a lot of courage to do what you did yesterday, and he'll think a lot of you for doing that. Who knows, he might try to keep you on permanently here. How would you feel about that?'

Mari didn't know how to reply. She'd promised her family that as soon as Bryn was working again, she'd give up working at the pit, but the truth was, despite having a tough time with Dan the previous morning, after that, she'd quite enjoyed working with Duggie. Since working with the man, the shifts had appeared to fly by as he related funny tales to her and told her some silly jokes. Yes, she was beginning to enjoy her work and the camaraderie it brought with it.

\* \* \*

But the following morning the four troublemakers were waiting at the pit entrance for her. One stuck his foot out as she passed and Mari felt herself flying through the air before falling heavily with a bump, landing on her hands and knees. It hurt so bad that tears began to well up in her eyes. Those rotters had chosen to do that when no one else was around too.

'Oooh, how clumsy of me!' the man who had stuck his foot out said in a mocking tone of voice while the others laughed.

Mari pulled herself to her feet, glaring at them until one of them was forced to turn away.

'Stop it, Pete, he's only a young lad...' one of the men who looked older than the others said as the laughing ceased.

Then Pete, stepping forward, said, 'You forced our friend out of his job. He's lost it because of a whippersnapper like you!'

'That's not true!' Mari stuck her chin out in defiance as she felt a small trickle of warm blood run from her nose. Wiping it on her sleeve, she sniffed. 'He was so drunk he fell asleep during the shift, and I didn't know what to do. So I found someone else to work with and the foreman questioned me when he saw me elsewhere. What else was I supposed to do?' She felt angry now at the whole situation, none of which was any of her own doing.

Pete's mouth, which had been open with surprise at the way Mari had answered him, snapped shut.

The four men filed past her as they headed towards the cage, then one of them stopped and turned to look at her. 'You'd best keep away from us – we don't like informers!'

Mari stood and watched them walk away; she'd wait for the

next cage to go underground. She feared standing too close to any of them for fear of what they could do to her.

'Hey, what's happened to you?' a voice from behind called.

She turned to see Duggie, standing behind her with a concerned look on his face. She explained what had just occurred.

'Bullies is what they are. Come on, I'll get you over to the foreman's office to check you're all right.'

Mari shook her head, knowing she'd only cause more trouble by alerting Mr Roberts. 'No, there's no need, honestly. My nose has stopped bleeding now.' She didn't tell Duggie that her knees hurt badly where she'd fallen, and she'd probably scuffed them, just in case they wanted to examine her, and they asked her to strip off. Then it would become evident she wasn't a boy at all.

Duggie sucked in a sharp breath through his teeth as he shook his head. 'If you're sure, Lew. Come on, you'll be working with me again today. But if I catch any of those fellas bullying you, I'll go to the foreman's office myself and report every single one of them!'

It was good to know that Duggie had her back, but she realised he wasn't going to be around all the time, so she'd best keep herself alert to any impending danger.

* * *

'But that's appalling what happened to you, Mari,' said Bobby with a look of concern on his face. It was a couple of days later and she was back working at the shop for a spell. Bobby had called in to purchase some washing soda for his mother and the shop was empty, while Mrs Jones was taking a well-earned break in the back room.

Mari lowered her voice. 'I haven't told anyone about it, not even my brother. The only person I've confided in is Duggie; he has my back at that place, and Big Al too.'

A shadow darkened Bobby's face and he went to say something but hesitated.

'What's the matter?'

'Haven't you heard?'

'Heard what?' Mari blinked.

'Al's wife has the cholera. That's probably why he's been taking time off from the pit – and given the foreman some cock-and-bull story that he's been ill himself. Probably wanted to stay home to help his wife.'

Mari's hand flew to her mouth. 'I'd no idea. I haven't heard anyone speak about him of late. I thought he was sick himself but would return to work any day.'

'From what my father told me, he's been taking care of his wife. Also, although he doesn't seem to have the sickness himself, he's probably afraid if he returns to the pit it might spread it if he has it too.'

Mari nodded, open-mouthed. She'd been banking on Big Al returning to protect her against those bullies, but of course it was more important that he care for his wife and keep himself safe.

'Look,' said Bobby, flashing a guarded glance in her direction. 'Don't mention any of this to anyone at the pit, will you?' She shook her head. 'It might be that he's spinning them some yarn about being ill himself to keep his own job. If the powers that be find out he's stopping off from work to care for his wife, they might sack him.'

'That's so wrong,' said Mari. 'He's a good worker.'

'He might be a good worker but, according to my father, he's not getting any younger and workers at the pit are ten a penny. You can see in a way why those bullies as you call them despise the new lads that come in and work on a casual basis. They're fearful of losing their jobs.'

'I suppose.' Mari nodded. She honestly hadn't looked at it that way before.

The shop doorbell tinkled, and an elderly lady entered with a big smile on her face, so Mari made to leave the counter to attend to her.

'I'll see you later!' Bobby waved and, by the time Mari had approached the customer, the doorbell was tinkling once again as he left the shop.

What a to-do though, poor Al having to care for his wife like that. But that was the sort of man he was: someone who looked out for others, wanting to protect them at all costs.

* * *

When Mari arrived home after helping at the shop, she was surprised to see Glenda sitting near the fireside, nestled beside Bryn, and he was holding her hand. Were those tears in the young woman's eyes? Mam quickly ushered Mari into the scullery before she had the chance to say anything.

'What's going on, Mam?'

Her mother looked deep into her eyes and after taking a breath said, 'It's all come crashing down.'

'I'm sorry, I don't understand.'

'Why should you, *cariad*? What adults do sometimes makes no sense whatsoever. Glenda arrived here about half an hour ago – sobbing her heart out, she was. It appears that the reason she's not paid a visit to Bryn since his pit accident is because her father has forbidden her from doing so.'

Mari frowned, feeling confused by the situation. 'I don't understand?'

'You will. The reason he stopped her from seeing our Bryn is because of your father's behaviour. He thought it not decent she come here after your father ran off with that floozy. I suppose he's thinking of his position as a chapel deacon.'

'But that's most unfair to judge Bryn by our father's actions!' said Mari, fury flooding her veins. 'Bryn hasn't done anything; he's not the one who has gone off with a woman, is he?'

'No, he's not,' said Mam, shaking her head. 'But some people are like that. He probably sees Bryn as an apple that might not have fallen too far from the family tree. What I mean is he might consider it as, *like father, like son!*'

Mari's hands flew to her face. 'But that's despicable for Bryn to be blamed for our father's behaviour.'

'I know.' Her mother shrugged in a defeated fashion. 'Anyhow, Glenda is here without her father's knowledge. She's come to explain, that's all. They've both been in tears in there. Anyone can see the deep feelings that pair have for one another. I was just about to prepare tea for them when you arrived home. I'll pour it now, so you can take the tray in for them – I don't want to break down in front of them both. But this is breaking my heart, it is.'

Mari nodded wordlessly. It seemed to her that there was no answer to the situation her brother and Glenda found themselves in. But that father of theirs had caused a lot of trouble for the family yet again.

## 11

It was just a few days later that the word came in the shop: Big Al's wife, Maud, had sadly passed away. Mari really felt for him and intended to call around to see him to pay her respects.

'I'd hold back on doing that if I were you,' advised Mrs Jones. 'We don't know if cholera has left the village yet.'

'But I've only heard of it at that house in Lewis Square and at Al's house,' she said.

'It's not as simple as that though, Mari. You just never know. Maybe Al even has it himself.'

Mari doubted it, not if Al had been well enough to take care of his wife, but nevertheless, she nodded in agreement. Maybe she'd wait a week or two. At least there appeared to be fewer cases of the disease in the village of Abercanaid than there was in the bustling surrounding area of Merthyr Tydfil. It was a large industrial town that brought people to work in the ironworks from far and wide. There was overcrowding in some areas such as the China district of the town and in some of the boarding houses where people lived cheek to jowl. At least Abercanaid was a quiet little village with a small population in comparison with that heaving iron metropolis.

'You're missing him at work, are you?' Mrs Jones asked as she placed a jar of raspberry jam on the counter. She often made jars of preserves for folks, which were for sale on the shop's counter – they quickly sold out; no sooner would she place them there than someone would enter the shop and a jar of pickled onions or marmalade would take their eye. She made the jars look ever so pretty with frilled blue and white or red and white gingham lid covers she also made herself.

'Yes, I am missing Al dreadfully, Mrs Jones. Duggie was good to work with an' all but he's going to be off from work for a week or two on annual leave, so goodness knows who I'll be working with next!'

Mrs Jones bit her bottom lip and, looking thoughtful for a moment, said, 'So, I suppose you're a bit scared you might encounter those bullies again?'

Mari nodded, then blew out a hard breath. It was no good denying it; that last time they'd goaded her had shaken her up. The scabs from falling on her knees were still there. Any physical scars would heal but not the mental ones.

'Yes, I am petrified, to be honest with you, Mrs Jones.'

'Look,' said her employer, softly, 'do you think you ought to tell your mother and brother what's going on? I bet if they knew they'd want to do something about it.'

'That's the problem though. Bryn might try to somehow get himself over to the pit and thump them. I can't have that. He's doing well at the moment.'

'I guess you don't want anything to impede his progress?'

'No, I don't. And if I tell Mam she'll only worry her guts about it all and try to stop me working at the pit. Not only that, but if

Bryn goes rushing to the pit and causes a scene there's always the chance my identity will get discovered in the progress. Those men and the foreman might wonder why Bryn is so worked up about someone bullying Lewis Lloyd when it's none of his business to begin with!'

'It's a dilemma for you, Mari, it really is.' Mrs Jones placed a hand of reassurance on her shoulder and, looking into her eyes, added, 'I don't know what the answer is. But do me one small favour, won't you?'

Mari nodded.

'If anyone hurts you again, you'll tell someone about it, won't you? If not your brother or mother, then the foreman?'

Mari nodded but she didn't really mean it, as wasn't it her informing on one of the men that had got her into this trouble in the first place?

* * *

Glenda had decided she'd still call to see Bryn against her father's wishes, so she had to be careful not to get caught out. Mari realised the girl would hate lying to her parents, but she had a friend who lived in upper Abercanaid, so it seemed feasible that sometimes she could leave the house with a basket of baked items such as a fruit cake or a loaf of bread as a gift, which the Evans family were most grateful for. Glenda's family weren't short of a bob or two. They lived in a large house near the canal bank. It wasn't as big as the Davenport one but nevertheless it made all the mineworkers' street houses and cottages look very small in comparison. The family didn't have any servants as such working for them except for a handyman who kept the garden tidied up and who did general repairs. Mr Harper was a busy accountant who often attended meetings or took the train to Pontypridd or Cardiff.

'I've kept away from Bryn for far too long,' explained Glenda when she arrived at the house that evening, her beautiful cornflower-blue eyes filling with tears, which she blinked away. Then she turned to them all and said, 'I hope you can find it in your hearts to forgive me...' She exchanged a loving glance with Bryn.

There was a short pause and then Mam broke the silence by saying, 'Of course we do, Glenda. You're always more than welcome in this house; you know that. I've prepared a little tea for us all, just a few ham sandwiches and such, and I thought we'd have coffee to wash it down with and I've baked some *bara brith*.'

'Oooh!' exclaimed Bryn. 'We really are honoured. I can't remember the last time we tasted coffee in this house.'

Mam chuckled. 'It is a special occasion after all. Now remove your shawl, Glenda, and come and be seated at the table.' All filed into the scullery where the table was set with Mam's best white lace tablecloth, the one she'd been gifted when she'd wed. The only trouble was the man she'd married was no longer head of the house. Now Bryn had taken his place and sat where once their father had. Despite how he'd treated her of late, Mari couldn't help shedding a little tear realising that the family were now all moving on without him but, in moments of sentimentality, she needed to remind herself that it was he who had first moved on from them.

\* \* \*

Mari was due to work the first of another three day shifts at the pit in the morning and was relieved that she was placed to work with William, the young lad Big Al had introduced her to. William was very welcoming, offering to show her the ropes.

He explained that the ponies were used to pull the drams of coal and needed to navigate the low tunnels. He told her that they were taken to the surface in the summer months on a rotation system where they were put out to grass. They needed to wear blinkers to protect their eyes and to prevent them from becoming startled by anything. They could be quite dangerous to work with if care wasn't taken, as one young lad had become crushed and almost lost his life. Fortunately, he escaped death but was unlikely to work ever again. William's official job title was 'ostler' and he, along with a couple of other lads, took care of the pit ponies. They needed to feed and groom them and guide them in and out of the mine. It was the ostlers who took care of their well-being. Now, one of the usual lads was ill, so someone was required to help and, luckily for Mari, she'd been chosen by the foreman. Although she was happy working with William and the ponies, she did realise she might encounter one of the bullying men. And what would William be able to do if they set on her again? He was only a young lad himself.

He introduced Mari to a pit pony called Brandy who was twenty years old. Brandy had worked underground for seventeen years, and he described her as being as wily as a wolf and as crafty as a fox, as she was able to navigate some tricky tunnels, took commands well and had even given birth to a few foals over the years. When that happened, William explained that the pregnant mares were sent to pasture for a while and when their foals were old enough, usually from three years old, they, in turn, became pit ponies.

Mari thought it a little sad that these beautiful creatures spent so long in an alternate world beneath ground, but then again, as William had explained, they knew no different and were often treated better than other ponies who lived on farms or were kept as pets. Every day he had an apple or two in his pocket for them and from what Mari could see, the lads treated them well. But those heavy loads they transported must have been hard toil for the poor beasts of burden.

'The ponies return to the stables after a shift where they are unharnessed to have a little walk, drink and are fed a bit of corn and rested for the next shift. That's how it works,' said William as he patted Brandy's neck with great affection. Brandy surprised her by snorting her appreciation, and it was then Mari realised that there was a lot of love between the two of them.

'Why was she named Brandy?' Mari asked.

'Rumour has it that originally she was owned by a group of Romany gypsies who lived on the Merthyr side of the Aberdare Mountain, in the woods. Her original owner was supposed to like a nip of brandy, and the name stuck. Well, that's how it was explained to me by one of the older ostlers...' He paused for a moment. 'Nice man he was an' all, but he perished in last year's pit explosion...'

Mari nodded. 'That's dreadful.' Gingerly, she patted the horse's mane.

'She likes you – I can tell,' said William approvingly.

'Why do you say that?'

'Because she doesn't take to everyone. She seems to sense the nature of folk. Some of the men here have treated her harshly in passing and she even bit one of them!' Mari chuckled. 'They weren't laughing, I can tell you, and they've kept away from her ever since.'

'I don't blame them, but it sounds to me as if this old girl has got a lot of sense!'

'You're right there. I should have added she's as wise as an owl!'

* * *

Mari found it interesting learning about the ponies. The other stable lad's name was Garth, and the other three ponies were called: Rufus, Sally and Moll. But the one that had taken her heart most of all was Brandy. If she could, she'd be happy to work in the stable every day. It was hard work though as the stalls needed mucking out and it could get a bit whiffy. She also had to watch where she was standing sometimes, as there were small piles of horse dung hither and thither, but there was an intense satisfaction in cleaning those stalls and providing the ponies with fresh hay and water.

'William,' she said later, 'do you think I ought to buy some apples and carrots and things for the ponies?'

'Good heavens, no!' He chuckled. 'I don't pay for the apples in my pocket. There's a supply of that sort of thing at the end of the stalls in a cupboard if you need them; they're in a couple of old sacks. Don't overfeed them though or they get quite lethargic.'

'Oh, that's good to know. I had worried I'd have to pay for supplies myself and it's hard enough for me to help feed my family as it is, ever since my father left us...' She bit her lip realising what she'd said. Now he'd want to know more.

'Oh, that's dreadful, Lew. You're not alone in that. There was a man what was working here, a collier, who left his family to go off with a fancy piece. By all accounts they're living hand to mouth now because of him. His name is Gwynfor Evans but don't tell anyone I told you, will you?'

She shook her head, feeling herself grow hot. To think he was referring to her father. But to tell him so would give her identity away. There were too many who worked at this pit who would have known him, including that group of bullies.

* * *

As William led Brandy down the low, dark tunnel with Mari in tow, she felt a shiver course down the length of her spine. This was one part of the mine she'd not entered before and quite suddenly it felt extremely cold, chilling her to the bone. Then there was a dripping sound, and they waded through a big puddle.

'This section is a bit dangerous by here, so take care, Lew,' William warned.

The tunnel had narrowed now so that Mari could reach out and touch the pieces of coal jutting out from the wall.

William turned and said, 'I've forgotten something. I need to return to the stable. Can you remain here with Brandy and just keep her calm?'

Mari, feeling confident of doing that, replied, 'Yes, of course.'

But when William had departed, she began to feel wary.

To keep herself calm she stroked Brandy's mane and whispered in her ear, 'You're all right with me, girl. I'll look after you.'

Brandy nuzzled Mari's face with affection.

There were voices headed towards them in the distance and a feeling of dread washed over her when she recognised the voice of the man who had got nasty and pushed her – it was Pete! What was she to do now?

*Please hurry up, William! Surely, they won't set on me with you around?*

As the two men approached, Mari turned her head to the side.

'All right there, William?' one said.

'Aye,' replied Mari and they went on their way. She breathed a sigh of relief that they hadn't recognised her in the dark. All they

e their own miner's lamps and they hadn't shone them in
and for that she was grateful.

en William returned, he said, 'Sorry to have left you like
ut I forgot a carrot for Brandy and sometimes navigating
narrow tunnels and the loud, echoing sounds in this part of
mine can make her a little on edge, so I usually divert her
ntion by giving her a little something.'

'D... does that usually w... work?'

'Yes, it does. But what's the matter with you, Lew? Your voice
ounds a bit shaky? Were you scared of being in the dark?'

Mari was about to say yes, when she decided to tell the truth.
No. There are a group of men who are giving me some bother
since I've been working here... two of them just passed me by but
luckily in the dark they assumed I was you.'

'Oh, I know the fellas you mean. There's five of them, right?'

'Yes. I ended up reporting one of them to the foreman
recently as he was drunk and falling asleep, so now they blame
me for him having lost his job.'

'That won't be the main reason for it though...'

'How'd you mean?'

'One in particular has been doing that for a long time now
and becoming bold with it; he's been getting away with murder.'

'Oh, I see. But that group of men seem to dislike us casual,
new boys anyhow.'

'Aye, they do. It wasn't the same for me when I started here, as
I came to work with my brother and was taken on full-time as his
butty to begin with. Then it was suggested I be taken on as a
stable boy. I'm glad that happened to me as I wouldn't have it any
other way,' William said with satisfaction.

'I wish I could work with the pit ponies all day.' Mari sighed.

'I can't see that happening, sorry. Jimmy, the lad who's off
work, will be back any day now. He's not going anywhere any

time soon. 'Course I'd love to have you work with me, Lew. If it were up to me...'

Mari nodded. Why were things going so wrong for her right now? She thought when she'd started work that first day that Big Al would always be around for her. But then she felt bad for thinking that way, as poor Al had problems of his own right now. He was a grieving widower, who'd lost the love of his life.

## 12

The first real thought Mari had about the approach of Christmas was when she returned to work at the shop a few days later. Mrs Jones had ordered extra supplies of sacks of flour and sugar, along with jars of dried mixed fruit and various spices.

'I thought I'd better get these in as we're running out and some folks are a little late making their Christmas cakes. I know from experience Mrs Mullins and Mrs Howells will be banging on the shop door on the first of December or thereabouts before I've even opened up. They do it every year. Though by rights...' she said, stroking her chin, 'it's best to bake a Christmas cake well in advance. Gives it time to mature, see. Also nice to feed it with a drop of brandy now and again. That way it's not too dry when it comes to eating it!' She turned towards the counter to face Mari. 'Has your mother baked her Christmas cake as yet?'

Mari shook her head as she huffed out a defeated breath. 'No, and I don't think she intends to either. I don't think any of us are in the mood to celebrate this year with how things are...'

Mrs Jones nodded. 'I quite understand, *cariad*. But there's nothing any of you can do about the current situation regarding your father and his, er...' She appeared at a loss for the correct words for a moment before saying, 'His *lady friend*. So, if I were you lot, I'd enjoy it as best you can.' She paused for a while to place a jar of mixed spice on the shelf behind her.

Mari was just about to sweep up the floor as the delivery man had brought some muck in on his boots and there was a long line of muddy footprints from the door as far as the counter, when Mrs Jones carried on.

'I tell you what we could do. When we have some quiet time later, how about we bake a Christmas cake together, you and I? In the back room, and then in a few weeks it will be a nice surprise for all the family. Especially if you help to bake it.'

Mari nodded, though she found it hard to get excited about mixing all the ingredients with a wooden spoon, especially as her arms were aching something rotten from loading up the dram with coal at the pit, but if it cheered up Mam and Bryn, then the effort taken would be worth it. Though Bryn was a lot happier these days since being reunited with Glenda, so it would be for Mam and the younger children really.

'Thank you, Mrs Jones. You're ever so kind to me.' Mari smiled. If only working at the pit was as nice as working at the shop. She'd enjoyed working with the ponies but realised she could end up working with anyone on her next shift, as Jimmy would return to his usual stable lad job. She had a sudden thought. 'Any news about Big Al, I mean Mr Probert?'

Mrs Jones chuckled at the nickname but then her face took on a serious expression as she nodded sombrely. 'Well, I've heard from his neighbour who calls in here that he's not so good.' She held the palm of her hand to her chest. 'His wife was his whole world. He absolutely doted on her.'

Mari felt a lump in her throat at the thought of the big man being so upset. He was such a lovely, caring man and she guessed he must have been a good husband to his wife and father to his kids, unlike her own father.

As if she could read her mind, Mrs Jones looked at her and asked, 'Have any of you seen or heard from your father since he's back living in Abercanaid?'

Mari shook her head. 'No. It's strange. You'd think we'd have seen him by now.'

'No one has mentioned him or that Blodwyn one to me of late. It's as if they've both gone to ground. I haven't seen him going into the pub either. Not that I go inside those places of perpetual sin, mind you.' She sucked in a sharp breath and shook her head. 'Oh no, I don't. They're the work of the Devil those are. Many a man or woman who enters one of those places might as well head straight to Sodom and Gomorrah!'

Mari was quite taken aback by the vehemence in the tone of the woman's voice. 'Why do you think that, Mrs Jones?'

'Because when the drink is in, the wit is out. Drunken fools they are...' Then she lowered her voice, as all became clear why she thought that way. 'My late husband, Edmund, he started off our married life sober but after a so-called friend of his persuaded him to join him at the pub for "a quick pint" as he put it, my Edmund was never the same afterwards. He took to going there every night after work, sometimes staggering home in the small hours. Then it got so bad, he'd leave me alone in the shop on the pretence of going "on business to Merthyr" when I knew it really meant he was off to the pub again. Took over his life it did. In the end his liver must have been as pickled as a walnut! I reckon that's what polished him off. And all because his friend asked him if he fancied a quick pint one night!'

'What happened to his friend? Did he have a problem too, Mrs Jones?'

'That's the best of it. He could just have a quick pint now and again. Oh no, his missus had no problem with him if she wanted him home. If he hadn't asked him to go for that drink, my Edmund would still be alive today, I reckon.'

Mari very much doubted that. Mr Jones would probably have found a way to drink anyhow, she reckoned, but was savvy enough not to relate any of that to her employer. But nevertheless, she did feel deeply sorry for the woman. It must have been lonely for her when the shop was closed or at times like Christmas when others were having a high old festive time with their families. It gave her an idea to ask Mam later if she might invite her for Christmas Day, to join in with their festivities.

* * *

'Make a wish!' urged Mrs Jones as she supervised Mari, sprinkling some extra cinnamon in the large porcelain bowl with the other ingredients.

Mari turned from the scullery counter to face the woman. 'But I thought that was only for a Christmas pudding, not for a cake?' She furrowed her brow with confusion.

'No!' said Mrs Jones in a firm tone of voice. Then she smiled. 'In our family it was always a tradition that everyone who got to stir the cake mix got to make a wish. I'm talking about when I was a young girl, of course. I had two elder sisters who joined in to take a turn as well as my mother and aunt. It was a family tradition amongst the womenfolk, I suppose. Course, it doesn't happen any more.'

Mari raised her brows. 'How is that, Mrs Jones?'

'All my family are deceased now: my mother and aunt died many moons ago and both my sisters have since passed away too.' She cast a glance at Mari. 'Don't look so concerned, *cariad*. I have lots going on in my life these days with running the shop. I'm far too busy to feel alone with all the people flooding through the shop door of a day!'

Thinking for a moment, Mari smiled and softly said, 'Would you like to stir the cake and make a wish right now then, Mrs Jones?' Even though the woman was putting a brave face on things, she couldn't help thinking there must be some moments when she felt alone in the world without her husband or family.

Mrs Jones chuckled. 'Why, indeed I would!' she said, taking the wooden spoon from her hand. Mari watched as the woman stirred the mixture and then closed her eyes firmly shut as she made a wish, then opened them again.

'What did you wish for, Mrs Jones?'

'That'd be telling!' The woman laughed as she tapped the side of her nose with her index finger. 'To be truthful, I'd better not tell you as it might not come true if I do.'

'Oh!' Mari felt a little taken aback by the woman's furtive behaviour. But she didn't mind too much as Mrs Jones often reminded her of a young girl, with her sense of humour and yearning to have fun even at her age. Baking a Christmas cake together had obviously revived happy memories for the woman.

The shop bell tinkled, which brought their merriment to an end. Mari headed off to attend to a customer as Mrs Jones placed the large cake tin in the oven to bake. Soon the delicious aroma of dried fruit soaked in brandy, containing cinnamon and citrus peel, permeated the air, drifting through to the shop floor.

Yes, there was no doubt about it. Mari planned to ask her mother tonight if Mrs Jones could join them for Christmas dinner rather than spend the day alone.

\* \* \*

'What do you want to ask her for?' Mari had summoned up the courage to bring up the subject of inviting Mrs Jones for Christmas Day later that evening, but her mother seemed cross with her as a frown embedded itself deeply on Mam's forehead. 'As far as I'm concerned, I can go without any sort of celebration at all this year!'

Mari swallowed hard and then let out a little sigh. She hadn't been expecting that sharp retort from her mother. 'Because she's been ever so good to me, Mam. To us all, really.'

Bryn glanced up from the copy of *Hard Times* by Charles Dickens he'd been in the middle of reading in the fireside armchair. He often became so absorbed in a book that he seemed to block out all that was going on around him but the mention of his sister's kind request to their mother was enough to prick up his ears. 'It's true though, Mam,' he said. 'Mrs Jones is keeping us going with food provisions during a difficult time...'

Their mother's eyes flashed as she straightened up. 'But our Mari has to work for those few eggs and loaves of bread, or whatever! The woman doesn't even pay her a decent wage for her time.'

What on earth was the matter with Mam? She seemed more on edge than usual this evening. Mari exchanged a concerned glance with her brother as their mother turned to exit the room for the scullery.

'Leave her to me,' whispered Bryn. 'She had a bit of a set-to with that Blodwyn one earlier today.'

'Oh!' Mari's mouth gaped wide open, and she snapped it shut. She hated seeing her mother get upset about anything, particularly if it was something to do with their father. She drew nearer to Bryn and lowering her voice said, 'So, what happened then?'

'It appears that Mam was brave enough for once to venture down to the village on her own, for the first time since Dad took up with that flighty piece. It was most unfortunate I suppose but when she called to the bakehouse to purchase the bread, Blodwyn was already inside.'

Mari frowned. 'But how did Mam realise it was her anyhow? None of us know her. I thought she'd never set eyes on her before, just her mother.'

'She hasn't. Apparently, she heard another customer refer to her by that name and by the furtive glances they were both giving Mam, it drove her to erupt and cause a right old scene.'

Mari shrugged. 'It had to happen sometime, I suppose. She's been too good about things since Dad left us in the lurch.'

Bryn nodded with understanding. 'I think you're right. Anyhow, better you wait a while before approaching Mam about Mrs Jones again. Allow the dust to settle for a while. I'm sure she'll be more amenable given enough time. Mam is just too angry now and rightly so.'

*The trouble is she's angry with the wrong people*, thought Mari.

* * *

A few days later, Mari was standing with the other colliers waiting for the cage to return so they might be lowered into the ground. The cage was raised and lowered several times before a shift and she tended to remain back until one of the last journeys into the bowels of the earth. She disliked being crowded in. It was just so stifling being surrounded – also she feared those bullies. As she stood there, she heard one of the men whose voice she recognised.

'Well, well, well, the wanderer returns!' His words had a sarcastic tone to them, and she realised it was one of the troublemakers.

Thinking they were talking to Big Al, who might have

returned to work, her head whipped around. But to her great shock she saw it was her own father who was being spoken to. He had returned to the pit after all this time. She'd not set eyes on him since the night her brother was taken ill, and one of her last memories was of him slapping her face. What if he saw her? It was not quite daylight yet.

She surged forward to get on the next cage.

Wary now, she thought maybe it would be best if, after she got through the shift, she stopped working at the mine completely. Luckily, she was put to work with Duggie again and the shift went by quite quickly. She'd almost forgotten her father was now back underground. She supposed he had to earn a living and, despite all his faults, he had been a good worker, so no wonder the foreman had taken him back on, with a warning no doubt after the way he'd left so suddenly.

Duggie had been feeling a little unwell, so he left Mari's side for a while, and she decided to take the opportunity to have a little break to eat her bread and cheese, which Mam had packed for her early that morning. She was just about to take a bite when one of the troublemakers discovered her. It was Pete, the ringleader, the one who had tripped her up when she'd hurt herself. A shiver coursed through her body as he sidled up beside her.

'What you got there then, sonny?'

'B... bread and ch... cheese...' Her teeth were chattering now as there was no one else around. *Duggie, where are you when I need you?*

'Hand them over to me now!' he growled as he stretched out his hand in her direction. From the way his eyes gleamed, she could see he meant business.

But then she thought, why should she, so she said, 'No! Go away and leave me alone!'

He drew nearer and she inhaled strong fumes of alcohol and tobacco. 'What did you say, *bachgen drwg*!'

'I am not a bad boy!' she shouted at him, fired with feelings of being treated unfairly. 'I work here the same as you do, though probably I work a damn sight harder than you!'

Roughly, he grabbed her by the collar of her jacket, forcefully shaking her. 'If you worked that hard, you wouldn't be wearing your jacket, little boy! You'd be stripped off to the waist like the other colliers. Remove your jacket and shirt, lad!'

Mari gulped. If she did so, he'd see that her chest had been bound up with a bandage and if he removed that, it would be evident she was a girl who shouldn't be underground at all.

A resinous voice emanating from behind the man came to her defence. 'Leave him alone, Pete. He's only a young lad!'

*Dad!*

Pete released her collar, causing her to tumble backwards, and she looked up at both men. Her father was now dragging the man away to have a few sharp words with him, and then he returned to kneel beside her. 'Are you all right, lad?'

She nodded, hoping he wouldn't recognise her in this garb and with the flat cap pulled over her eyes.

'Good, come on then, let's get you on your feet. You've no need to worry about bullies like him. I'm going to inform all the other men to watch out for him with you new lads...'

As he spoke, Mari's cap fell to the ground; it had got displaced when Pete had shaken her like that and now, under the lamplight, she watched her father swallow and then his eyes enlarge.

'Mari, is that you?'

'Y... yes, Dad.' She began to sob and, before she knew it, she was in his arms, and he was holding her tightly as she wept.

'But why, how are you doing this? This is no place for a young girl!'

When she'd finally composed herself, sniffing, she said, 'When you left us, our Bryn had an accident underground and couldn't work, a crush injury...' She was so unsettled at seeing her father again that she began to tremble all over.

'You're not afraid of me, are you, Mari?' said her father with disbelief in his voice.

She thought back to that time he had slapped her face, and in that moment realised it was not fear she felt right now but relief at seeing him again after being abandoned. 'No, Dad.' She shook her head. 'It's just I'm surprised to see you after all that's gone on lately. It's been an awful time for us as a family ever since Bryn got injured.'

'Aye, I just heard about that from one of the other men,' he said, nodding his head sadly. 'But he's on the mend now?'

'Yes, he is, though not fit enough to return here as yet. Anyhow, I wondered how I could help, so first I started working in the shop for Mrs Jones. She couldn't afford to pay me any wages, but she gave me some food in return to help us over a lean time. But our Bryn gave me the idea one day saying if I dressed as a boy that maybe I'd get a job underground. It was only meant as a joke though.'

'And you took him seriously?' her father asked in an incredulous tone of voice.

She sniffed loudly. 'Yes. I only wanted to help everyone out.'

'Oh, my dear child.' He hugged her close again. 'This is all my fault that I've put you in this position. If I hadn't gone off so suddenly like that you wouldn't all be in such a pickle right now. And your mother? How is she?'

'She's coping after a fashion, but it was hard for her when Bryn had his accident.' A big lump had formed in her throat, so she swallowed it. 'But why did you leave us all, Dad?'

He shook his head. 'I can't explain it, love. Something took over me and, to be truthful, as soon as I arrived in London, I wondered what I was doing there and felt I should be back home with you all, but by then it was already too late to alter things.' The regret in her father's voice was evident.

Mari wondered what he meant by 'too late to alter things' though.

'So, why are you back in Abercanaid then, Dad?'

'My friend, er, that is, er, Blodwyn, was missing her mother and had a yearning for home. I did have a job lined up in London, but the cholera is raging in a big city like that. We thought it best to return and face the music, as it were... I've been meaning to pay a visit to you all, particularly to your mother and now to Bryn too after hearing about his accident.'

'Oh! I don't know if either of them would like that right now,' she said softly, then added brightly, 'but Tommy and Nerys would.' Even if her mother and Bryn didn't want to see him ever again, she knew her younger siblings would. They missed their father dreadfully.

'There's something your mother needs to know about...'

Before her father had the chance to explain further, Duggie appeared, so Mari quickly replaced her cap on her head.

'Hello, Gwynfor,' he said good-naturedly as though genuinely pleased to see her father again. 'I'd heard you were back at work just now; one of the fellas told me.'

'Aye, couldn't keep away from the ruddy place!' Her father chuckled.

'I see you've met Lewis, then? Otherwise known as Lew?'

'Oh, aye. We've just had a conversation. He was being bullied by that Pete. We need to keep an eye on these young lads.'

'I'm with you there,' said Duggie.

'See you both later then!' Dad smiled at them and winked at Mari.

It had been wonderful seeing her father again but what was she supposed to say to her mother and Bryn about the encounter?

\* \* \*

Mari didn't see her father again during the shift and was still muddling away to herself whether she ought to inform her mother and brother about unexpectedly seeing her father today, but when she came up in the cage and stepped forward to walk through the pit gates at the end of her shift, Dad was waiting for her. It was dark now after a twelve-hour shift and he looked more hunched over than normal. It was usual for him to have his evening meal with the family and then sometimes nip to the pub for a couple of pints, but she had the feeling that he didn't do that these days. He would be going back home to the new woman in his life – she was his family now.

'Come on. I'll walk you back home, "Lew",' he said, smiling. She'd never known her father to be so kind and thoughtful towards her, not since the days he took her walking up the mountain to see those glorious daffodils.

'All right, Dad,' she said gratefully. She often feared walking home alone in case any of those troublemakers followed her and set upon her in the dark – there were plenty of bushes and shady corners they might hide behind to lie in wait for her approach.

'And when we reach home, you are going to go inside and tell your mother I need to speak to her, all right?'

Had things soured so much between Blodwyn and Dad that he wanted to return home to them all with his tail between his legs? And more importantly, would her mother want him back anyhow?

'Yes, Dad. But if you want to make a good impression on her, why don't you clean up a bit first, make yourself presentable?'

'There's no time for that,' he said with some urgency. 'I must speak to your mother this very evening before it's too late...'

Mari nodded, surprised by the urgency in her father's voice. Whatever could be so pressing he had to turn up right after his shift at the pit? The only thing she could think of was that he so desperately needed to return home. After all, he'd returned to work, maybe he wanted his old life back. That would make sense, wouldn't it?

* * *

When Mari turned up at the house, she left her father outside the front door while she entered the back way and left her mucky boots in the understairs cupboard.

'Mam!' she called out. It was up to her now to pave the way for her father to speak to her mother.

'Sssh!' said her mother, putting her index finger to her lips, her eyes wide. 'Bryn has gone to bed for a nap. He went out for a little walk earlier to see how his leg would hold up and it's taken it out of him, but he managed well. He's doing all he can to get himself fit for work again.'

Mari nodded with understanding. 'Where are Nerys and Tommy?' She lowered her voice.

'They're upstairs playing quietly in the bedroom; I've warned them not to wake Bryn. Is anything the matter?'

She shook her head. 'There's someone outside the front door waiting to see you...'

She had toyed with telling her mother who that someone was, but her father had told her not to say in case she flat-out refused to speak with him.

Mam angled her head to one side, frowning. 'It's not that hawker trying to sell his pots and pans again, is it?' she asked, tutting loudly.

Mr Loveday was an Irish hawker who travelled from town to town selling all sorts. Mam had bought several things from him in the past, but the last time he'd visited, she reckoned he'd over-charged her for a frying pan and a saucepan. It hadn't been until he'd long gone that she'd worked out the sums in her head and, to her despair, realised it might be some time before he ever headed in her direction again, and by then, he'd have forgotten all about what he'd charged her in the first place as he kept no records.

'No, it's not Mr Loveday.' Mari was bursting to say who it was stood outside the door.

'Well, I haven't got all day to play riddle-me-ree, so I'd better check it out.' She seemed a bit perplexed but walked to the front door and, drawing it open, almost immediately closed it again as though she'd seen a ghost.

But Dad was too quick for her as he jammed his hobnail boot in the doorway.

'Look, Mavis,' he said, 'I need to see you about a particular matter. We can talk out here if you don't want to let me in.'

'And have all the neighbours earwigging, no ruddy fear!' she said, drawing open the door to allow him access while Mari bid a hasty retreat to the scullery where a delicious-smelling stew was bubbling away on the stove in a large pan.

Not knowing what to do and not wishing to intervene, Mari kept an eye on the stew and laid the table for supper. She wondered if her mother might invite Dad, but then she heard footsteps overhead and the sound of raised voices. It was Bryn! No doubt hearing their father talking to Mam had disturbed his rest and now it sounded like he was telling him he had to go.

What on earth was going on? She, herself, had only just made it up with her father and she hoped the rest of the family would too, but all that commotion sounded far from any sort of reconciliation.

Suddenly the scullery door burst open as Tommy and Nerys rushed towards her. Her sister had tears in her eyes and Tommy's bottom lip was quivering.

'What's going on, our Mari?' Tommy finally asked.

Mari opened her arms to hug her siblings. 'I don't know,' she said. 'But we must keep out of it. All I know is that Dad came here with me tonight as he's back working at the pit and walked me home. Then he wanted to speak to Mam...' She didn't tell them she'd been hoping he'd left that Blodwyn and was going to come home. Maybe that's what it was: he'd asked to come back but Bryn didn't want him to return?

There were more loud voices and what sounded like Mam pleading with Bryn, then the front door slammed shut, and Mari heard her mother crying loudly, almost wailing, and then fast footsteps on the stairs as though she'd taken herself off to her bedroom in floods of tears.

The scullery door thrust open as Bryn stood there staring at them all, his eyes hard and dark like flint. 'I suppose you heard all that?' he said, looking at Mari. She nodded at him.

'I heard fighting but not what anyone said. What's going on?' Her voice sounded shaky to her own ears.

Bryn looked at his younger brother and sister and there was a softness in his voice. 'You two go and sit in the living room for a few minutes, while I talk to your sister.'

Tommy and Nerys didn't need asking twice. They rushed out of the room as though glad to be away from any conflict.

Then Bryn looked at Mari and he gritted his teeth. 'Our father has been here!' he yelled.

'Yes, I know. He walked me home from my shift at the pit.'

Bryn furrowed his brow. 'He waited for you by the pit gates? How on earth would he know you're working there? It's such a well-kept secret...'

She shook her head. 'He didn't know. They've taken him back on to work there and I encountered him underground. Of course he recognised me. He seems to have changed though; he wishes to make amends.'

Bryn's eyes widened with disbelief. 'Amends, my foot! He's just upset our mam.'

'By asking to come home?'

'No, it was something far worse than that. That's why I sent the kids out, but you're old enough to know...' Bryn paused for a moment before saying, 'He's only gone and got his floozy up the spout!'

'Spout? I don't understand?' Mari shook her head, wide-eyed with confusion.

Bryn let out a long sigh. 'Pregnant! She's having his bloody baby!'

## 13

It was some time before Mari felt able to utter a word. 'A baby? That means we're having a new brother or sister? No wonder Mam is so upset. Dad didn't mention anything like that to me...'

'Yes, a brother or sister but what will that child be though? More than a brother or sister for us, a bleeding bastard that's what!' Bryn spat out the words as though they were venom.

'That's not a nice thing to say about an innocent baby,' Mari chastised. 'Using a swear word like that!'

'Sorry.' He sighed. 'But it's a well-known term for a baby that's born out of wedlock. It is the correct word even if it's also used as a swear word. And you're right, of course, it's not the child's fault, is it? It's our own dear father's and that loose wench from Pond Row.'

Mari fought to stem the tears that were threatening to run like rivulets down her cheeks. No wonder their mother had taken herself off upstairs. She would be heartbroken to hear that news. It was bad enough their father betraying the woman he'd married and his family too, but to be given the news that a birth was imminent would be devastating for her.

Glancing at the stove and the freshly laid table, Bryn said, 'Well, we're all going to need to eat, baby or no baby. So, make Mam a cup of tea and take it up to her. She'll not want to come back down right now, and I can't say I blame her. Save her some stew an' all. And you might want to get yourself cleaned up a little first, Mari!' He shook his head.

In all the hullabaloo, she had forgotten she hadn't even washed her face and hands or changed out of her work clothing. But life had to go on. They'd be all right if they all stuck together, wouldn't they?

\* \* \*

Following a restless night, Mari finally managed to drift off into a fitful sleep, but when she rose from her bed to prepare herself for another day at the pit, there was no sign of her mother pottering around in the scullery as she usually did. The fire in the living room hearth had gone out too. Maybe she'd decided to have a lie-in. Thinking it best to go check on her, she went to her bedroom to find her, but when she opened the door, she felt a sudden pang of sickness as fear took over. Her mother's bed was empty. Normally when her mam rose, the first thing she did was make her bed, but it appeared as though she'd had a restless night; both pillows had been tossed on the floor and the bed covers flung back so that the bed's under sheet was on show.

Panic-stricken, Mari opened Bryn and Tommy's bedroom door. She did not wish to frighten her younger brother, so she went over to Bryn's side of the bed and gently shook him.

'Wassup?' He stirred drowsily.

'It's me – Mari...' she whispered. 'It's our mam. She's not in her bed and I have to go to work soon if I want to keep this job.'

Alert now, Bryn sat bolt upright and roused from his sleep.

'Go downstairs. I'll just put something on, and then I'll be with you,' he said, glancing at their brother's sleeping form beside him. Tommy, so far, had not stirred an inch, happily in the land of Nod, oblivious to any of the upset, and that was the way Mari wanted things to stay.

Eventually, Bryn staggered downstairs, partially dressed in his old comfortable trousers and carpet slippers, and he'd pulled on an old woollen jumper. His hair was messed up where he'd been sleeping.

Keeping his voice low, rubbing his eyes, he asked, 'Have you checked the privy?'

In all honesty, she hadn't. Now she felt a fool. That's where their mother might be and, foolishly, she'd woken her brother from his sleep without checking there first. He had difficulty sleeping sometimes too, following memories of the accident and various aches and pains that overtook him during the night, so if their mother was there all along, he wasn't going to be best pleased.

Dashing out of the back door, she went to check the privy, which was shared with the Marshalls' house next door, to find it empty, the door wide open as though someone had just made use of it.

Turning, she was surprised that her brother had followed her this far and she shook her head. 'Mam's not in there...' Her stomach was now churning at the thought of what had happened to their mother. She blamed herself for not telling Mam the truth in the first place that it was Dad at the door. If she had, then maybe she'd have refused to speak to him, and this wouldn't be happening right now. But then again, word had a way of getting out and eventually someone would find out that Gwynfor Evans's trollop was with child.

'Look, you've got to get to work,' Bryn said, laying a hand of comfort on her shoulder. 'Try not to fret. Have your usual breakfast and I'll go in search of Mam.'

'But Nerys and Tommy?'

'They won't be awake for a while yet. I can have a little scout around and maybe call to Mrs Griffiths's house. That's where she goes when she needs to talk to someone.'

Mari nodded but she wasn't totally convinced their mother would make her neighbour's house the first port of call, particularly at this time of the morning. But then again, the menfolk in their house would be up early for work, so it might make sense that the woman would be up and about anyhow.

By the time Mari was ready to leave for the pit, Bryn was by the back door, out of puff and pale. 'I've called to Mrs Griffiths's house. She's not been there but she said she'll keep a lookout for her.'

Mari nodded, then her eyes fixed on the mantel clock. It was a quarter to six. She needed to get a move on if she was to arrive at work on time. Another thought occurred to her: how would she possibly face her father today, knowing what she now knew?

\* \* \*

Thankfully, Mari didn't run into her father until towards the end of the shift as she'd been assigned to work on a new coal seam with a man called Morris Armstrong. The man was a good worker who lived up to his surname and she was pleased that Morris was a quiet sort of a fella who put his back into his work. But even so, her thoughts kept drifting towards her mother and the niggling feeling all wasn't well.

Her father finally found her towards the end of the shift, and he asked Morris if he might have a quiet word with 'Lew'. If the man thought it odd, then he wasn't saying so, but her father led her a good distance out of the seam until they were out of earshot of any prying ears.

'I'm glad I found you...' he said. 'I've been worrying all night long about your mother. I take it you've heard the news?'

'I have now, yes. But, Dad, I don't know how she really took it as she disappeared upstairs after you called and when I got up for work this morning, there was no sign of her in your... I mean, her bedroom.'

Mari felt bad about slipping up and saying 'your' to her father, as he obviously was well aware it was no longer his bedroom nor ever likely to be again. She watched him rub his chin.

'So, your mother wasn't even there to set you off for work this morning?'

She shook her head. 'I woke Bryn up and he went straight to Mrs Griffiths's house, as he reckoned she might be there if she was upset. But no joy, she wasn't there. He said he'll carry on looking for her while I'm at work.'

Dad sighed. 'Hopefully, she just took herself off as she was so angry about things and will have returned by the time you get home. She used to do daft things like that when we were first married.'

'Maybe, but you didn't tell her then that another woman was having your baby?'

'Er, no.'

Even though they were underground, she guessed her father's face must be flushing bright red beneath all the caked coal dust on it.

'I'd better get back to work,' she said solemnly.

'Don't worry,' he reassured her. 'If your mother's not back by the time you return home, I'll help look for her.'

Mari nodded but her father's reassurance provided little comfort.

\* \* \*

When the work day was finally over, her father walked her back home again. It had been difficult to endure the rest of her shift as the hours seemed to drag on with Mam constantly on Mari's mind. When she and her father arrived at the house, they were both met by a frantic Bryn on the doorstep.

'Is Mam back home?' was the first thing Mari asked.

He shook his head. 'I went to search for her with a couple of men earlier, but no one has seen her. I've half a mind to contact the police.'

'Now there's no need for that yet, lad!' said their father.

'Don't you "lad" me!' snarled Bryn as he drew back his arm and formed a strong-looking fist.

'Please don't,' said Mari, frightened now. 'It's not going to help anyone if you punch our father, especially not Mam.'

'It would make me feel a damn sight better though!' Bryn growled, but then he unfurled his fingers, dropped his arm to his side and let out a laboured breath.

'Look,' said their father, 'I'll nip to the pub and see if I can summon up some of the men to form a search party. The temperature will drop significantly overnight. We have to find her.'

Bryn nodded, but then said, 'If we couldn't find her in daylight though, what chance does your search party have in the middle of the night? Particularly when those sorts have been swigging the ale!'

Dad just shrugged. 'Have you any better ideas? By the time we inform the police and they, if they're willing, form some sort of search party, it might be too bloody late. There's not enough of them working anyhow. Who knows the layout of the land more than the colliers and farmers who live in this area?'

Bryn forced a smile. 'I'll join you then. Mari, take over here and look after the kids.'

'All right.' She had a feeling there'd be little sleep for anyone that night.

\* \* \*

There was little Mari could do when the men had left the house other than to ensure her younger brother and sister ate their evening meal and were settled into bed. Thankfully, neither had a clue what was going on, nor how serious it could possibly be. The weather was turning colder with the threat of snow, so it was imperative that Mam be found as soon as possible and brought back home where she belonged. Mari managed to stave off the children's questions about their mother's disappearance, saying that she'd gone to help Mrs Griffiths out as the woman wasn't at all well with a winter 'bad chest', which she was prone to. That latter part was true, but not the part that she was ill right now. Mari could have bitten her own tongue off for lying like that, as didn't the Good Book say it was wrong to lie and honesty was always the best policy? But, in this case, she didn't think a small white lie would harm her siblings and afterwards she'd ask God for his forgiveness. But for the time being, all her prayers and petitions to the Almighty were to bring their mother safely back home to them.

God must have heard her fervent prayers that night because a couple of hours later, when Nerys and Tommy were tucked up in bed and fast asleep, Mari heard the front door click open and urgent voices headed towards her. Rushing from the armchair by the fire, she watched as her brother and father escorted her mother over to the hearth.

'Sit down there now, Mavis,' her father was saying, his voice gentle and with such a loving tone it belied his philandering ways. The way he was looking at his wife told Mari without a shadow of a doubt that he still loved and cared for the woman he'd married eighteen years ago.

Mam's face looked deathly pale and her eyes sunken in their sockets; her mouth was slightly gaping, but she listened to what her husband said, sinking into the armchair then warming her hands in front of the fire.

Bryn fixed his concerned gaze on Mari. 'Go boil the kettle and fetch Mam something hot to drink right away,' he commanded.

Their father nodded. 'Aye, good idea and see if you can add a tot of whisky to it.'

Mari bit her lower lip. 'I don't think there's any left. Bryn, you drank a lot of it after your accident.'

Shamefaced, Bryn shook his head. 'I'd forgotten that. I wish I hadn't drunk every drop as now there's none left for Mam.'

Thinking on her feet, Mari forced a smile. 'I'll ask Mr Marshall if he has any.' Mr Marshall was one of their neighbours and well known for liking a tipple at night at home. He wasn't one for frequenting alehouses, but he swore a glass of something alcoholic kept his constitution in order.

'I don't think he drinks whisky though,' said their father, thoughtfully.

'But Mrs Marshall might have some brandy to feed her Christmas cake – that's similar!' Mari brightened up, thinking of the time Mrs Jones mentioned the brandy for her Christmas cake. 'If not, I'll call to the shop, as I know Mrs Jones definitely has some to feed hers.'

'All right then!' said Bryn, also brightening up now.

Mari was in luck as Mrs Marshall did have a little brandy to spare and when Mari explained it was needed for shock for her mother, she poured some into a teacup. There was no use lying about Mam going missing like that as word would get around anyhow – after all, a search party had gone out looking for her. But, still, Mari refrained from telling the woman *why* her mother had left home. It was all too much for her to take in that her husband had fathered a child to another woman.

Once Mam had been handed a glass with a tot of brandy to warm her up, the colour returned to her face and hands, but she continued to stare into the flames of the fire, almost as though mesmerised by them.

Bryn took Mari to one side. 'I think it will take some time for Mam to return to herself,' he whispered. 'Meanwhile, try to get something hot inside her. Is there any of that stew left from yesterday?'

Mari nodded. 'Yes, there is.' She lifted her head to look intently into her brother's eyes. 'But where did you find her?'

He cleared his throat. 'We didn't. That man you used to work with, Big Al, found her near the pond that borders the pit.'

The pond was used to feed the colliery – Mari knew of it well as in the summer Bryn used to take her there to see the wildlife that surrounded such an industrial, dirty area. The pond in summer was teeming with butterflies, dragonflies and the like, and she once saw the odd frog hopping around there.

'B... but why would Mam go there of all places? And in the middle of the night, too?' She swallowed the lump that had formed in her throat.

Bryn shook his head. 'I don't know for sure, but I can hazard a guess.' He blew out a hard breath. 'S... she wanted to take her life, maybe?'

Mari began to shudder, and big sobs engulfed her body as her brother took her into his strong arms. All the while, she guessed he'd be giving their father an evil stare over her shoulder.

She became aware of their father stepping towards them. 'Maybe this might help,' he said softly as he stretched out his hand. Mari and Bryn broke apart to stare at him. There, in his palm, were several silver coins, obviously his recent payment from that day from the pit.

'You can keep your thirty pieces of silver!' snarled Bryn as he knocked his father's hand, toppling the coins so they fell onto the flagstone floor, clinking, and some of them spinning like whirling tops until finally they stopped.

Mari stood there open-mouthed as her father stooped to retrieve them. Fixing her gaze on him, she could see the tears brimming in his eyes.

'Keep your betrayal money for that wanton whore of yours and that bastard she's conceived!'

Mari couldn't believe her ears. 'Stop it!' she yelled. 'This isn't helping Mam one little bit!' She pointed her finger towards their mother. Mam now had her head in both hands as she began to weep, and Mari rushed over to her to take her into her arms. Looking up at her father now, she said, 'Dad, you'd better go and take that money with you, as it's causing upset here in this house. Though I know you mean well.' Then she fixed her gaze on Bryn. 'Go and warm that stew for Mam while I comfort her.'

Without another word, her brother nodded weakly and began to walk off to the scullery, while their father stood up from where he'd retrieved the offending coins and dropped them into his trouser pocket. He laid a hand on his wife's shoulder and appeared about to say something but stopped himself. He just nodded and, with a sad expression on his face, let himself out through the front door.

## 14

Mari dreaded turning up for work at the shop again as she realised word would have got out about her mother going missing and her father getting that Blodwyn one pregnant. Oh, wouldn't Marguerite Thomas have a great time chewing over that. She wouldn't get away with much if Mrs Jones was around though, but she could just imagine the high-handed housekeeper relating the tale to the staff at the house where she worked. But Mari needn't have worried as when she turned up for work there a couple of days later, Mrs Jones hadn't even heard about what had gone on until Mari told her.

'I hope no one finds out about it though,' she added.

'I can't promise you that gossip doesn't fly around this village,' Mrs Jones said, 'but what I can promise is that anyone who mentions it in here shall have a sharp slice of my tongue; I can assure you that much!'

That thought conjured up a strange picture in Mari's mind, which made her stifle a giggle. The trouble was she had hoped to invite the woman to join them for Christmas dinner, but how could she now? Mam wasn't in any fit state to host a festive feast with an additional guest. Bryn had promised to keep an eye on her whenever Mari wasn't around, but he couldn't keep a constant eye on their mother, especially at night while they all slept. Mari had saved up a little money that she had intended contributing towards Christmas but now she realised it might be put to a better use by getting the doctor out to give Mam a once-over – see if he might provide a professional opinion on her state of mind.

When she'd told Bryn that, though, he'd just scoffed. 'She's a woman scorned, that's all,' he'd said. But Mari thought it was much more than that. She'd seen Mam looking sad before, but this was something else. She no longer got herself out of bed early in the mornings; it was as if it was now an effort to drag herself out of bed at all. She slept a lot, having no inclination towards her household chores whatsoever. It was as if the light had diminished from her life. And that light had been extinguished by the man she'd chosen to marry.

\* \* \*

Later that afternoon during a quiet spell at the shop, Mari was surprised to see Bobby enter the premises. She hadn't seen him for such a long time. He was there on an errand for his mother, and Mrs Jones, sensing the two needed to catch up with one another, sent them out the back for a glass of her home-made lemonade. She was such a perceptive lady.

Mari found herself telling Bobby all that had gone on lately and it was some time before he closed his mouth and swallowing said, 'I had no idea, Mari. I mean I knew that your father was back in the village but didn't think he'd have the, er...'

'Gumption to go back to working at the pit?' she offered. It was good to speak to someone who understood her and her position.

'Well, yes.' He nodded. 'It would take some guts to return there after all that's occurred.'

'I suppose,' she admitted reluctantly. 'I hadn't thought of it that way.'

'Particularly as he'd be returning to a lot of ribbing from the men. So, you got to speak to him then?'

'Yes. For once, he seemed like a loving, caring father but then he went and spoiled it all after he walked me home.'

'How so?' He scratched his chin.

She went on to tell him about her father turning up at the house, how Mam was so upset she went missing overnight. About the men her father rounded up and how a search party set out to find her.

'It's a wonder you've not heard anything?' she finished, omitting to tell him about Blodwyn's pregnancy for the time being.

Bobby shook his head. 'I honestly hadn't, but then again, Dad doesn't go to the pub much these days. Most of his tales come from customers at the market stall in town. So, what happened then?' He tilted his head to one side, digging his hands deep into his trouser pockets.

Mari sighed. 'Thankfully, she was found safe and well but not until later the following day. She was perishing cold and a bit dazed and confused. She's not been herself since. Bryn has to keep a close eye on her when I'm at work.'

'I should think so an' all,' said Bobby. 'I'd go spare if that happened to my mother and my father was the cause of it. Though I can't see Dad doing anything to hurt her, as he worships the ground she walks on.'

Mari nodded. At least the pair were happily married, not like her parents. What a mess. They carried on speaking for some time. Mari felt so at ease in Bobby's company, she almost forgot she might be needed on the shop floor. So, finally, letting out a little sigh, she said, 'I'd better return to work. I heard that bell tinkling again. We get busy around this time of the day.'

Bobby nodded. 'Aye, I need to get back home to Mam. I promised her I'd chop some logs up for the fire later.'

She smiled at him. 'It's been nice catching up, Bobby,' she said, barely in a whisper.

Then quite unexpectedly, he lowered his head and pecked her on the cheek. She was so taken aback that she felt her colour rise and hoped her cheeks hadn't turned bright red. But then, Bobby turned his back to walk away from her. Maybe he was a little embarrassed too by his impetuous action?

By the time she returned to the shop floor, Mrs Jones seemed pleased to see her as quite a queue had formed. And a woman Mari knew as 'Mrs Brown' was arguing over the last loaf of bread left on the counter with Mrs Williams who lived just across the street from the shop. Mari stood there open-mouthed as both women continued to bicker about who had laid their hands on the loaf first, until Mrs Jones said decisively, 'Since neither of you is going to back down' – she was referring to their staking a claim each over the crusty bloomer loaf – 'then I am going to donate it to a poor family living in this village who need it more than you two!'

She roughly tore it away from their hands to their astonishment and placed it under the counter.

Both women stared at the other and blinked.

'Well, really!' said Mrs Brown as Mrs Williams nodded in agreement and huffed out a dissatisfied breath. It was comical how after arguing over the loaf, both women sided with one another as they agreed they'd never set foot in the shop ever again.

'But you've lost two customers by there!' Mari sighed when they'd departed, Mrs Brown slamming the door behind them.

Mrs Jones shook her head and laughed. 'They'll be back with their tails between their legs. They need this shop more than I need their custom.'

Mari nodded. 'I suppose you're right, Mrs Jones.'

'Trust me, dear, I am.'

Mari had to admire the elderly woman's resilience; she took no nonsense from anyone and that included rude and selfish customers.

\* \* \*

By the time Mari returned home from work that evening, her mother seemed more settled and was reading a book by the fireside, while for once, Bryn was keeping an eye on the evening meal cooking on the stove.

'How are you this evening, Mam?' she asked as she removed her bonnet and hung it on the hook on the back of the living room door, along with her shawl. Her hands were blue with the cold, so she began to warm them by the fireside.

Her mother fixed her gaze on her and smiled. 'I'm feeling so much better,' she said. 'I don't know what came over me that night...'

'You had a severe shock, Mam. It wasn't what you were expecting to hear.'

Her mother nodded her head. 'Yes, you're quite right.' Then she swallowed hard. 'I think the worst of it was that I thought your father, when he said he'd come to tell me something, was going to ask for forgiveness and that he wanted to come home. I thought, you see...'

'That he'd left Blodwyn?'

'Yes. Silly, aren't I?'

'Oh, Mam, you're not silly at all. It's plain for all to see that you still love him, and I believe in my heart that he still loves you too...'

Mam raised her eyebrows. 'You do?'

'Yes, I do. But it seems obvious to me that our father has got himself in somewhat of a pickle. He's ended up with a woman and a baby on the way and he doesn't know what to do next...'

There was the sound of the scullery door slamming and then Bryn appeared in the doorway, his eyes almost bulging out of his head. 'Don't you go feeling sorry for him, Mari!' Bryn shouted. 'Nor make excuses for that monster!'

'I... I'm not.' Mari shook her head. In fact, her brother was now reminding her of Dad, of his quick temper. They were more alike than Bryn would care to admit.

'Why are you putting foolish notions in our mam's head, then?'

Mari sighed. 'It just seems obvious that he still cares about her.'

'Well, even if he does, that man is not to step another foot over this threshold, you hear?'

Reluctantly, Mari nodded, fully understanding that they didn't even own the house – it was a rented property, so Dad didn't have much say in it anyhow. It wasn't as if he owned it. Even if a lot of his money had gone towards the rent over the years, that was all dead money. But then again, it might be argued that Bryn in recent years had paid his share of the rent too.

Bryn lowered his voice. 'Sorry, I shouldn't have shouted at you like that, but I'm so angry about that situation. If Mam hadn't been found by Big Al the other night, then who knows what might have happened to her?' He spoke almost as if their mother wasn't even present.

Finally, Mam, looking back and forth between them both, said, 'Look, there's no harm done physically to me. I'm on the mend. The rest of the family are still together, and we've got a roof over our heads and food in our bellies, so that can't be bad, can it?'

'I suppose not,' said Bryn. 'We have one another.'

Never was a truer word spoken, thought Mari.

## 15

Over the following week, Mam built her strength up day by day, until Mari felt she was in a good enough position to put the idea of Mrs Jones joining them for Christmas once again. To her surprise, Mam agreed to it.

'What do you think made Mam change her mind?' Mari asked Bryn later that day.

Placing the palms of his hands on her shoulders and looking deep within her eyes, he replied, 'It's you what it is, our Mari!' Then he smiled at her and planted a kiss on her cheek.

Mari frowned. 'Me? What have I done to persuade her?'

'You just have a way with folk, that's all. You even seem to have won our father around recently...'

'Well, he does seem to have changed and is much more caring towards me than before he left us.'

A flicker of pain crossed her brother's face, and he huffed out what sounded like a hard breath. 'Aye, maybe, but we still need to take care. We don't want him moving himself back in here with that floozy one and rocking the boat! Our mam has got used to him being away, I reckon.'

'I don't think so!' Mari shook her head. 'I don't think she ever will.'

Bryn didn't say any more; instead he changed the subject. 'So, Mrs Jones will be joining us for Christmas dinner, eh? Maybe she'll donate some stuff from her shop for the feast?'

'I expect she will, as she's a generous soul.'

'You don't fancy approaching Mam about Glenda joining us, do you?'

'I would do that for you, Bryn – you know it – but it's my understanding that her father doesn't want her coming here?'

'Aye, you're right enough. He doesn't want us courting one another. He's taken a strong dislike to me. He assumes I'm up to no good and he wants his precious daughter kept pristine white for marriage.'

'Bryn! What a thing to say!' Her brother could say some right shocking things at times.

'It's true, isn't it? I've not laid a ruddy finger on her in that sort of way, Mari. I respect her too much and I'd like for us to wed someday, I would...' He stroked his chin.

'But?'

'But.' He sighed. 'I haven't got the finances to afford to marry her right now, have I?'

Mari supposed not. 'You will have someday, especially if you go back to work.'

'When will that be, though?'

'You've made good progress with that leg of yours. You're walking with a stick now; you weren't doing that a month ago.'

'That's true.' He shot her a disarming smile. 'Nevertheless, if I do get a job, I still can't wed really, as I'll be the breadwinner to keep this family going.'

'That won't be forever though. It won't be too long before Tommy's working himself in a few years' time.'

Bryn grimaced. 'Don't I know it! I don't want any filthy coal pits for our brother though. Oh no. He's a good scholar.'

Mari had to admit he was. Bryn had been complicit with her working underground, but to be fair to him, it was on the understanding it would be on a temporary basis only and not for good. Whereas Nerys was a little bit flitty and scatty at times regarding schoolwork, Tommy took his homework seriously. He'd even stay indoors to complete it before joining the other lads outside, putting up with some gentle ribbing from them in the process. Tommy wasn't like the other boys in the village with their rough and tumble. In some ways, he seemed far too delicate for this world. Mari wondered, if Bryn had had the chance, would he have ended up a scholar himself? He was so intelligent, and it seemed that Tommy was following in his footsteps. Bryn was wasted at the pit.

'Aw, don't worry, Bryn. One day you and Glenda will be together as man and wife.' An idea occurred to her. 'Instead of inviting her to dinner on Christmas Day where she'd be missed from her home, why don't you invite her for afternoon tea in between Christmas and the New Year? That way she can always tell her father she's gone to visit a friend; she won't be missed as much.'

'That's a good idea, Mari. Nothing to say that she and I can't have our own Christmas celebration on another day, is there?'

'And on the afternoon she comes here, I'll take Tommy and Nerys out somewhere. Maybe for a long walk or to visit Bobby and his family. Maybe Mam will come too.'

'I don't think Mam would be happy with me being alone in the house with Glenda, mind you.'

'Does she have to know? No one does, but me, you and Glenda.'

'That sounds like a plan!' His eyes glittered with excitement.

Whatever happened this Christmas, Mari was determined they'd all have a good time after the horrendous past few months.

* * *

There was a surprise caller at the front door a few days later. 'Now who on earth can that be?' Mam frowned as she flounced off to answer.

'It wouldn't be Glenda, would it?' Mari asked, glancing at Bryn.

'No. I'm not seeing her until tomorrow. Her father is at home this evening, so she'll have to stop there.'

'You don't think it's Dad, do you?' She chewed her bottom lip.

'It better not be!' Bryn placed both palms of his hands on the arms of the chair as though ready to heave himself out of it.

But then hearing a voice she recognised, which most certainly was not their father, Mari gasped. 'That sounds like Big Al!'

Mam was now escorting Alwyn Probert, who had removed his flat cap, into the living room and asking him to take a seat. Bryn, who was midway getting out of his seat, made the offer, but Al said, 'Sit yourself down, Bryn. How are you feeling since the accident?'

Bryn smiled. 'A lot better, thank you. And a big thank you too for finding our mother that night.'

Al seemed to blush and, wringing his cap in his hands, said, 'It was nothing. I was glad I was able to help, that's all.'

Mari was about to rush over to him with delight but then she remembered he wouldn't recognise her as herself, so thinking better of it, she just smiled and nodded.

'Sit yourself down by the fireside, Mr Probert,' Mam ordered as he'd still not sat down. She gestured towards the empty chair opposite Bryn. It wasn't as comfy as the one he was in, but it would suffice.

Al nodded gratefully and sat, placing his cap on a nearby low table.

'I daresay you'd like a cup of tea, Mr Probert?'

'Aye, thank you very much, Mrs Evans. And how are you feeling now?'

Her mother's eyes lit up. 'I'm feeling so much better.'

'That's good to hear.' Al was smiling. 'Hopefully you've made a good recovery and will get back to full health soon enough.'

Their mother nodded and then made her way to the scullery.

Al stayed a good hour, chatting to Bryn about the pit and, when they discussed returning to work, Al said he hoped to return within the next week or so. It was obvious from the worn expression on the man's face that he'd had a lot to contend with lately, and Mari so wished she was able to chat to him as 'Lew', but that just wasn't possible. But still, she reminded herself, when he was back at the pit, she'd get that chance.

Al got along well with Mam too and she seemed at ease in his presence. It was good to see her eyes sparkle for a change, as the light had long since dimmed. Al seemed to bring something out of her mother with his jovial, easy manner.

If there was some sort of panacea for Mam's ills, then encountering Al seemed to be it. He left the house buoyed up himself with a promise that he'd call again soon. One good thing was that Bryn obviously liked and respected the fellow. And Mari, well, she thought he was the bee's knees.

* * *

When Mari returned to the pit the following day, there was no sign of her father, and she feared asking anyone where he was lest questions be asked of her. She figured maybe he was ill, and she'd see him there in a day or two, but when he failed to turn up for his shift the following day, curiosity got the better of her.

'Rumour has it he's left Abercanaid again,' said Duggie, when she questioned him about it. He shook his head. 'I thought he'd returned to make a go of it, but obviously not. I'm guessing the gossip in the village got too much for him. Sad, really, as he was a good worker and well respected by the other colliers here.'

For the first time in a long while, Mari felt sorry for her father and she turned away and choked back a sob, in case Duggie noticed how upset she was. She didn't know how she'd get through the rest of the shift as she felt like breaking down weeping. Weeping for them all, the whole dreadful situation. Maybe it was the way Bryn had knocked the money out of Dad's hand that had done it. He'd exhibited an iron will towards their father, giving the impression that they were all right on their own and didn't need his help.

But that simply wasn't true.

As she walked home after her shift that night, without her father by her side, she looked up at the sky as white flakes began to fall from on high. The first snow of winter. Thankfully, her shifts for this week were over for the time being, but she was needed at the shop the following afternoon. But by the time she got into her bedroom that night and took a peep through the curtains, the snow had fallen so thick and fast that she just knew it would settle overnight.

* * *

The sound of voices down below drifted towards Mari and she turned over in her bed to see Nerys still fast asleep beside her. That girl could sleep on a clothes line. Smiling at the scene before her, she arose from her bed and, placing her bare feet on the linoleum, which was freezing cold, she winced. She grabbed her dressing gown from the peg on the back door, wrapped it around her shivering form, slipped into her carpet slippers and then took another peek out of the window, gasping to see the winter wonderland out there. Everywhere was carpeted in glistening, virginal snow and it was still coming down. She even noticed icicles had formed from the eaves of the house as the window frosted over, creating white fern-like patterns. How on earth could she get to the shop today? She reminded herself she had her work boots; they'd help keep some of the cold out, but what if the snow seeped through? Water sometimes leaked through the soles if she was standing in a puddle underground.

'The snow's drifted up as far as the back door,' she heard Mam telling Bryn. 'I need to get out to the privy.'

'Don't worry, there's an old shovel in that cupboard under the stairs,' he was saying.

'If you can clear a path to it as soon as possible,' she urged.

Mari hoped her brother would get a shift on as she needed to pee too. Thankfully, Bryn was more able on his feet these days, so he went off to locate the shovel. 'I'll clear a path for Mrs Grimes to get to hers, too,' he said.

Mrs Grimes was their elderly widowed neighbour who lived next door but one.

'There's good you are to us all.' Mam smiled. She seemed to have perked up a lot since that visit from Al Probert the other day.

\* \* \*

'I wasn't expecting you in here today!' Mrs Jones exclaimed when Mari turned up at the shop that afternoon. 'You're looking perished, *cariad*.'

The truth was Mrs Jones was right. It had taken Mari ages to trudge through the high level of snow to get to the shop and now her fingers and toes felt like icicles. It was hard work to even reply to the woman.

'I c... couldn't let you down again...' Mari said, huffing out a breath.

Mrs Jones angled her head to one side and smiled warmly at her. 'Don't think I don't appreciate the effort taken to get here, but I insist before you begin work that you take a seat in the back room by the fire and thaw out. And I'm going to make you a hot drink!'

Mari smiled gratefully at the woman. 'But what about your customers?' she protested, thinking she was taking the woman from the shop floor.

Mrs Jones threw up her hands. 'What customers? No one's been through that door for well over an hour apart from yourself.'

So, for the next twenty minutes, Mrs Jones and Mari sat by the fireside with a hot cup of cocoa, nibbling on a home-baked Welsh cake each. Mari's thick woollen stockings were draped over the ledge of the fireplace, steaming away alongside her damp leather boots. Meanwhile, the woman had loaned her a warm pair of carpet slippers as they both had similar-sized feet. Mari's woollen shawls were draped over two chairs near the fire to dry out.

'So, you're telling me your father has left Abercanaid again?' Mrs Jones asked incredulously.

'Sounds like it. One of the men working at the pit told me. I didn't say why I was asking where he was though, obviously.'

Mrs Jones nodded. 'Very wise. From what you've told me though maybe it was the final straw for your father when he offered that money to you all and was rejected. Maybe now he feels he's no longer of any use to you children and your mother. After all, you're all surviving without him.'

Mari nodded. 'The funny thing is for the first time in a long while, I can actually see another side to him.'

There was a moment of retrospection while Mari watched the dancing flames in the hearth, listening to the logs spitting and crackling away. It felt comforting as she cradled the warm cup of cocoa in her hands.

'Oh, Mrs Jones,' she said finally as she jolted back to reality. 'I've been meaning to ask if you'd like to spend Christmas Day with us.'

The woman beamed and then she nodded. 'That would be lovely, Mari. But does your mother mind?'

'Not at all. She brought the subject up herself.' Which was only half the truth as of course Mari had approached her mother about it not the other way around. Mam had initially been against the woman coming for dinner on the big day but now, Mari realised that Mam's agreement with having Mrs Jones as a guest that day was sincere. Before that she'd just felt down in the dumps and hadn't wanted a fuss made with anyone let alone Mrs Jones. But since Al had rescued her and become a regular caller at the house, she seemed to have sprung back to life.

'And I can bring that Christmas cake we made...' Mrs Jones was saying. 'And I'll bake some mince pies too. Oh, it will be smashing. I haven't been a part of a family Christmas in years!'

Realising she'd made Mrs Jones's day, Mari smiled to herself. It was worth her trudging through the snow after all just to give the woman that invitation alone.

\* \* \*

The snowfall had finally ceased and Mrs Jones, after only a couple of people graced the shop with their custom, stood and sighed. 'It's best you go home now, young lady!' she declared.

'But are you sure you don't want me to stay to help out?' Mari protested, not wanting to leave the woman in the lurch. 'I don't mind stopping on a while longer.'

Mrs Jones smiled at her. 'I know that, *cariad*, but we might well get snowed in here if it starts up again. I'll be all right, as I have heat and a comfy chair in the back room and plenty to eat and drink in the shop. Your mother would have my guts for garters if you got stranded here overnight!'

Mari chuckled. 'I very much doubt it, Mrs Jones. She allows me to work underground in those conditions after all.'

'I suppose so, but that's through necessity, it's not to be forever. How is your Bryn these days anyhow? Any chance of him returning to the pit?'

Mari smiled. 'The doctor called the other day to examine him and said he's seeing a great improvement and that my brother should be able to return to work sometime in the middle of January. I don't know though...'

Mrs Jones frowned. 'Don't know what, Mari?'

'I get the feeling that maybe he's developed some sort of fear of going underground again after what happened to him. He was buried in that fall for some hours.'

'Hardly surprising, is it?' Mrs Jones raised her silver eyebrows.

'Yes. If it happened to me, I don't think I could return. I just try to put all of that out of my mind when I go to work there. The reason I know this is not because he's said anything to me or Mam, but our Tommy has heard him having bad dreams at night, thrashing around in the bed, and once he shouted out for help and fell out of bed, which frightened Tommy half to death.'

'That's understandable. He was probably half asleep himself

when he heard Bryn. Must have been so scary for him.' She paused for a moment and, dipping her hand into her pocket, handed Mari a silver shilling.

Mari gasped. 'But I can't take this off you, Mrs Jones.'

'You can and you will, Mari. You've worked hard for me, and I can afford it on this occasion.'

'Oh, thank you.' Mari smiled through her tears and then she planted a kiss on the woman's soft cheek.

'Go on with you. Get off home now and take a couple of those bloomer loaves from on the counter. They'll be a little stale by now but all right if dipped in a bowl of soup or stew, or your mother can use them to make a bread-and-butter pudding.'

Mari nodded and went to put on her stockings and boots, which had dried nicely by the fireside. She wrapped both shawls around her shoulders and returned to the shop floor. Mrs Jones had packed the two loaves into a wicker basket and covered them in a muslin cloth for her to carry home.

\* \* \*

Darkness had fallen just as Mari arrived at the house. She entered via the back door as her boots and feet were wet through once again. She placed the wicker basket on the scullery table and removed her boots, placing them in the hearth, and her stockings to dry on the back of a nearby wooden chair. She removed her shawls and did the same with those, then stood by the fireside holding out her hands near the flickering flames as life returned to her frozen digits. From the living room, she heard the sounds of laughter and the unmistakable voice of Al Probert. Had Al arrived here to see her mother or her brother? Maybe both? Whoever it was, it cheered her to hear everyone in such high spirits.

'Glad you got home safely,' greeted her mother as Mari entered the room.

Big Al nodded and smiled as she approached. 'Hello, Mari.'

'Good evening, Mr Probert.'

Al stroked his bewhiskered chin. 'It's been on my mind for some time now,' he said thoughtfully, gazing up at the ceiling. 'I'm trying to think who you remind me of.'

Oh no! Here it came. She just knew he was going to say he realised that she'd been 'Lewis Lloyd' all this time. Exchanging a worried glance with Bryn, she held her breath.

Then Al said, 'Ah, I know who it is now. She's a sweet young girl who lives in my street, about your age, Mari. But her hair is long and yours is short.'

Mari breathed out a quick sigh of relief. 'Really, Mr Probert. What's her name?' She blinked.

'Violet Morgan.'

'That's a pretty name,' enthused Mam. Of course, she and Bryn must have realised what Mari must be thinking.

Later, when Mari was helping her mother to lay the scullery table, she asked what Al was doing there.

'Mr Probert very kindly brought us a sack of potatoes. Wasn't that nice of him? Trudged through all that snow he did. The man's as strong as an ox.'

Mari didn't doubt it for a moment. She decided that when Al left after joining them for supper, she'd have to have a word with Bryn – Al had mentioned he was returning to the pit next week.

* * *

'I think I better give up working at the pit now that Mr Probert is returning to work next week,' Mari said later that evening. 'He'll soon work out who I really am after visiting here. I could easily slip up if I forget and go back to being Mari when I'm working with him.'

'I've thought about that too,' said Bryn thoughtfully, 'but I'm confident that he'll not give you away to the others.'

'It's not that that's bothering me.' Mari sighed.

'What is it then?'

'It's the fact he might be forced to keep my secret. It could cost him his job.'

Bryn sucked in a sharp breath between his teeth. 'You do have a point there, Mari. There's only another month or so to go until I return to work, so perhaps it's best you no longer go to work at the pit. We'll manage until then. Mam has said she's going to take in washing again now she's feeling brighter.'

Mari nodded. 'And I'll carry on helping at the shop.'

The truth of it was that it wasn't just because Al would be returning to the pit that caused her concern, it was because her father was missing from it and now from all of their lives.

Why did he have to leave now when she was getting on with him so much better than before? Finally it had felt like he was becoming a real father to her. But the reality was, she knew the answer to that in her heart. It was all Bryn's doing. He'd rather oust their father and encourage the recently widowed Alwyn Probert to visit their mother than allow Dad to set one foot over the doorstep ever again.

## 16

Mari fretted that if she didn't turn up for work on Monday, the foreman might come looking for her, but then she reminded herself that 'Lewis Lloyd' didn't exist. If he should try enquiring at the Rhydycar area where she'd told him the boy lived, no one would know who he was. She had a feeling if she'd gone to tell the man she no longer wished to work underground, he'd question her further. She was a good worker that he'd not want to lose. But then she risked breaking down and telling the man the truth. No, Bryn was right, honesty wasn't the best policy in this matter. Lewis Lloyd would now have to simply cease to exist.

It would be nice to go back to being a girl full-time but for now she had to make do with wearing that mob cap at the shop, and when out and about around the village she wore a bonnet to cover her shorn locks. Her hair would grow soon enough, Mrs Jones said, then by the time spring arrived it would be a tidy length.

But at the moment, spring seemed a long way off. They were still in the throes of winter and the chapel was preparing for a Christmas carol concert in the run-up to the big day itself.

Al Probert had even carved and painted some wooden figures for a nativity scene, complete with Mary and Joseph, the three wise men, a shepherd, various cattle and the baby Jesus asleep in his crib. The choir were busy practising for the concert and the one with the lovely soprano voice was her brother's young lady, Glenda. Oh, she looked and sounded like an angel when she sang, and Bryn was so proud of her.

After chapel that Sunday morning while her mother was speaking with the minister, Al took Mari to one side. 'I'm going back to work at the pit tomorrow,' he said.

Mari nodded. Why was he telling her this?

Al continued. 'I'm looking forward to seeing my little butty again after all this time. I've missed Lewis; he's a good worker.' The way Al was looking at her – with a twinkle in his eye – brought her up sharp.

'Y... yes...' she stuttered.

'Look, Mari,' he whispered, surreptitiously glancing around as the congregation departed slowly out through the large wooden front doors where the minister waited to shake hands and exchange a few words with his flock. 'I know you and Lew are the same person.'

Mari gulped. 'But how would you know that, Mr Probert?' she asked, wondering how to respond.

'I've known for some time, Mari.' He let out a long breath. 'Don't get me wrong, as far as I'm concerned, no one else working at the pit has worked it out, but when I called to your home after checking on your mother after she went missing, I noticed your hair was very short for a girl...'

'But I might have had head lice,' she protested.

'It was more than that though, even though your voice wasn't as deep as when you were performing as Lew, it was the way you spoke, your mannerisms too.'

'So, what do you want to do now, Mr Probert? Report me to Mr Roberts? As I'll deny it!'

'Sssh, steady on!' He placed his index finger to his lips. 'I'll do nothing of the sort. You're a good worker but the coal pit is no place for a young girl in my opinion. Were you put up to it by Bryn by any chance?'

Mari shook her head. 'No. He and Mam didn't know anything about it until after I'd gone underground. They were both shocked of course but I asked could I continue working there and earning money until we could manage again.'

'I see,' he said with some sympathy. 'Look, if you want to return to the pit tomorrow, I'm happy to work with you again and my lips will be sealed as to your identity, but it will be strange knowing I'm working with a young girl and not a lad.'

Mari shook her head. 'I talked it over with my brother and he thinks we can manage without my wage from the pit. The doctor says he can return to work in around a month's time.'

Al huffed out a breath. 'I see,' he said, looking relieved. 'Well, if there's any way I can help your family out, then I will.' He smiled and patted Mari on the head.

Mari deliberated for a moment. 'There is one thing you can do for me...'

'Oh, yes, and what might that be?' Al asked, his eyes widening.

'Please could you inform Mr Roberts that Lewis Lloyd has finished working at the pit? Tell him he has to stay home to care for his sick mother or something like that. I hate the thought of just leaving everyone in the lurch as Mr Roberts has been kind and very fair towards me, especially over the bother I've been getting from that group of troublemakers.'

'Right you are, Mari. Now I better get on as my daughter is cooking a big Sunday roast today.'

Mari heaved out a sigh of relief. At least she wouldn't have to face those bullies any more.

'Does your daughter live at home with you?' she asked.

Al shook his head. 'No, both my children are grown up now. I've lived alone since my wife passed away. My daughter and her husband have lodgings with her parents-in-law and my son works at the Cyfarthfa Ironworks. He lodges with a very nice lady on the Brecon Road.'

While Bryn lingered at the chapel to have a word with his beloved, Mari made her way home with Mam, Nerys and Tommy. On the walk, she thought what a nice man Al Probert was. Pity her mother hadn't married him years ago, as he'd have treated her so well. Her thoughts turned to her father for the time being and she wondered what he was doing right now.

\* \* \*

'I, for one, am glad you're not going back into the bowels of the earth, Mari!' Mrs Jones declared as she placed an assortment of bread loaves on the counter just before they opened the shop for the day. 'Many a time I've worried about you getting hurt down there...' She bit on her bottom lip before adding, 'Or even worse.'

'I know, Mrs Jones. I did worry myself at times, especially when those men caused problems for me. But I will miss it. I liked working with Mr Probert and would have looked forward to working with him again.'

Mrs Jones smiled and angled her head to one side in a sympathetic fashion. 'It's good you came clean with him when he questioned you, mind. Though you will be seeing him again by the sounds of it, the way he's calling to your house lately.' She arched a knowing eyebrow, which made Mari think the woman had guessed that maybe the man was sweet on her mother.

'Yes, it won't be the same relationship I had with him under-ground though, will it?'

'Maybe not, but you're still the same person, aren't you? Believe me, there was a lot of "Lewis Lloyd" in you anyway!'

Both chuckled and then the doorbell tinkled as the first customer of the day emerged through the door.

Business was brisk and the banter with customers friendly but then, after the shop had emptied and during a quiet period, the door burst open and Marguerite Thomas marched up to the counter. Seeing her there, Mrs Jones rushed over to serve her, but Mrs Thomas brushed her off. 'I want the girl to serve me!' she said sharply.

Mrs Jones exchanged a worried glance with Mari, who nodded at her as if to say, *'It's all right, I can deal with this one!'*

Mari swallowed. There was something in the woman's eye that told her today she was not to be messed with! A warning, perhaps?

Mrs Thomas extracted a long shopping list from her basket and instructions were given as to the weight and size of various items required for the Davenport house. 'Half a dozen eggs, a quarter of Indian tea leaves, a small pat of butter, two ounces of shag tobacco' – Mari knew this was for Mr Davenport himself who smoked a pipe – 'a green cabbage...' And on and on the list went. The requirements of which Mari wondered if they would all fit into the two wicker baskets the woman had brought with her. But when it became evident they wouldn't, Mrs Jones offered two of her own baskets and a loan of Mari herself to help the woman transport said goods to her employer's home.

Now Mari realised she was in trouble as she'd be walking along with the woman without Mrs Jones, or any other customers present to protect her. She did briefly consider apologising for her previous outburst, but that really went against the grain.

Marguerite Thomas had insulted her family, so, consequentially, never in a million years would she apologise to that stuck-up old trout – never!

But it was to be her undoing as Mari trudged along, awkwardly in silence in the woman's wake, Mrs Thomas carrying the lighter two of the four baskets. They had now approached the canal bank itself, and Mari was struggling with her baskets as they contained heavier items like the potatoes and even a small bag of sugar. She wondered why Mr Davenport hadn't sent his coach to pick up such heavy items. But then she figured that maybe he was on some pit business today; he appeared to be a very busy man who often attended meetings sometimes with the Crawshay family themselves, who owned the coal pit. Maybe he'd gone to their ancestral home, Cyfarthfa Castle!

By now Mari's arms were aching and she paused for a while, placing down her heavy loads on the towpath. She took a deep breath and let it go. *Soon – this too shall pass*, she thought. But as she stooped to retrieve both baskets, she failed to see Mrs Thomas dropping hers and approaching her from behind with an angry look on her face.

'As I suspected!' she yelled, roughly snatching Mari's mob cap from her head and holding it aloft between her thumb and fore-finger as though contaminated. 'You've hardly any hair; that's why you're covering it up, you filthy little scroat! You've got head lice, haven't you?'

'No, I have not!' Mari yelled back at the woman as her hands flew to her head, which was cold and bare now as she felt the little tufts between her fingers.

*How dare that old crone try to humiliate me! She's probably hoping some passer-by will see me.*

In temper, Mari flung both baskets on the ground, causing a couple of potatoes to dislodge from one basket and roll across the slush-covered towpath. Then thinking better of it, she said in a normal tone now, 'You are correct, of course. I'm crawling with the things and fleas too! Those are hopping all over me!' She began to scratch herself in a mocking fashion as she walked towards the woman while Marguerite's mouth popped open at her impudence.

'Get yourself away from me!' the woman cried with fear now, dropping the offending article on the ground. 'I can manage myself from here!'

Laughing to herself so much that her sides ached, Mari retrieved her cap, placed it back on her head, turned and walked away. It wasn't much further to the big house for her to go, though Mrs Thomas would have to make two trips with all those baskets. She'd have to hope no one came along in the meantime to steal them away.

When Mari arrived back at the shop, Mrs Jones wasn't best pleased with her.

Mari's laughing almost turned to crying. 'I'm sorry, Mrs Jones, but that woman insulted me again calling me "filthy"! She snatched the cap from my head and said it was as she suspected, I have head lice. So, I pretended I did have them, and fleas too!'

Mrs Jones pursed her lips. 'I'm afraid you've played right into her hands by telling her that. You should have denied such a thing. Now it'll be all around the village and no one will want to step foot in this shop. I'll lose custom over this!'

Mari's shoulders began to shake and then, to her horror, her eyes misted with tears. She hadn't wanted to upset the elderly lady for all the world.

* * *

When Mari called to Bobby's house later that day, he was full of sympathy for her.

'Don't be too hard on yourself, love. No doubt Mrs Jones was just angry in the moment.'

'But I've never seen her that way before, Bobby. It shocked me. She reckons now that word will get around the village that I'm lousy with nits and fleas and no one will want to buy anything from the shop for fear of catching something from me!'

'That's silly that is.' Bobby folded his arms as he leaned up against the back door of the house and with a lopsided grin said, 'Who is going to believe that hoity-toity hag, anyhow?'

Mari chuckled at Bobby's description of the woman. 'I suppose you're right. Not many like her, that's for sure. That day I had words with her, I got a round of applause and pats on the back from all the other customers in the shop.'

'Well, there you go then.'

It felt good and all making light of the situation with Bobby. He never failed to cheer her up at her lowest moments. She hesitated for a couple of seconds before saying, 'I've packed it in at the pit...'

'Oh?' He raised a curious brow. 'Why's that? Can't say I'm not relieved, mind you. Every shift you worked there I worried my guts about you.'

'You did?' She blinked several times and then released a breath while Bobby nodded. Then she added, 'Big Al, I mean Mr Probert, told me he knew I was "Lewis Lloyd"!'

Bobby's eyes widened with surprise. 'How'd he work that out?'

'He said he realised when he started calling around to our house to visit Mam. That one day he noticed I had nothing on my head, and he was surprised to see how short my hair was. It must have got him thinking as he then noticed other things.'

Bobby nodded knowingly. 'Probably your little ways and such like!'

She smiled.

'If you ask me, part of you was Lewis Lloyd anyhow.'

'I suppose.' She glanced at the back door. 'I assume your tea will be ready soon?'

'Aye, it's the same time every evening!'

'Same with our house. It used to be on the table bang on time when Dad was living at home or woe betide!' She wagged a chastising finger at him and laughed, causing him to smile. 'But now it doesn't seem to matter if it's a few minutes early or late.'

Bobby's forehead creased into a frown. 'So, word has it that your father has left the village then?'

'Yes, I think it got too much for him when Bryn rejected the money he was offering us and told him to leave the house. Maybe it's best they've both gone, probably back to London I reckon.'

'Oh no, love!' Bobby said suddenly. 'Didn't you know?'

'Know what?'

'Blodwyn is still here, living in the village. Talk has it she's moved back in with her mother.'

'Well, that is odd indeed.'

'Why do you say that, Mari? Perhaps your father just got fed up with her and wants to show you all he's left her for good.'

'But you don't understand, Bobby. This isn't common knowledge, so keep it to yourself, but Blodwyn is having my father's baby!'

He gulped. 'She's pregnant by him? There's a rotter leaving her with a bun in the oven like that!'

Up until recently, Bobby had never bad-mouthed her father at all, but now he seemed disgusted with his behaviour.

'I can't believe he'd do a thing like that,' said Mari, slowly shaking her head.

'He did it to your mam and the rest of you, didn't he?'

Bobby's words washed over her like an ice-cold bucket of water. He was right. Her father had left at the first sign of trouble instead of sticking it out. He'd left another child high and dry, and this one was an innocent baby who had not even had the chance of life yet. In that moment she cursed her father's name. Bryn was right about him. What was she to do now?

The sound of Mrs Brewster calling Bobby in for his tea drifted towards them, so turning she said, 'Thanks for listening.'

'Will you be all right, Mari?' His eyes looked full of concern.

'Yes.' She nodded as tears blurred her vision. And, blinking them away as she unlocked the back gate to walk home along the canal bank, she realised she'd be passing Pond Row where Blodwyn resided with her mother. She wondered what she would be doing right now. The young woman had more in common with her mother than anyone realised. And for the first time ever, Mari felt deeply sorry for her.

* * *

That evening, Mari toyed with telling her mother and Bryn that Dad had left his new love behind in the village, abandoning both her and their unborn child, but then something inside her pulled her up sharply. *No, whatever you do, don't tell them. The time isn't right. Instead, go and pay Blodwyn a visit yourself to see how she's coping.*

After all, Bryn would only gloat about the situation and say that Blodwyn had got what was coming to her. Mam, on the other hand, would probably get most upset by it all. She'd have to see her husband's former mistress and young child living in the village soon enough. Mari shuddered at the thought of poor Mam walking into one of the shops to see the young woman buying something and cradling her young infant in her arms. It would remind her of when her own children were young only a few years back. She'd feel a range of emotions, not just betrayal at that. He'd replaced her with a younger woman in his affections. Was she prettier than Mam? Mari wondered. Was that what the attraction was? Mam was still a good-looking woman for her age, but lately, she looked well worn and exhausted from all she had to do. Not since Mr Probert had decided to call though – his presence was a good thing; it perked her mother up no end.

\* \* \*

'You're quiet tonight, Mari!' Bryn exclaimed after they'd eaten. Mam had gone for a well-deserved sit-down by the fire as Mari had promised that she and Bryn would help clear the table away and wash and dry the dishes, the two younger members of the family having gone upstairs to play.

Mari hesitated.

'Cat got your tongue?' Bryn teased.

She shook her head. 'I've just had a trying day, that's all.' She related the tale of what happened with Mrs Thomas, telling him pretty much what she'd told Bobby.

Bryn's reaction wasn't the same though. Whereas Bobby had made her feel better about herself, Bryn was provoking and said, 'Well, you've only got yourself to blame for making out that you have head lice! And I agree with Mrs Jones. She can do without losing the custom!'

Now Mari was sorry she'd mentioned the incident, but she'd only done so as his question had prompted a response, and she didn't want to tell him the main reason for her upset was more to do with the fact her father had abandoned yet another child.

Why was Bryn so off this evening, she wondered. He'd been

in good spirits at the chapel only just yesterday seeing Glenda. Maybe it was something the young woman had said to him?

He said no more to her about the situation and left midway through drying the dishes, leaving her to it. Typical of him leaving the job half done.

When she'd put everything away, she went to sit with her mother in the living room.

'All right, Mari?' Mam asked.

For a moment, she felt like blurting everything out as she hated keeping secrets. It was bad enough working down the pit, keeping her secret from the other men and boys, but withholding information from Mam made her feel guilty. Yet, how could she shatter the peace by telling her mother the woman she resented was still in Abercanaid and soon she'd see her and the baby around the village? For the time being, she said nothing. Instead, just made small talk with her mother.

But then Mam looking her squarely in the eyes said, 'I've known you long enough to know there's something up. There's something you're not telling me, isn't there?'

Mari nodded and then it all came out in a torrent. How Bobby had told her Blodwyn hadn't even left the village with her father, that she was still here and that in time Mam would see the young woman with her husband's infant in the village. Abercanaid was a small place as villages went. There was no way on God's green earth that both women wouldn't encounter one another at some point. And even if it were possible to keep both women apart, then the gossip and muck-spreading would surely find its way to her mother's ears. There was no getting away from it: Dad had left a right mess behind in his wake and the villagers themselves would see no problem with spreading it around. One name in particular sprung to mind for Mari.

Mam's response wasn't what she was expecting. 'Oh Mari,' she said gently. 'Thank you for telling me, but if you hadn't, someone else would have made it their business to. You have no worries, believe me. You've done the right thing. Though it's no surprise to me your father leaving, it puzzles me he's left both Blodwyn and his unborn child behind.'

Mari nodded in agreement.

The living room door opened suddenly. 'Who's left?' Bryn looked at the pair.

'Your father has. Your sister said he's gone and left Blodwyn behind.'

Bryn let out a scornful laugh. 'Good enough for her. Now she really will have a bastard to care for!'

'Bryn!' scolded their mother. 'There's no need for that sort of talk. After all, that child when it's born will be your half-sister or - brother.'

Bryn's face reddened. 'It will be no sister or brother of mine; I can assure you!' Then catching Mari's eye, he said, 'How'd you come by this information, anyhow? That's what I'd like to know. Shop gossip, is it?'

Mari shook her head. 'No, Bobby told me.'

'Bobby!' Bryn threw up his arms. 'What does a young lad like him know?'

'He knows enough about it!' Mari's chin jutted out in defiance; Bryn's attitude was annoying her of late.

'That Blodwyn one couldn't afford the rent to that house they were living in on her own though,' said Mam, now narrowing her gaze. It was almost as though since Bryn had entered the room, he'd completely changed their mother's mind and now she doubted Mari's story was true at all.

'Well, from what Bobby told me she's no longer living at that house and has moved back in with her mother!' Mari said sharply, annoyed that her brother was upsetting the apple cart, and her version of events was not to be believed.

Mam's mouth gaped open. It gave Mari no pleasure that that piece of information had taken the wind out of her sails.

Slowly her mother's mouth closed. 'That makes sense,' she said, staring into the flames of the fire.

Even Bryn was silent now. He half expected the story to be tittle-tattle but what Mari knew, and her brother didn't, was that she trusted Bobby and what he said implicitly. The lad wouldn't want to hurt her for all the tea in China.

\* \* \*

The following morning when Mari arose from bed, after having a little lie-in, as there was no work at the shop for her that day, she was surprised there was no sign of her mother. The fire in the hearth was lit though and the kettle felt like it had not long since boiled. So wherever Mam was she'd not long left the house. For a moment, Mari was concerned in case her mother had gone missing again like when she'd discovered Blodwyn was pregnant, but then she reassured herself that Mam would hardly have lit the fire and gone to the trouble of making herself a cup of tea before leaving the house if that were the case. The remnants of tea leaves discarded at the bottom of a cup were near the sink.

Sighing to herself, she lifted the kettle and placed it on the hearth to boil. Tommy and Nerys would be up soon. Bryn was still slumbering upstairs; she'd heard his gentle snores as she passed the boys' bedroom.

Taking a cup of tea alone by the fireside gave her time to reflect. A lot had happened these past few months: Dad leaving them all, Blodwyn's pregnancy, working at the pit and the shop, and now Dad leaving the village alone with none of them having a forwarding address. Tears stung Mari's eyes when she thought back to last Christmas when they were still a family. Her father hadn't been all that nice to her back then, but at least they were all still together.

When he'd returned to Abercanaid that time and she'd encountered him underground, he'd seemed to have warmed towards her. Maybe Blodwyn had softened his heart somehow. But Bryn had made it blatantly clear when her father had offered them that money that he was having none of it. As, in truth, her brother was the head of the house now and that must surely have broken her father's heart, just like her mother's was broken.

## 17

When their mother returned home about an hour later, Bryn and Mari eagerly waited to see what she had to say. It wasn't like Mam to leave the house so early, as the children would usually run errands for her to the village shops.

'Where have you been?' Bryn narrowed his eyes as he watched their mother lay down her wicker basket on the kitchen table.

'Just out to fetch a few provisions,' she said, gesturing at the basket with her hand. She hesitated for a moment. 'But while I was out, I decided to call on Mrs Parry, Blodwyn's mother.'

'And was she home?' Bryn frowned.

'Yes, she was.'

'And her...'

'Daughter?' Mam shook her head. 'Mercifully I was spared the embarrassment of seeing her after that upset at the bakehouse.'

Mari nodded knowingly as she watched their mother undo the ribbons of her bonnet and place it beside the basket on the table. Then she removed her shawl and, after shaking it as though warding off some sort of evil spirit, laid it over the back of a chair. She patted down her hair.

'She was very helpful to me actually.'

'How?' asked Bryn as he took a step forward.

'Well, she made me a cup of tea for one thing. It's a bitterly cold morning.'

'For heaven's sake, Mam. I want to know did she give you any information about our father?'

'Yes, yes, she did.' Mam sighed and then took a seat at the table. 'You'd both better sit down.' There was a tone to their mother's voice that told Mari Mam was about to tell them something of great importance.

Mari and Bryn exchanged curious glances with one another, and both sat at the table, Bryn sitting opposite while Mari sat beside her mother.

'Mrs Parry gave me this.' She dipped her hand inside her basket, producing a buff-coloured leaflet, which she set out on the table before them, smoothing it out with the side of her hand. From what Mari could make out – the leaflet was upside down – there was a drawing of a ship on the front of it.

'What is it?' she asked her brother, who could read it the right way up, watching as he inhaled deeply and then let out a low whistle, the sort of whistle that told someone they were amazed by something.

'Go on, read it out to your sister then...' Mam urged.

Bryn swallowed and read:

'*Welsh Emigration Office, Liverpool. Those persons from Wales who intend emigrating to America or Australia are hereby informed that we book Passengers, either per Steamers or Sailing Vessels, at the very lowest rates in Liverpool...*'

Mari glanced at her mother and then toward Bryn whose complexion had turned very pale as he read further on. But somehow, she wasn't taking it in. It was almost as though it were all a dream, and she'd wake up at any moment.

'It goes on to say,' he continued, 'something about cautioning against paying any deposit money or instalments to any agent in the area as some are defrauding said emigrants.'

'What's an emigrant?' Mari blinked.

'It's someone who leaves this country to settle elsewhere,' said her brother, laying down the sheet of paper on the table. He scratched his head then fixed his gaze on their mother. 'So, it looks like he's done more than leave his home town; he's left or is leaving his homeland too?'

'Looks like it,' said Mam. 'According to Mrs Parry, Blodwyn found this leaflet the day he left Abercanaid. Her daughter wanted to go after him. Somehow find a way to get to Liverpool.'

'You think she wanted to stop him leaving?' Mari asked.

'Possibly so,' said Mam, forcing a smile now. 'But her mother talked her out of it as I think if she found him in Liverpool, she'd have tried to go with him, and as those sea journeys are so long, particularly if he chose Australia, her life and the baby's too might be at risk.'

All three sat in silence as they tried to comprehend what had gone on. Then finally Bryn said, 'So, when did our father actually leave Merthyr, Mam? Do you know?'

'According to Mrs Parry, about a fortnight ago, so he's well on his way somewhere by now.'

Mari felt a tightening in her gut as she realised about a fortnight ago was not long after Bryn had banished him from the house.

For her father to leave Wales for some other place overseas, it was unlikely in Mari's mind that he was ever coming back. She was shaken out of her reverie as Bryn interrupted her thoughts.

'But what I don't understand, Mam,' he was saying, 'is how

our father had enough money for his passage? Did Mrs Parry explain that? How he scraped enough money together?'

Their mother shook her head. 'To be truthful, that didn't even occur to me at the time. I was so stunned by what the woman told me...' She bit her lower lip as though considering something. 'Your father does have an uncle who is not short of a bob or two.'

'Oh? Who's that then?' Bryn asked as his eyes rounded like a pair of saucers.

'Uncle Tegwyn from Cefn Coed.'

'I've never heard mention of him before!' Bryn narrowed his eyes suspiciously as he exchanged glances with his sister.

'Me neither!' Mari shook her head. 'Our grandfather's brother?'

Mam nodded at the pair. Their grandfather had passed away when Mari was two years old, so she had no memory of him. The only brother she knew was their great-uncle, Ifor. He was getting on in years and they rarely saw him.

'Tell us about this "Uncle Tegwyn",' said Bryn, eager to know more about the man.

'I don't know that much about him myself other than he was the black sheep of the family, by all accounts.'

'Didn't you ever get to meet him?' Bryn frowned.

'Just the once. He didn't attend our wedding but...' Their mother's eyes glazed over for a moment as though it was all too much for her, as her mind slipped back to a time in life when she was most probably at her happiest, before everything she'd ever known had soured.

'But what?' Bryn angled his head to one side with curiosity.

'But I did meet him at your grandfather's funeral.'

'And what was he like then, Mam?' Bryn persisted, causing Mari to shoot him an angry glance. Couldn't he see that Mam was near to tears right now? It had undoubtedly been a trying morning for her, no matter how light she tried to make of it.

'A quiet man from what I could tell. A man of few words.'

'How'd he make his money, then?' Bryn asked gruffly.

'By buying and selling properties in the town. He rented some properties out to folk but was known as being a mean landlord. Some of the places were in dire need of repair too. That's what your father told me.'

'Well, I can't see it being him who loaned money for Dad's passage to America,' Bryn said, raising his voice.

'He had a soft spot for your father though.' Mam's voice sounded croaky now.

'Why was that, Mam?' Mari asked.

'Suppose it was because he never wed or had any children of his own. He lives with his housekeeper, but I don't think he's a happy man; he can't be. All that wealth and now with your father gone, no one to leave it to! All the money in the world can't buy you happiness!'

'Oh, I don't know about that!' snapped Bryn. 'If I had money, I could marry Glenda and give her a life she's accustomed to. Maybe her father would respect me then!'

The mention of money had obviously struck a chord with her brother, yet he had turned down the money offered to the family from their father as he viewed that as 'blood money', a false recompense as a way to serve his penance.

'You could always ask Uncle Tegwyn if he's given Dad money for his passage, Mam,' said Mari in a soft tone of voice, not wanting to upset her mother for all the world, but some questions needed answering.

'I suppose I could, but I won't,' said their mother with a note of finality to her voice. 'Your father's made his decision to leave us all, even his new woman and unborn child. Nothing's going to change about that. So, let's get cracking. Bryn, go outside to the coalhouse and bring in a bucket of coal to bank up the fire, it's perishing today.' Her eyes fixed on Mari. 'There's some vegetables and onions in my basket, get peeling. I'm going to make us a warming stew today.'

Mari nodded as she watched her brother head towards the back door. The best she could hope for now was word from her father via a letter. But would he bother contacting any of them ever again? And most importantly of all, where had he gone to and why?

\* \* \*

It was a few days later before Mari received an inkling where her father might have gone and why, when Al Probert turned up at the house one evening asking to speak to them all as a matter of great importance. It was then Mari realised it must be about their father.

Al's face was a deathly shade of puce as he explained word had got to him via another collier, whom he did not name, that Gwynfor Evans had left Wales for America. So, not Australia then. Mari realised it had to be one of the two places mentioned on that blessed leaflet.

Al went on to explain that another miner had accompanied him. The pair were headed for Pennsylvania where Welsh coal mining skills were in demand and highly sought after. So much so, that any Welsh miner who had half-decent skills would likely be put into a position of authority, made a manager even.

When Al had related the tale, much to everyone's astonishment, he added, 'So, you can understand the attraction for your father. He'll be paid far more than he would working at the pit here in Abercanaid and, eventually, possibly given a lot more responsibility to boot. He's one of the best there is, is your father, a very skilled fellow indeed.'

Mari didn't doubt it. She snuck a quick glance at Bryn, who was scowling in the corner.

Al continued. 'I've half a mind to go there myself.' He chuckled nervously, as though to make light of the situation.

'The sly bastard!' Bryn shouted, causing their mother to lift the edge of her pinafore over her face, disgusted with her son's bad language in front of Mr Probert. In all the time Mari had worked underground, she'd never once heard Al cuss or lose his temper. He was mild-mannered but, even so, the men respected him.

Noticing Tommy and Nerys emerging through the door, Mari quickly ushered them out of the room. 'Go and play outside, you two, until I call you for supper!' she advised. There was no way she wanted either of them subjected to what was being discussed. It would only serve to upset both, particularly Tommy who was highly sensitive and missed his father dreadfully. And, being their father's favourite, surely Dad must miss him dreadfully too? All of them really. She'd seen the look in her father's eyes that last time he'd called to the house – the longing and regret in them. It was so obvious he'd wanted to make amends to them all, but Bryn had put paid to that.

When she returned to the room, Mari noticed that Al was now seated beside their mother on the couch while Bryn was stood, staring out of the window as though the answer to why their father had fled lay there – somewhere in the far-off distance, over the mountain and far away.

'I'll boil the kettle for tea, shall I, Mam?' Mari asked, trying to sound bright and breezy, but a lump had formed in her throat and was threatening to choke her.

Mam nodded, forcing a smile.

* * *

Before Al left, Mari managed to have a quiet word with him.

'Did you tell the foreman Lewis Lloyd can no longer work at the pit, Mr Probert?'

Smiling, he patted her head. 'You've no worries on that score; there'll be no comebacks for it in any case as to all intents and purposes Lewis Lloyd no longer exists.'

'What about those bullies who were causing trouble for me, though?'

Al's face flushed. 'Well, er...' He coughed. 'I do have to warn you that one called Pete reckons he's going to track down Lewis Lloyd and give him a good hiding.' Mari drew a sharp intake of breath. 'But...' Al smiled. '...how can he possibly do that when there is no longer a Lewis Lloyd out there?'

Somehow, despite what Al said, it did little to reassure her. She'd made some enemies there at the pit and she'd also made one in the village as herself: Mari Evans.

# 18

Once the initial shock of discovering what had happened to her father wore off, life began to settle down again for Mari and the rest of the family. If her mother had shed any tears about Dad going off to America, then she'd done it in private, for Mari had not witnessed any since the day her mother had visited the Parry household and been given that emigration leaflet. Indeed, Mam seemed to be thriving, with Al Probert paying regular visits to the home. Unfortunately, that didn't stop the village gossips now turning their attention towards her mother and Al.

It was while she was working at the shop that she heard Al's name mentioned by a tall, sour-looking woman. Mrs Jones referred to the woman as 'Mrs Sherbet Bonbon', which highly amused Mari as it wasn't the woman's real name, but Mrs Jones couldn't pronounce it properly and it was a double-barrelled name too. The woman called into the premises a couple of times a week for 'something for her husband's tea' as she put it.

This day Mari began to feel quite uncomfortable as the woman spoke to another in the corner of the shop behind the palm of her hand. She'd already heard the Probert name mentioned but what came next brought her up sharp. She purposely began to tidy up, sweeping the floor, a job that was usually left until the end of the day.

She was sweeping behind the woman now who was not aware of her presence.

'And his wife not dead a six-month as yet!' she said in a stage whisper.

As Mari drew nearer, she could see the look of horror on the other woman's face, her eyes enlarged as she coughed as though to warn Mrs Sherbet she was being overheard.

But the woman was in her stride now and she continued. 'That poor wife of his isn't cold in her grave yet and he's sniffing around a married woman like that!'

Mari gently tugged on the woman's shawl. 'Er, Mrs, you've forgotten something...'

The woman turned on her heel to be faced with Mari, whose face was full of fury. 'I h... haven't forgotten anything, I was just about to leave...' she said, her voice trembling now.

'Oh yes, you have forgotten something. You've forgotten the part where Mr Probert had to finish his job at the pit to take care of his very sick wife and how upset he was when her body was lowered into the earth, realising he and his children would never see her again. You've also forgotten the part about him being one of the nicest, kindest people to live in this village who will help anyone out. And most importantly of all, you've forgotten the part where he minds his own bloody business!'

A pink flush crept over the woman's face and her hand went to her throat as her mouth popped open from the shock of being put in her place.

'You ought to put that hand over your mouth instead or better still get someone to cut that evil tongue out of your head!' Mari shouted.

A flurry of footsteps behind them alerted Mari to that fact that Mrs Jones had come rushing out of the back room, but instead of taking Mari's side, she roughly pulled her by the arm and, apologising to the woman, said, 'I'm sorry about that. Please take anything you'd like from the shop as way of compensation.' Then turning to Mari she said, 'Go out to the back room now and put the kettle on to boil.'

Mrs Sherbet lifted her chin and, shaking her head, said, 'I do not want anything any longer from you or your shop, Mrs Jones. Not until you get rid of that impudent, foul-mouthed assistant of yours. That outburst was most uncalled for.'

The woman who had been the recipient of the gossip spewing from Mrs Sherbet's mouth nodded her agreement, and Mari turned from the trio and headed off to the back room.

When the women had departed, Mrs Jones flicked the shop sign on the door to 'Closed' and went to address Mari in the back room.

Mari had already boiled the kettle with the hopes of having a refreshing cuppa, but as the woman stood in the doorway, shaking her head and pursing her lips, she realised that wouldn't be forthcoming.

Mrs Jones folded her arms. 'I'm sorry, Mari. This is the second time you've insulted a customer in the past couple of weeks. I warned you when it happened to Marguerite Thomas, it might cause me to lose custom. That wasn't the first time with her either. That first time I could forgive as she insulted your family and the other shop customers who witnessed it liked the fact you put her in her place, but you should have left it at that. With time, she returned to the shop as she had little choice – I expect as Mr

Davenport likes his couple of ounces of tobacco from time to time. But the second time, when you told her you were lousy with nits and fleas, was unforgivable. She's not been back here since as no doubt you gave her the impression that this shop is hopping with fleas and all kinds of filth! I used to get a regular large order every week for goods from Mr and Mrs Davenport. They were my best customers in this village – but now, no more! Some other establishment has secured their custom instead, thanks to you!'

Mari's heartbeat quickened as her mouth dried up with anxiety. She glanced at the kettle on the hearth as it puffed out plumes of steam.

'And then you insulted Mrs Shirley Babcock-Brown!'

Mari gasped. For once Mrs Jones had remembered the woman's real name and recited it correctly. It was evident that her anger had caused her mind to focus sharply on the task in hand.

'But I only answered her back as she was running down Mr Probert, tarnishing his good name and my mam's too.'

Mrs Jones frowned. 'What do you mean?'

'Well, she insinuated that Mr Probert hadn't waited all that long before calling on my mother and, as she put it, his wife wasn't cold in her grave yet! And it was as if she was making out my mother is a hussy, when she's nothing of the kind. My mother is a good, God-fearing, respectable woman who works her fingers to the bone for her family.' Mari swallowed hard.

Mrs Jones tilted her head in a show of understanding. 'I do understand, you know. But you must take all sorts if you want to work at my shop. You need to develop a thicker skin, Mari. What you should have done when you'd heard that pair gossiping was to come and tell me about it. I'd have stopped it in its tracks. Now it might be better if you go home, and I'll see if I can limit the damage done on this occasion before you return here to help me again.' She wagged a warning finger in her face.

Tears were close to the surface for Mari. She hadn't even got to tell the woman how her father had set sail for America yet and it was unlikely she'd ever set eyes on him again. In truth, maybe it was that situation that had made her feel so helpless and caused her to retort so sharply towards the customer. She felt she no longer had the strength to stand up for herself – she'd obviously exhausted all Mrs Jones's supply of sympathy.

Nodding, Mari sniffed. Then she pointed at the kettle on the hearth. 'It's boiled now, Mrs Jones.'

She turned her back on the woman to fetch her shawl from a chair and walked out through the shop door. She'd hardly ever used the back entrance but today it seemed fitting as, in her employer's eyes, she'd done a very bad thing, and she wondered if the woman would ever forgive her for it.

\* \* \*

A couple of days later, Mari was on her way to the village, being mindful how she walked. The wet ground had quickly turned to ice overnight, as the temperature had plummeted. So certain areas were treacherous underfoot. Even the canal had begun to ice over, and bargemen had to use wooden sticks to break the ice.

Today, Mari was on a mission to purchase bread from the bakehouse, deciding it wise to keep away from Mrs Jones's shop to allow the woman time to simmer down. She'd had the opportunity to reflect on her behaviour this past couple of days and she felt she'd let the elderly woman down. Why on earth hadn't she bit her tongue to stop herself responding so savagely to that gossip's harsh comments? Still, there was no use fretting about it now. She'd been sent to fetch two large loaves of bread and once that was accomplished, she intended to make herself useful by helping her mother with the housework.

As she neared Pond Row, she noticed a young woman with a red thick flannel shawl wrapped around her head and shoulders leaving one of the houses with a wicker basket over the crook of her arm. As Mari watched the woman walk along, she realised she must be unaware of how icy the conditions had become as her feet went from under herself and she slipped on her backside. She appeared to be having a hard time pulling herself back on to her feet as there was nothing for her to put her hand on to pull herself up. No wall or tree for her to cling on to.

Walking carefully towards her, Mari called out, and laying her basket on the icy ground said, 'Here, let me help you.' She stretched out her hand towards the young woman.

It was then Mari noticed the rounded belly beneath the woman's skirt. She was pregnant. It had to be Blodwyn!

Looking up at Mari through a pair of clear blue eyes, Blodwyn forced a smile. 'It's my own fault for rushing like that. There's not much food in the house this morning and I wanted to get some bread in and some other shopping as my mother's not at all well.' She clutched her stomach as she spoke.

Although this was the young woman who had stolen her father's heart, Mari felt a pang of sympathy for her. She was just another young person not that much older than herself, who also wanted to help her mother.

Pulling Blodwyn to her feet, Mari huffed out a breath. 'Look, I have to go to the village for bread myself, why don't I pick up a few things for you at the same time?'

Blodwyn brushed her skirt down. 'That's very kind of you, er...? Sorry, I don't know your name?'

Mari deliberated on whether she should lie but decided honesty was the best policy. 'It's Mari, Mari Evans.'

She watched as the young woman opened her mouth as

though about to say something but then closed it again. Finally, Blodwyn spoke. 'You're Gwynfor's daughter!'

Mari nodded. 'And I'd already worked out who you are.'

'Oh!' Blodwyn said as her hands flew to her face as though she were somehow disarmed by this knowledge. 'You must really hate me?'

'No, I don't.' Mari shook her head. 'I don't even know you to hate you. You must know someone personally before you can do that, mustn't you?'

Tentatively, Blodwyn nodded. 'I suppose you do.'

'Even my mother doesn't hate you. She's just upset at what's gone on lately with my father behaving so strangely. That's why she had words with you. But it's all for nothing really, as in the end, my father abandoned us all, even that baby you're carrying. He turned his back on his unborn child.' She glanced at Blodwyn's swollen stomach.

Blodwyn's lip trembled, and then to Mari's horror, she began to weep. 'I... I don't know how we're going to cope with another mouth to feed...' She was trembling all over, her shoulders beginning to shake.

Mari reached out to touch the woman's hand. 'Don't you worry yourself; we can help you out,' she heard herself saying, and was relieved in that moment that Bryn wasn't in earshot, as he'd have had a lot to say about Mari's kindness and willingness to help the young woman. In her brother's eyes, Blodwyn was as much to blame for things as their father was.

Mari retrieved both baskets from the ground and then she escorted the woman safely to the front door. Blodwyn handed her a silver shilling and told her what was required in the way of shopping.

'I won't be long,' Mari reassured, shooting her a smile. 'Now go indoors and keep yourself warm.'

True to her word, Mari returned later with the basket of provisions, and she donated one of the two loaves she'd bought for her own family to Blodwyn and her mother.

'I've never known such kindness.' Blodwyn sniffed as Mari handed her the full basket, dropping the spare change into her open palm.

In the background, through the open front door, Mari noticed Mrs Parry reclining on the couch near the fireside. It appeared to be used as a makeshift bed, with a pillow placed beneath her head and a couple of woollen blankets draped over her. No doubt it was warmer for the woman to sleep near the open fire downstairs.

'If you need any help with anything at all, you only need to ask.' Mari smiled. 'You know where we live, don't you?'

Blodwyn nodded as she subconsciously rubbed her free hand over her stomach, the one that wasn't gripping the basket. 'Thank you, Mari.' Quite naturally, Blodwyn leaned forward to peck a kiss of gratitude on Mari's cheek, before closing the door behind herself.

Who'd have thought today she'd be helping the young woman out and would even receive a kiss from her? Not Mari, that was for sure. The day had already taken a strange turn, and it wasn't over yet.

* * *

When Mari arrived home, her mother was waiting for her on the doorstep. 'How come it's taken you this long to fetch two loaves of bread?'

'Sorry, Mam. I'll explain when I get inside. I'm f... freezing out here.' She hoped her mother hadn't been standing on the doorstep for all that long awaiting her return, she'd hate to have put her in an overly bad mood.

Her mother took the basket from Mari's grasp. 'There's only one loaf in here, not two like I asked you to buy.'

Mari shook her head. 'I know.'

'They'd run out again, had they?'

'Er, no. I gave one of them away to someone.'

'Gave the loaf away? We've not got any food spare to give away to folk. We're struggling as it is. You should understand that!'

'I do, but I'll tell you all about it now. Is Bryn at home?'

'He's outside in the backyard, chopping up logs for firewood. Why?'

'I just thought I'd only tell you, as Bryn will get angry.'

'All right.' Her mother relented. 'But this had better be good.'

Once inside, Mari felt her body begin to thaw out as she splayed her fingers by the fire. By that time, Mam had deposited both bread and basket in the scullery and returned to the living room, closing the door behind her.

'Pass me your shawl,' she said.

Mari removed the shawl from her shoulders and passed it to her mother, who hung it up behind the door and then returned by her daughter's side.

'Well, what happened?'

Mari explained the situation, hoping all the while her mother wouldn't be cross with her.

But after she'd spoken, Mari was pleasantly surprised when her mother said, 'You did the Christian thing there, Mari. Well done, I'm proud of you, *cariad*. I don't like the sound of Mrs Parry being ill like that. I'll call to the house later and take a bottle of tonic to build up her strength.'

Mari nodded; she had no idea what ingredients were in that

bottle but there was always one spare in the cupboard. Mam swore by it for all manner of ailments.

* * *

Later that day, without Bryn's knowledge, Mari and her mother visited the Parry household and were glad that they did. When Mam saw the blanched-looking pallor on Mrs Parry's face, the sunken eyes and laboured breaths the woman struggled to take as she reclined on the couch, she became concerned. It was apparent that no amount of tonic medicine they brought was going to help on this occasion.

'What your mother needs is to see a doctor.' Mari's mother looked at Blodwyn.

The young woman opened her mouth as though about to say something but then closed it again. 'I... we don't have enough money to pay for a doctor's visit,' she said helplessly as she rubbed her stomach.

Mari, knowing that neither did they have enough money either, whispered in her mother's ear, 'Shall at least one of us stay here to help out?'

Mam nodded. 'I'll stay,' she said, forcing a smile, and then turned back to Blodwyn. 'That fever needs to break; your mother must sweat it out. Have you enough coal here to bank up that fire?' She glanced at the hearth where the pitiful flames seemed to be on the verge of extinction.

Blodwyn nodded. 'There's some in the coal scuttle and more outside in the coal cwtch. We don't usually have this much coal but Gwynfor got a couple of sacks delivered here – before he left us.'

Mari exchanged glances with her mother. It sounded as though a lot of planning had gone into her father's scheme to escape Abercanaid. He'd realised he would be leaving and had at least thought to pay for some fuel for Blodwyn and Mrs Parry, but of course, he'd made no more provision than that, otherwise there'd be money to pay a doctor's fee.

'Sort that fire out for us, Mari, will you?' Mam asked. Mari was quite used to starting and banking up fires in her own home, so she set to work. Then turning to Blodwyn, Mam said, 'Do you have any more blankets in the house?'

'There's some on my bed, I'll fetch them now.'

Within the hour the fire was nicely ablaze, and Mrs Parry well covered in blankets and several shawls. Mam set about making a nourishing broth for the woman from leftover chicken bones, onions and carrots. Mam was very resourceful like that, having the ability to make something tasty from next to nothing and eking it out for several days. She had to be, these days, as money was in short supply.

As time wore on, her mother turned to Mari. 'You'd better get back home now, love, before it gets dark. The kids will be needing their supper. There's some lamb cawl left in a saucepan in the scullery. You can make that stretch if you make some dumplings to go with it.'

Mari raised her eyebrows. 'You're stopping here then, Mam?'

'Yes, I am.' Her mother nodded with conviction. 'For as long as it takes. If we had the money, I'd pay to fetch the doctor myself...'

Mari couldn't help thinking that if her father were still here, then there'd be money for her to fetch the doctor. And to think her brother had knocked all the money out of his hand like that! It would be most welcome right now in the Parry household. What a dreadful mess her father had left behind in his wake.

'What am I to tell Bryn though? I mean about where you are?'

'Tell him the ruddy truth!' Mam said with a gleam in her eyes.

'These people need help from someone, don't they? And I'd not be doing my Christian duty if I turned my back on them.'

*No matter who they are!* thought Mari as she nodded obligingly at her mother. Bryn wasn't going to be best pleased, of course he wasn't, but what other choice did they have?

* * *

Darkness was beginning to fall as Mari walked back home, when she noticed three men walking towards her. The voices sounded familiar to her ears and she stiffened as a chill coursed down her spine. It was three of that group of five men from the pit who had treated her so badly. For a moment she was Lewis Lloyd again and she imagined them pushing her and trying to trip her up as she passed by. The loudest voice was of that one called Pete; he was speaking about some woman in a derogatory fashion.

'Panting for it, she was!' he boasted to his mates. He chuckled as he dug his hands into his pockets and kicked a stone from the canal towpath. 'Couldn't get enough of me!'

Mari realised they were probably on their way to the pub. She'd need to brave this one out so she could get home before dark.

'Hey, what do we have here?' one of them shouted as they noticed Mari approaching.

Mari's heartbeat quickened as she froze to the spot. If she attempted to run off, they might try to make a sport of it. Whatever she did, she realised she must show the men no fear.

'Perhaps this one might pant for it too?' Pete said, laughing maliciously in front of his mates. No doubt he was out to impress them.

One of the men, as though weighing things up said, 'Best leave her be, she's only a young girl.'

Pete stepped in front of Mari to block her path, causing her to take a shuddering breath. 'Aw, I don't know about that,' he said, letting out a low whistle. 'Bet you've got a nice figure beneath that dress of yours.' Then he lunged forward, but the man who had stood up for her dragged Pete away.

'Use your head, man,' he advised. Then, looking at Mari with sympathy, he said, 'Go on. Quickly on your way, love, before it gets dark.'

Mari nodded gratefully but the way Pete was still leering at her, as his friend held him at bay, began to anger her. The actions of that group of bullies came back at her swiftly, and now, she felt angry – angry for herself, for Lewis Lloyd and for the other young colliers like him who had been at the mercy of that mob.

'I don't think my brother would be too happy with what you've been suggesting towards me!' she said, facing up to Pete as his eyes widened with astonishment. 'He knows you very well, and so does my father.'

The men glanced curiously at one another.

'And who might they be?' asked the man who was prepared to let her go on her way.

'Gwynfor and Bryn Evans,' she said, jutting out her chin in defiance.

Pete began to laugh nervously. 'Well, your father has buggered off from Abercanaid by all accounts! So, he can't say much, can he?'

'No, but her Bryn's still around and I wouldn't like to tangle with him. He's got a temper on him, that one,' said the man as he let go of Pete. 'Big Al is calling regularly at the house too, I've heard.'

Pete reached out as though to make a grab for her and then he put his hand down by his side. 'You haven't had a chance to blossom into a fully grown rose as yet, darling. You'll keep!' he sneered, eyeing her with contempt.

Then, laughing, he walked past her in the direction of the pub with his friends following behind. He stopped and turned to give one last glance in her direction, which made her shiver with fear.

Mari heaved out a sigh of relief, but she could have kicked herself for choosing to defend and identify herself like that. She should have just carried on walking and got away from him when she had the chance; that way there'd be no further dramas. That quick temper of hers had got her into too much trouble of late and now she wished she'd said nothing at all.

## 19

Mari arrived at her door, anxious and out of breath, as she'd lifted her skirts to run all the way home following her ordeal. It seemed to her that it was Pete who was the ringleader. He'd caused her plenty of trouble lately. The rest of the men weren't as vindictive as he was. She seemed to sense they'd calm down if it weren't for him and maybe would treat the new lads a whole lot better. Pete was a troublemaker who loved stirring the pot. *I hope you get your comeuppance someday soon, lovely boy!*

She was just about to open the front door when it was opened from the inside. Having thought it would be Bryn stood there, she was surprised to see it was Al Probert and he had a look of concern in his eyes.

'I thought I heard footsteps,' he said, then looking behind her, added, 'Hasn't your mother returned with you, Mari? Bryn left here a while ago in search of you both. I think he thought your mother might have gone missing again, so I offered to stop on here and watch the kids. They're upstairs playing.'

Mari thanked him and then shook her head as she crossed

the threshold, Al stepping to one side to allow her to pass. 'Mam's all right. It's nothing like that.'

Once inside the living room, she removed her shawl and bonnet, throwing them on the armchair near the fireside. Then she explained what had occurred, both with Blodwyn and her mother, and later with the men from the pit.

'I'm sorry to hear about that, on both counts of what you told me, Mari. About Mrs Parry, I think your mother has done the right thing in the circumstances. Now about the other thing...' He shook his head. 'I don't think you need to worry any further about Pete and his cronies.'

Mari frowned. 'But why do you say that?'

'Look at it this way, not one of them had a clue you were Lewis Lloyd – they didn't recognise you!'

'I know that,' said Mari, her voice full of exasperation. 'I'm more concerned now with being in danger as myself, in case that Pete recognises me again.'

'I doubt he will, Mari.' He pointed towards the armchair. 'You were wearing your bonnet, which would have covered part of your face, and it was beginning to get dark. You don't think you're the only young woman Pete accosts, do you?' Al's eyes seemed to bore a hole in her soul as he spoke with such conviction. 'He's at it all the time with various women and girls from the village, some old enough to be his mother! By the time he's had a few beers at the pub tonight, he'll have forgotten all about you. And you said one of the men took pity on you?'

'He did,' she said, sighing audibly. 'He just wanted for Pete to leave me alone and the other said nothing.'

'Well, there you are then. I bet if either of those two are with him and they even recognise you, they'll not mention it to Pete. You can rest assured. In any case' – he huffed out a breath – 'now this is unofficial news so keep it to yourself for the time being...

Word has it that Pete and those other cronies of his are going to be dismissed from their duties for good soon enough! First thing Monday morning, to be precise!'

Mari gasped. 'But how do you know that?' she asked, blinking in disbelief.

'I overheard the foreman talking to Mr Davenport in the office the other day. He reckons he knows what's going on and he has enough information to hang the blighters! Not really send them to the gallows, of course, but to make things tough for them if they try for another job elsewhere – their names will be muck in these parts! Especially as the higher-ups know what's been going on. Mr Roberts said he wouldn't even give them a character reference either, so maybe their best bet would be to begin again in Pennsylvania with the other Welsh miners; that's if they'll take them without any references, of course!'

A slow smile crept across Mari's face. 'This is such good news that I feel like shouting it from the rooftops!' she said, then looking at Al, carried on, 'But I know I can't do that. At least not for the time being.'

'Not until it's official, Mari,' he said, tapping the side of his nose with his index finger. 'Those agitators are going to get their comeuppance at long last! Maybe young lads can begin work at the pit without anyone causing problems for them from now on. Not only that, but Mr Roberts will be on his guard now if anyone tries to do such a thing again in the future.'

Mari nodded. As she considered the fact that those bullies might possibly end up in Pennsylvania, a thought occurred to her. 'Do you want to go yourself, Mr Probert? To Pennsylvania I mean, like my father?'

Al vehemently shook his head. 'No, not me. Never. I was only making light of things when I mentioned that the other day.'

'But you don't have any ties now and your children are grown up.'

'That may be so,' he said, stroking his chin, 'but there are other reasons I'd like to remain in Merthyr.'

Mari smiled, realising that one of those reasons was undoubtedly her mother.

\* \* \*

When Bryn returned home about half an hour later, Mari explained to her brother what was keeping their mother.

Bryn frowned and was about to go off on one when Mari stopped him mid-sentence. 'Now I'll hear no more of this. Mrs Parry is extremely sick, and someone needs to help her. It's not the woman's fault what happened between our father and her daughter. And it's not that unborn child's fault either. So, stop it!'

Bryn fell silent for a while, then he began to chuckle. 'Why, our Mari, aren't you a force to be reckoned with lately!'

She had to admit, she was.

\* \* \*

The following day when her mother hadn't returned from the Parry household, Mari went in search of her. Tentatively, she knocked on the scuffed wooden front door at Pond Row, which caused one neighbour to peep through her curtains. No doubt Blodwyn's and her father's shenanigans of late had caused many a raised eyebrow in the vicinity. And poor Mrs Parry would have been the one who bore the brunt of it all, as her home had been turned into a hotbed of sin. A flood of sympathy for the woman coursed through Mari's veins.

It was a couple of minutes before the door was opened and it was Blodwyn who was standing there with dark rings beneath her eyes.

'I... is my mother still here?' Mari blurted out. It hadn't been that long since Mam had been unwell herself and had gone missing, so her concerns were founded for her mother.

Blodwyn nodded. 'You'd better come in,' she said, opening the door a fraction more to allow Mari access; no doubt she didn't want to allow too much cold air into the room as there was no passageway – the door opened directly into the living room.

Mari's eyes searched the room until she saw her mother in the corner, stood over an old, shabby table. She was measuring something from a yellow and silver tin onto a large spoon.

'What are you doing, Mam?' Mari asked as she approached.

Mam turned. It was evident she'd hardly slept a wink all night; she looked exhausted. 'Sssh,' she warned. 'Mrs Parry has just dropped off to sleep. She's been up coughing all night long. I'm just making a mustard poultice to apply to her chest. This sweating-it-out thing though appears to be doing the trick. She's even managed to drink some of the broth I made her.'

Mari blew out a breath of relief. 'Oh, thank goodness for that.' She watched as her mother added a large spoonful of flour to the mustard powder.

'I could have done with you earlier, mind, my girl.'

'Oh?' Mari frowned as she watched her mother make some sort of paste by slowly adding water to the powder in the bowl and stirring it with a fork until it was the right consistency. There was an old crepe bandage by the side of the bowl and Mari guessed her mother would apply the paste to that and place it on the woman's chest. She'd seen her do that before when her father had had a chesty cough last year. Whether it really worked or not,

Mari didn't have a clue, but sure as eggs were eggs, a couple of days later, Dad was up out of bed and sitting in his favourite armchair and by the following week was back working at the pit.

'Yes,' her mother continued, 'I had to send Blodwyn down to Mrs Jones's shop for the mustard powder. She didn't have any for sale, but thankfully, she kindly gave us some of her own.' Her mother gestured towards the yellow and silver tin, which was still open. 'Anyhow, when Blodwyn explained to her what happened and that I was here helping, she gave her a message to pass on to you...'

Oh no! Mari could feel her colour rising now and her eyes darted around the shabby room. A sheet of wallpaper was peeling off around the window and for some reason her eyes focused on that. Mrs Jones must have told Blodwyn what had happened with her being cheeky to those customers and had probably sent a message to say she wasn't to return to the shop any more.

'Well, you tell Mari what Mrs Jones said, Blodwyn,' Mam said, smiling.

Mari's eyes slowly averted from the peeling wallpaper and she moved her gaze to Blodwyn's face. The young woman was stood to the side of the hearth with her hand over her swollen stomach.

'I don't know what she meant by this,' said Blodwyn, 'but she said to let you know that she has now limited the damage done and you can return to work at the shop on Friday.'

Mari felt a sense of intense relief wash all over her. *Thank you, Lord!* she said inwardly.

'What on earth did she mean by that though, Mari?' Mam asked.

Thinking on her feet, Mari said, 'It must be as she had a bit of a flood in the back room. She had been considering closing the shop for a day or two to clean up.'

'Well, it's open again now,' said Mam brusquely. 'That's the trouble with that shop being down in a bit of a dingle so close to the canal,' she said, fully believing Mari's story.

Of course, what Mrs Jones must have meant is that she'd made amends to the customer. Maybe she'd offered her some free provisions. Realising what it must have taken for Mrs Jones to forgive her, her heart went out to the woman. This year, she was going to ensure Mrs Jones had the best Christmas Day ever at their home.

Mari offered to take over from her mother so she could go home and rest up, but Mam refused.

'No, I'll stop here until I'm satisfied that Mrs Parry is out of danger,' she said. 'What you can do for me though, Mari, when you leave here is to pick up some provisions. Another loaf of bread and some eggs and bacon, if you will.' She dipped her hand into her skirt pocket and handed Mari a shilling. 'Get the best price you can, mind you, as this is my final shilling for the time being.'

Mari nodded, feeling guilty she'd left work at the pit now. It was a few days before Christmas and Bryn wouldn't be returning until January. She'd ask Mr Probert if it might be a good idea if Lewis Lloyd made another appearance at the pit to get them over Christmas.

When she arrived at the shop, Mari thanked Mrs Jones for giving her another chance and told her she wouldn't mess up again. She explained the family were down to their last shilling, so very kindly the woman gave her the eggs and bacon for nothing as she reckoned she owed her for the last shift she'd worked. All she had to do was purchase a loaf of bread from the bakery, but Mrs Jones insisted on giving her a loaf free of charge too, saying it had been there on the counter since the previous day, but Mari didn't believe that for a second. To her, the loaf felt fresh and springy. Still, beggars couldn't be choosers, and she was very grateful for her free bounty that day.

The next time she saw Al Probert, she was determined to ask if he might put a word in with the foreman to get back to work, to tide them over until mid-January when there'd be another wage coming in from Bryn.

'I can stay a while to help out,' Mari said to her mother, once she'd returned to Mrs Parry's house.

Her mother shook her head. 'You go home and see to your brother and sister. I'll stop here a while longer until I'm certain Mrs Parry is over the worst of her fever.'

Mari frowned. 'So, what do you think it is then, Mam?'

'I'd say it's some sort of chest infection. Sounds like bronchitis to me, the way she coughed so harshly throughout the night, right exhausted she is an' all.'

Mari touched her mother's forearm lightly, and her mother steered her to one side as Blodwyn carried some crockery on a tray into the scullery.

'Between you and I,' Mam whispered, 'I don't know what will become of them even if Mrs Parry gets over this.'

'How'd you mean, Mam?' Mari wrinkled her nose.

'They've hardly a penny between them and Blodwyn says they owe the rent man a fortnight's rent money.'

Mari's hand covered her mouth. Then dropping her hand to her side, she said, 'So that means they might be forced out onto the street, I suppose?'

Mam nodded, her eyes scanning the room for fear Blodwyn might overhear their conversation. 'It might mean the workhouse for them both. And that will mean that poor baby she's carrying will be born there.' Tears welled up in her mother's eyes. 'What that man has done to us all,' she said shakily as she dabbed at her eyes with a handkerchief.

No matter what people said about her father, or no matter how harshly he'd treated her in the past, Mari found it hard to despise him. The tenderness she'd received from him when they'd recently reunited had been real; she was sure of it. She'd seen it in his eyes, heard it in his voice. It seemed to her he was now running away from his responsibilities, escaping it all for some reason only he knew. Maybe it was more than he could deal with? But one thing was for certain: all this mess was of his own making.

* * *

Before returning home, Mari called to Al Probert's house in the village to explain everything to him – her plans to return to the pit, especially now they needed the money as much as ever.

Al rubbed his chin in contemplation. 'I'm sorry, Mari. Now that I know who you really are, a girl and not a boy, I couldn't allow you to return to working underground. I wouldn't feel right about it.'

Mari shook her head sadly. 'Please, Mr Probert. The doctor said my brother can return to work at the pit around the middle of January if he's walking all right by then, but I can't see it myself. I've watched him and although he can safely put one foot in front of the other, he's still limping badly.'

'I know,' said Al, looking at her with sympathy in his eyes. He paused for a moment. 'I did say I'd not like to get you a job working below ground again, but how about above it?'

Mari frowned, angling her head to one side. The man was making no sense whatsoever. 'What do you mean?'

'Well, I could enquire about a tip girl job for you? The money won't be quite as much but it's decent enough, plus there will be less risk to your health overall.'

She folded her arms. 'But I was led to believe those jobs are hard to come by.'

'Not if you have the right contacts!' He chuckled. Then he tapped the side of his nose. 'You just leave it to your Uncle Al!'

Mari laughed but then her expression became more serious. 'I'll have to square it up with Mam and Bryn, though,' she said.

'But of course. We wouldn't want you to do anything behind their backs now, would we?' His voice had a tone of mischief and she realised he was referring to her not telling them the first time she'd disguised herself as a boy.

'What if they refuse, though?'

'I doubt they will. It's a whole lot safer sorting out drams of coal on the top than it is working below, even if you do have to put up with some choice language!' He pursed his lips and shook his head. 'Some of the cuss words from those tip girls are enough to turn the air blue. They'd put a navvy to shame!'

Mari could only hope Mam and Bryn would be happy with this suggestion, as she'd hate to get Al into any trouble on her behalf.

* * *

Mam finally came home that evening with a promise to Blodwyn that she'd return early next morning to check on her mother. Apparently, her efforts had paid off as the woman's fever had now broken and her bouts of coughing were less frequent and less harsh. Mari allowed her mother to rest up in the armchair for an hour or so before broaching her with the plan Al Probert had come up with.

'I don't know whether you should go back there to work now you've left the pit, Mari,' Mam said, shaking her head as Bryn looked on from the other armchair.

'But she'd be safer working on the top with the other girls,' Bryn chipped in.

'Safer is debatable, Bryn,' said their mother. 'I've still heard of some dram accidents up on top: your father told me about one or two.'

Bryn exchanged a knowing glance with his sister. 'It'll only be for a couple of months until I'm walking properly again,' he said. 'Then there'll be no need for our Mari to work at the pit ever again. We'll manage on my wage.'

Mam nodded. 'Let me sleep on it,' she said and then she closed her eyes for a moment.

Bryn pointed at the door to the scullery, beckoning his sister to follow him and, understanding his intention, she complied.

'Look,' he whispered as he closed the door behind them, 'I know Mam's not that keen for you to return to the pit, but you will be all right on top. I know some of the girls and although they get a bad reputation from time to time, most are salt-of-the-earth types. They stick together and look out for one another. You're more at risk from some of those men beneath ground who dislike the new lads being employed there.'

Mari smiled with understanding. She'd never confided her fears in Bryn about that group of bullies for fear he should stop her going there.

Letting out a long breath, she said, 'Yes, I'll manage if Mam will agree to me working there again.'

'That's the spirit,' he said, slapping her on the back. 'Mam's exhausted right now. She'll be different after she's rested tomorrow.'

Mari had to agree that helping at the Parry house had been wearying for their mother who was already fatigued from all she had to do in her own home, never mind anyone else's.

'Is Glenda still coming here between Christmas and the New Year?' Mari asked hopefully.

Bryn nodded. 'Yes. She hopes to. Are you going to come and watch her singing in chapel at the carol concert?'

'Yes, I'm looking forward to it. Mr Probert has just finished painting the nativity scene he carved, it's beautiful.'

Bryn stared into the distance, and she realised his mind was somewhere else. What was he worried about? Or was he thinking about their father, maybe?

\* \* \*

A couple of nights before Christmas, Nerys and Tommy seemed keyed up as Mari helped them change into their nightgowns and put them to bed.

'I can't wait for Christmas Day!' Tommy yelled, jumping on his bed.

'I hope I get a new doll this year!' said Nerys.

Mari didn't have the heart to disappoint them, but she knew full well that there wouldn't be much for either of them this year as their mother simply couldn't afford it. If Dad was still with his family, there would have been modest gifts for them all, but now, food on the table, fuel for the fire and making the rent payment were the most important things of all. Even if there were no gifts this year, they'd all be together. They had more than most and were rich in that respect. At least they'd have ample for Christmas Day, as Mrs Jones had said she'd bring the Christmas cake she and Mari had prepared at the shop, and she'd iced it too, along with baking some minced pies. She also promised to bring other provisions along with her in payment for her Christmas meal, so they'd not starve.

Mari's mind turned towards Blodwyn and her mother. What

kind of Christmas would they have with the threat of losing their home hanging over their heads? There were many who would rather live on the street than enter the workhouse. Mam knew of a woman who'd hit hard times, and she'd ended up there and to their knowledge she'd never come out again. As far as her mother knew she was still there right now, unable to be a valuable member of society. As Mam put it, *'Her mind has gone.'*

Gone where though? Mari didn't have a clue, but it sounded like a madness had taken hold of the woman and never let go.

It was later that night that Mari heard her mother cry out. Feeling alarmed, Mari dashed out of bed and made her way, stumbling in the dark, to her mother's bedroom. By the time she'd got there, Bryn was already on his feet, and he burst through the bedroom door.

Stooping, he lit a candle by their mother's bedside to see what was going on. Mam was sitting up in bed staring at the wall. It was almost as though she was still asleep, yet she wasn't. Bringing both hands to her neck in a choking gesture, she seemed to be gasping for breath.

'Mam! You're all right!' yelled Bryn as Mari looked on in horror. 'You've been having a bad dream!' He sat now on the bed beside her and placed an arm around her shoulders. Then she seemed to relax and laid her head on his chest while she openly wept.

Mari had never seen her mother quite in this state before. Oh, she'd seen her upset – of course she had. She'd witnessed her tears on many an occasion, but they'd been silent tears as Mam was prone to holding them in. Often, she'd notice tears in her mother's eyes or a single, solitary tear coursing her cheek. She was stoic, so to see her mother crying this way as her whole body convulsed was quite alarming.

Finally, Mam composed herself and Mari handed her a clean handkerchief from the chest of drawers. Their mother began to dab at her eyes, then looking at her, Bryn said, 'What were you dreaming about, Mam?'

Sniffing, she replied. 'It was a horrible dream, more of a nightmare. It was about drowning. I could see this long stretch of water; the waves were choppy and rising high. Then for some reason I was in the sea and the waves were washing over my head. I tried to fight them and get my head above the surface but as soon as I did, the current dragged me down again.'

'No wonder you felt you couldn't speak when we came into the bedroom,' said Bryn as he exchanged a concerned glance with his sister. 'Thankfully, though, it was just a bad dream.'

'Can I get you anything, Mam?' Mari offered. 'A glass of water?'

Mam shook her head vigorously. 'No, thank you! I had enough water in that bloomin' dream.' She gave a wry chuckle. Then fixing her gaze on both of her children, she said, 'I'll be all right now, honest I will. I'm so sorry to have disturbed your sleep though. I must have had that nightmare because I ate a piece of cheese late last night. Well, I won't be doing that again in a hurry, I can tell you!'

Mam insisted that Bryn return to his bed and Mari said she'd stay and sleep in Mam's bed with her to keep her company. It was then she realised how sad it must be for her mother to wake up in the bed she'd shared with her father for the past eighteen years, to discover he was no longer there. Maybe she sometimes forgot about it and when she awoke thought he'd still be there. Maybe she'd reach out to him only to find a cold, empty space beside her instead.

\* \* \*

The following evening, Mari heard the strains of 'Oh Come, Oh Come, Emmanuel' being played on the organ as they approached the chapel, and she hoped they weren't late for the carol concert. She needn't have worried as, when they entered through the double doors, a group of people were still in the foyer chatting excitedly about the coming season, nodding and shaking hands.

Mari, her mother and her younger brother and sister took a seat in the back pew while Bryn walked confidently down the aisle to speak with Glenda, who was attired in a green velvet dress. It really seemed to set off her blonde hair, which lay loose in ringlets on her shoulders. Mari gasped when she saw the young woman, as she'd never seen her looking so beautiful. And, in that moment, she could see what her brother saw in her.

After Bryn had exchanged a few words with Glenda, he made his way to the back of the chapel to sit with his family.

Mam showed no signs of being upset further by her nightmare, though she had been particularly quiet that day as though she had a lot on her mind, which Mari put down to Christmas. She realised as today was Christmas Eve it could be a stressful time for ladies of the household. Mari scanned the chapel to see who was present. She noticed, about halfway down the aisle, that Al Probert was seated in a pew with his daughter and son-in-law but there was no sign of his own son, so she assumed maybe he was at work at the ironworks that evening. In the pew in front of Mr Probert was Marguerite Thomas and her husband. The woman was sporting a fancy bonnet on her head, all feathers and fur, which no doubt was a cast-off from Mrs Davenport. Mari smirked, all the while thinking how ridiculous the bonnet looked on the woman. At the thought of her turning and glimpsing her presence, Mari stiffened, not knowing whether

she would have any harsh words to say to her following the
service.

A tall Christmas tree stood near the pulpit, adorned with
small flickering candles, hanging pine cones and red and green
ribbons. It did look grand and all. And to the other side of the
pulpit was the wooden nativity scene Al had carefully carved and
painted. There were Mary and Joseph stood gazing in awe at their
baby son, Jesus, in his straw-strewn crib, along with a shepherd,
various cattle and three kings with their precious gifts for the
newborn babe. For the first time that season, Mari began to sense
the Christmas spirit. It was a time for reflection and forgiveness.
She wondered whether, if her father turned up right now, her
mother would take him back into her heart and home.

Her mind wandered back to the previous year's concert.
Things had been all right then. There'd been no mention of
another woman at the time, and the family had seemed united
with her mother and father sitting side by side in the pew. Then
they'd arrived early to sit near the front, but now these days, Mam
preferred the back so not all eyes were on her.

The minister entered from a door at the back of the chapel,
and he rose to the pulpit via a set of small steps. After welcoming
the congregation, he spoke about the gift of Christmas and the
importance of forgiveness.

'Well, that was a lovely concert.' Mam sniffed as she wiped away a
tear with the back of her hand.

Mari guessed her mother was so emotional as she too had
been reflecting on last year's concert when they'd all been
together.

'Yes, it was, Mam,' Mari said, then glancing near the pulpit where Bryn lingered to speak to Glenda, she added, 'Particularly that solo from Glenda.' The chapel choir had been singing 'Silent Night' and Glenda had got to sing a couple of verses on her own. The whole congregation had been silenced by the voice of an angel that evening.

'Yes, she has a fine soprano voice,' said Mam. 'Crystal clear. Simply divine.' Then looking at Nerys and Tommy, she said, 'Did you enjoy the concert, kids?'

Both nodded at their mother, but Mari could tell by the wistful look in Tommy's eyes he was missing his father. During the concert, she'd noticed him turning his head towards the chapel door as though in the hope of someone entering at the final hour. Initially, Mari had reasoned maybe her brother had thought Father Christmas would pay a surprise visit, but then she realised it was Dad Tommy was half expecting to see.

'Mince pies are about to be served in the chapel hall,' said Mam brightly. 'Shall we all have one? I've heard there will even be something special for all the children!'

That was enough to brighten up her brother and sister as, eagerly, they left the pew and ran down the aisle towards the hall. It was usual practice for some shop owners and other traders to donate sweets and even small toys for the children at Christmastime. Those people were usually chapel members who owned a business and were extremely wealthy compared to ordinary folk. But it was a treat for the children nevertheless who were entertained by a couple of volunteers who handed out the gifts and later played games and told them stories while their parents had a mince pie and a welcome cup of tea.

Christmas Eve had always been Mari's favourite time of the year. To her, it was better than the big day itself as the expectation and promise were far more exciting. Not that she didn't enjoy Christmas Day itself, far from it, but there was something very special about Christmas Eve. She sometimes wished all days felt like today. Though this year it was a bittersweet day for her, for them all really. But at least there was hope.

She took her mother by the arm as they headed for the hall and, smiling to herself, she noticed Al Probert making a beeline for them. There was no doubt about it, her mother had an admirer.

## 20

The following morning, Mari was up bright and early to help her mother prepare for Christmas Day. The fires needed lighting in the living room and scullery, which Mari attended to, sallying back and forth to the coalhouse, humping the large metal bucket heaped with lumps of coal. Thankfully, Bryn had chopped up logs for firewood the previous day. Once both fires were merrily dancing away, Mam brewed up a pot of tea and Mari toasted some crumpets with a long-handled fork in front of the living room fire. Crumpets for breakfast on Christmas morning, dripping in salted butter, were a tasty treat they rarely had the rest of the year.

'What time is Mrs Jones arriving?' asked Mam.

'I told her we'll be eating the Christmas dinner around one o'clock, so she suggested arriving about eleven, to help us out. Is that all right?'

Mam smiled and nodded. She wasn't as antagonistic towards the woman as she'd once been. Mari now realised her mother's pride had been wounded when the woman had offered help in the form of provisions from the shop.

'What time will Mr Probert be coming?' Mari asked her mother.

Mari noticed two pink spots appear on Mam's cheeks as they began to flush. 'I think he'll be here by midday. He's going to chapel first.'

They weren't going to chapel themselves, but Mari guessed Al was making a point of going on Christmas Day to spend some time with his daughter and maybe his son would be attending too, as the ironworks wouldn't be in operation on such a special day.

'After we've had breakfast, I'm going to put the goose in the oven to cook,' said Mam. 'I hope it'll stretch though...' she said, sounding doubtful. Al had gifted them the largest goose he could find at the poulterers in payment for being invited to Christmas dinner.

'I should think it will. It's the largest goose I've ever seen!' Mari blinked.

'Hopefully, it will, but we'll cook some extra veg just in case. I might fry some leeks in butter to make things go further. Leeks go very well with goose.'

Mari hadn't heard of that before but was prepared to try it.

'Now let me see, after the goose has gone in the oven, I'll make a start peeling the potatoes. You can wake your brother and sister for me and give them breakfast, though leave Bryn where he is. Let him have a lie-in.'

Mari nodded. 'All right, Mam.'

'Then when you've done that, you can help me with the vegetables. Later I'll put the pudding on to steam...'

'Come and sit down and have your crumpets, Mam,' chided Mari. 'Have a rest while you get the chance.'

Her mother met her gaze and smiled at her. 'You're right as

usual, *cariad*. Once Nerys and Tommy are awake it will be bedlam here!'

Mam had carefully hidden away their Christmas presents in the pantry. Al Probert had whittled a wooden boat for Tommy, and Mam had skilfully sewn a new rag doll for Nerys. She'd used various leftover scraps of material to make its dress, used strands of thick yellow wool for its hair and two bright blue buttons for the eyes. Oh, it did look good and all.

Mari had purchased a poke of peppermint creams for her mother from Mrs Jones's shop and, to make the package extra special, had attached red and green ribbons to it. For Bryn, she'd knitted a scarf as he'd lost his old one in the pit accident. For the twins, she'd managed to purchase a small picture book each from a market stall in the town. While she was there, she'd spotted a stall that sold second-hand jewellery and spied a lovely pearl brooch, which she'd wrapped in tissue paper for Mrs Jones. It wasn't a real pearl, as one of those would cost a fortune, but it did look pretty and to the untrained eye might appear expensive. Not worth much at all, but she hoped the woman would like it. She wanted her to have it as a token of her gratitude for all her help and kindness towards her and her family.

As if on cue, just as Mari had taken the final bite out of her crumpet, she heard the sounds of footsteps from above. 'The kids are awake!'

\* \* \*

Nerys and Tommy were thrilled with their Christmas presents and, following breakfast, Mari helped them get washed and dressed for the day ahead. Mam had instructed her that they were to change into their Sunday best outfits, and Mari was to do the same herself, once she'd finished helping her mother clean and tidy the living room.

Mrs Jones arrived promptly at eleven o'clock with a tin containing the Christmas cake she'd baked with Mari some weeks ago and some mince pies too. The cake had been stored in the tin ever since and fed with a tot of brandy every couple of weeks to keep it moist. Finally, it had been iced, and the elderly lady had tied a red satin ribbon around it, which set it off nicely.

'Thank you so much, Mrs Jones,' Mam enthused. 'I wasn't expecting anything from you.'

The woman smiled. 'Mari helped me with it.'

Mam blinked in astonishment. 'I had no idea.'

'We were keeping it as a surprise for you!' Mari was beaming now as she was feeling quite pleased with her accomplishment.

Bryn entered the scullery at that point. 'Why didn't anyone wake me?' he complained.

Mari turned her head and studied her brother. At least he was dressed, with Mrs Jones being here. She'd have been mortified if he hadn't been and it would have been embarrassing for the woman to see Mari's brother bare-chested, just wearing his vest and trousers, which he was prone to do on waking from bed.

'Come and see what Mrs Jones has brought us!' said Mam brightly. Nothing was going to spoil today for her; that much was evident.

'Oh aye, that looks lovely. Thank you very much indeed, Mrs Jones!' Bryn said, smiling as he inspected the cake, then he stooped to peck a kiss on the woman's cheek.

Mrs Jones blushed. 'It was the least I could do, and I did have a willing helper!' She gestured towards Mari.

'You helped with the cake?' Bryn's eyes widened as he looked at his sister.

'Yes!' Mari was feeling some sense of satisfaction that she'd played a part in that cake being baked.

'Well, I'll go to the foot of our stairs!' Bryn chuckled. 'I didn't realise I had such a gifted sister. You can bake all the cakes for us from now on!'

Mari realised that her brother was only teasing her. 'I think I could have a go at it,' she said proudly.

An hour later, Al Probert turned up at the house. 'Something smells good,' he said, sniffing the air, and then he handed over a dark bottle to her mother.

'What's this?' Mam asked.

'It's elderflower wine. One of my neighbours made it. I thought it would go down well with the meal.'

'That's so kind of you, Alwyn,' said Mam as she placed the palm of her hand on her chest. She was obviously touched by the man's generosity. 'But you've already bought us a goose!'

'It's no trouble at all. You'll be doing me a favour if we can share it between us, the adults present, that is!'

Mam nodded gratefully, and for a moment Mari thought Al was going to plant a kiss on her mother's cheek, but instead he made his way to the scullery where the table was already laid for the feast ahead. Mam had used her best tablecloth, the one she and their father had been given as a wedding present. It was fine white Irish linen and hardly ever used. Was this a sign that she was getting over losing him? This was the second time she'd used it in recent weeks. A couple of months ago, Mam would have got upset at the mere mention of the cloth, never mind it being in use on the table. In the middle of the table there was a centrepiece that Bryn had put together of a candle surrounded by holly and pine cones. Mari had never seen the table look so pretty.

Before they dined, Mam insisted on giving Al and Mrs Jones a nip of brandy from a bottle her neighbours had kindly gifted them. These days Bryn was pain-free though still limping a little but was no longer reliant on nips of brandy or a spoonful of laudanum.

'Ooh, I'll be getting myself merry after this!' said Mrs Jones with a twinkle in her eyes.

'That's the whole idea!' chuckled Bryn.

They all chatted amicably as a plethora of metal pots bubbled away on the hob in the other room, the children playing with their toys near the hearth. Mrs Jones was seated comfortably in Dad's favourite armchair, and no one resented her that privilege. The elderly lady worked hard to keep the shop going and the villagers well supplied with provisions.

* * *

The dinner went well, and everyone felt full to bursting afterwards. Al had promised that on his way home he'd check in on the Parry household to see how Blodwyn and her mother were doing. There were some leftovers from the dinner, so they were spooned into two porcelain bowls, the dinner itself in one and the other contained the pudding. After covering the bowls with tea cloths, her mother gave them to Al on a tray to take to the women.

Mam was kindness itself, Mari thought. She could have kept all that food, as it would take them through the next day, but her concern was for both women, two women that many in the village would not even bother with after all that had occurred. But her mother was not like that. Her initial anger at Blodwyn had quickly subsided. After all, Dad had done the dirty on them all in the end.

As Al stood near the front door about to leave, he glanced at

Mari and asked, 'Did you square things up with your mother and Bryn?'

She nodded. 'Did you ask about the tip girl job for me?'

'Yes, I did. You can start work there on the 31st of December if you wish? It'll be three days a week, sometimes four.'

Mari let out a breath of relief. All through dinner she'd wondered if Al would ever get around to mentioning the job. Now she'd be able to help the family again through a lean time until her brother was ready to return to work. Meanwhile, she was going to have to cover for him tomorrow on Boxing Day when he'd get to be alone at the house with Glenda, as she'd promised. Her plan was to get her mother out for a walk with the children for a couple of hours. Maybe they could call to see how Mrs Griffiths was doing as her pregnancy was advancing day by day and she wasn't getting any younger. Mam hadn't been there for a while. And after that they could check on the Parry household. The children were yet to meet Blodwyn and her mother, and as that baby the young woman was carrying would be their half-brother or -sister, it was important, Mari thought, for everyone to be on good terms. As yet, the children didn't have a clue there was a baby involved, though both had an inkling their father had a 'lady friend', as their mother had put it to them.

Mam, who had been in the scullery as Al hovered near the doorstep, returned, minus her pinafore as though she wanted a quiet word with him, so Mari left them to it, returning to the living room to join Mrs Jones, Bryn and the younger children. Bryn was playing some sort of card game with them and both children were giggling at his antics.

'Thank you for inviting me, Mari.' Mrs Jones smiled. 'For allowing me to share your Christmas with you. It's been a long time since I've had a family Christmas with anyone.'

Mari felt a lump rise in her throat at the thought of all the

Christmases the elderly woman had spent alone. 'You're welcome here any time, Mrs Jones,' she said, hoping her voice didn't belie how emotional she was feeling. 'In fact, Mam said she's going to invite you for Sunday dinner here sometimes as well.'

Mrs Jones nodded with appreciation. 'Your mother is a very kind woman. I'll have to be going soon before it gets dark, as I don't like being out when daylight has disappeared. Perhaps I ought to leave with Mr Probert?'

Bryn, who had caught the conversation, rose to his feet and approached her. 'Don't worry, Mrs Jones. Stay a while longer. Mari will brew up a cuppa for us and we can all enjoy a slice of your lovely cake, then I'll accompany you back home safely.'

Mrs Jones smiled. 'Thank you, that's so kind of you, Bryn.'

'I've got something for you,' Mari said, 'I meant to give it to you earlier. You too, Bryn. I didn't have time to give you both your presents, so I'll fetch them for you now.'

Bryn and Mrs Jones exchanged curious glances with one another as Mari left the room. She'd had time to give the twins their picture books earlier before everyone arrived and both had been delighted with those.

Mari returned with the gift-wrapped items. Mrs Jones was enchanted with the brooch, and she hugged Mari warmly. 'It was enough that you invited me to spend Christmas Day with you and your family,' she said as her eyes filled with tears. 'I wasn't expecting a present as well! I shall treasure this brooch; it's very precious to me, as it's from you, Mari!'

Mari's heart swelled with pride and pleasure to hear the woman say such a thing. 'I wanted to buy something special for you though, as you have been so good to me. Shall I pin it on your dress for you?'

The woman nodded gratefully. 'Oh yes. Yes please, Mari. It's beautiful!'

Mari carefully pinned the brooch onto the woman's dress, being mindful not to stick the pin in her finger. Once secured, she stepped back to admire it. 'It does look lovely on you, Mrs Jones,' she said, pleased with her Christmas purchase.

Then Bryn held up his scarf, admiring it. 'I love this, Mari. Did you knit it yourself?'

Mari nodded. 'It took me a long time, mind you.' She chuckled.

'Well, I never! How did you manage to keep it a secret? I've been at home for months!'

She shrugged her shoulders. 'I just knitted a few rows at a time when you were still in bed in the mornings or if you went to bed early.'

'I really appreciate it.' He smiled. 'I'll wear it for my first shift back underground. My old one is probably still buried beneath the coal...' he said with a note of regret to his voice.

Mari realised that the first shift back at work for Bryn would be the hardest. There were some colliers who would refuse to work underground ever again after an incident like that. It took some courage to return to the place that had almost killed you.

\* \* \*

The shop reopened in between Christmas and the New Year, and both Mari and Mrs Jones busied themselves keeping it well stocked. Her employer wanted to give it a good clean and tidy-up one day when trade was quiet, so they both donned old pinafores used for such tasks and, with damp cloths as well as dry dusters, set to work clearing the shelves and giving them a good, thorough wipe-down before replacing the stock.

'Oh, darn it!' yelled Mrs Jones. Mari heard a clatter as the old woman stooped to retrieve something.

'What's happened?' Mari asked.

'It's the brooch you bought me for Christmas. I can't have attached it to my dress properly this morning and, as I was leaning against the shelving, it must have got dislodged and now it's on the floor.' She held it up for Mari to see.

'It's all right,' she reassured her. 'Just leave it off until we finish doing this to keep it safe.'

The woman nodded and Mari watched her place it on the counter.

They were so busy that Mari thought no more of it. Several customers drifted in and out of the shop that afternoon, and she or Mrs Jones would leave the task in hand to attend to them while the other one worked. Finally, Mrs Jones said, 'Well, I think we deserve a break now, so I'm going to close the shop for twenty minutes. Mari, go and lock the door and turn the sign to closed; there's a good girl.'

Mari didn't need asking twice but, as she went to do so, Marguerite Thomas barged her way in through the door.

Noticing this brought Mrs Jones scurrying across the shop floor. If it had been any other customer, Mrs Jones might have told them to return later, but as it was Mrs Thomas, whom she was eager to please, she said, 'Put the kettle on, Mari. I'll deal with Mrs Thomas.'

Mari didn't mind too much as she'd rather keep out of the old crone's way. So, without even making eye contact with the woman or acknowledging her after their last encounter, she made her way to the back room to brew up.

Mrs Thomas seemed to keep Mrs Jones for some time, placing her order for the big house, but Mrs Jones was beaming when she finally showed up for her brew after locking the shop door behind the woman. 'Everything's all right now,' she enthused. 'Mrs Thomas gave me a big order for the Davenport house. Wherever the woman was getting her provisions from after the last falling-out, she's obviously decided my shop is a better bet!'

Mari was pleased for Mrs Jones of course and she felt responsible for the woman losing all that custom, but there was part of her that wished Mrs Thomas never needed to set a foot inside the shop again.

Feeling refreshed after a break, both made their way back to the shop floor and Mari unlocked the door and turned the sign on it to open.

'Oh no!' she heard Mrs Jones cry out, which brought Mari running to the woman's side, thinking she had injured herself.

'What's wrong, Mrs Jones?' Mari asked, her voice full of concern.

'It's my brooch! It's gone.'

'Where was it?'

'Just here on the counter...' She tapped the wooden counter with the palm of her hand but there was nothing on it.

'That's strange.' Mari wrinkled her nose feeling confused. 'Don't worry,' she said reassuringly. 'It can't have gone far. Maybe it slipped under the counter when someone placed their basket on here.' She dropped to her knees to fumble beneath it, but there was no sign whatsoever. Pulling herself to her feet, she said, 'You don't think anyone's taken it, do you?'

'No, certainly not!' said Mrs Jones. 'I don't like to think any customer who's been here today would do anything like that.'

'You never know though,' said Mari. 'Maybe one of those ladies is light-fingered. I mean, I know that brooch didn't cost a lot but it did look like a real pearl and I suppose the gilt edging might be mistaken for gold.'

Mrs Jones brought her index finger to her chin as she reflected on the various customers who had walked in and out of the shop that afternoon. 'No. I definitely can't think of any of those women being light-fingered at all,' she said with some confidence. 'I expect it will show up eventually. Maybe I placed it elsewhere for safekeeping and I've forgotten about it.'

Somehow, Mari couldn't see that. She had her own suspicions who had taken the brooch but for the time being said nothing at all – sometimes it was best to keep her thoughts to herself until she could be proved right, particularly when it came to Mrs Thomas.

* * *

It was a couple of days later when Mari attended chapel one Sunday morning with her mother and siblings that she realised her suspicions had been correct because there in her usual pew, seated beside her husband, was Marguerite Thomas perched like a duchess in what appeared to be a new cape, which was probably another cast-off from Mrs Davenport. It was unusually warm there that morning as the sun was shining on the windows and as she loosened her fur-edged cape, turning to glance behind her, Mari noticed the pearl brooch pinned to the high collar of her ruffled blouse. No doubt, she thought no one would notice it beneath her cape, but Mari had.

Mari gritted her teeth. The cheek of the woman taking Mrs Jones's brooch like that. She hardly heard a word of what the Reverend Bevan was saying in his sermon as she fumed so much about the injustice of it all.

Mari glanced at her mother, who seemed to be well into what the man was saying, something about it best being quick to forgive but slow to anger. Mari wished she could control her anger on this occasion and maybe she would have if the woman had stolen from her but because it was Mrs Jones she'd done it to, it made her see red. All right then, maybe she'd just do the right thing and ask her for the brooch back outside the chapel when the service was over, just to let the woman know that she knew.

Mam hadn't seemed to notice anything was amiss and after the service, which seemed to take longer than usual to end, she said to her mother that she wouldn't be straight home as she was going to call to see Bobby – which was the truth, but not until she'd spoken to that old crone first! So, Mam made her way back home with the kids in tow and Mari waited outside the chapel doors for Mrs Thomas to emerge.

Where was she? She was taking ages and the final stragglers from the congregation left, shaking hands and passing the time of day with Mr Bevan. Finally, last of all, Mr and Mrs Thomas came through the door and stopped for a while to speak to the minister. Now was her chance as Mr Thomas crossed the road to speak to a man on the other side of the street. Marguerite hadn't seemed to have noticed and appeared to have lost her bearings for a moment.

'Hello, Mrs Thomas,' Mari greeted.

The woman sniffed and looked down her nose at her as though she was something she'd trodden in and was now stuck to her shoe.

'I don't expect you wish to speak to me, but I wish to speak to you!'

She had the woman's attention now. 'Oh, what about?' Marguerite arched her well-defined eyebrows.

'About that very pretty pearl brooch you've got pinned to your blouse.' Mari watched as the woman's colour changed to a deep shade of coral and her eyes widened so the whites appeared to be on show. She'd definitely unnerved her.

'Y... yes, it is very pretty, isn't it?'

Mari nodded. 'Where did you get it from?'

'From my husband – it was a present.'

Mari folded her arms. 'Really? So, when he comes back over here and I ask him, he'll tell me that he bought it for you, will he?'

Marguerite drew a sharp intake of breath as though she couldn't believe what she was saying to her, but Mari persisted.

'Yes, I think he'll be surprised to hear that he bought you that brooch when you actually stole it from Mrs Jones!'

Marguerite looked horrified now as her hands flew to her face; she was on the spot and didn't know how to get out of it. Finally, she dropped her hands to her sides. 'Please, you mustn't say anything to him.'

'Then tell me the truth... is that Mrs Jones's brooch or not?'

'N... no, of course not! Someone else gave it to me, not my husband; that's why he mustn't know.'

Deliberating for a moment, Mari said, 'So if we take that brooch to the jeweller's and he looks at it through a magnifying glass, he won't see Mrs Jones's initials engraved on the back of it?' This was a total bluff on Mari's part, but she wanted the woman to think there was a way of proving the brooch belonged to Mrs Jones.

Defeated, Marguerite said, 'All right. I did find the brooch in the shop, but I didn't know it belonged to her.' She shook her head as though not knowing what to do now.

'Well, it does belong to her and the reason I know is because I bought it for her for Christmas and she loves it. She's been most upset that she can't find it.'

On hearing this, Marguerite began to fiddle with the offending brooch and appeared to stab herself with the pin until finally it was released from the neck of her blouse, and she handed it to Mari. It was evident it no longer held any attraction for her now she'd been found out to be a thief, and the woman probably quickly realised the brooch wasn't worth that much anyhow if Mari could afford it.

'Now, what I'm going to do is pretend I've found this at the shop when I go back there tomorrow morning and hand it back to Mrs Jones without telling her you took it from her.'

Marguerite nodded, grateful for this concession. She made to turn away, but Mari stopped her.

'Hang on a moment, there is one condition...' she said, now having her full attention once again. 'From now on when you enter the shop, you will treat Mrs Jones and myself with respect. If I ever as much as get a whiff that you're gossiping about anyone or my family, or take one more thing, then I shall let the whole of Abercanaid know what a dreadful person you are. How they have a petty thief and a nasty, vindictive gossip in their midst! Understood?'

Marguerite lowered her head and then nodded slowly. 'Yes,' she said meekly, and then she made her way across the road to stand with her husband, who was still speaking to the gentleman he'd crossed the road for. No doubt the woman was grateful for small mercies as Mari might well have told Mr Thomas that his wife was a petty thief! Even her employer might have been informed if Mari had a mind to do so.

It was a small but valuable victory and tomorrow Mrs Jones would have her brooch returned good as new and Mari would have the privilege of knowing that Mrs Thomas could never have one over on her ever again, knowing what she knew about the woman. She'd forgive but she'd never forget.

\* \* \*

On New Year's Eve, Mari was home alone resting before her shift that afternoon at the pit. For once, she could relax working there as she'd no longer be Lewis Lloyd, but now she'd be herself, as a tip girl. She didn't know any of the girls and women who worked on the top, to speak to as such. A few called into the shop. Some were women who popped in to purchase provisions, others were younger women looking for a little treat for themselves, maybe a poke of sweets or a small bar of chocolate. The younger women would always give their pay to their parents. The only ones who didn't have to do so lived independently in lodgings. None of the women or girls though could afford to splash around their money; every penny had to be accounted for.

On Boxing Day, Bryn had finally managed to see Glenda alone at home as Mari had engineered. The rest of the family were out of the house, as planned, visiting Mrs Griffiths, and then they called on the Parry household. Mam didn't have a clue that her eldest son had entertained his sweetheart alone under their roof. She probably wouldn't be best pleased if she were to discover that little piece of information. And Glenda's father would be livid if he found out!

Today, though, Mari was sitting in front of the fire, eating a bowl of lamb cawl, when there was a sudden and urgent-sounding knock on the front door. Muttering under her breath at having been disturbed, she laid down her bowl on the small side table and rose from the armchair to answer.

As she opened the door, she saw, there on the doorstep, a man of around her father's age. He wore a short tweed jacket, brown shirt and a bowler hat. Thinking he might be some sort of hawker, she said, 'I'm sorry, we don't need anything today!'

She was just about to close the door on him when the man spoke. 'Sorry, miss. I'm not trying to sell you anything. I'm a friend of your father's. May I speak with you?'

Thinking it was a trick to get inside the house, she narrowed her gaze. 'I don't know if my brother and mother will be too pleased about that. They'll be home at any moment.' Her chin jutted out.

'It's your mother I need to speak to...' he said. There was something in the man's eyes that told her he was being truthful.

She opened the door further to allow him access. It was true, her mother or her brother would be returning soon. Bryn had gone to meet Glenda secretly on the canal bank and her mother had paid a visit to Mrs Griffiths's home.

'You'd better come inside and wait,' she said reluctantly, sighing as he stepped over the threshold. He walked through the open door of the living room and, seeing her bowl of stew on the side table, said, 'I'm sorry I've interrupted your meal.'

There was something about how thin and scrawny the man appeared that told her he was famished. So, she said, 'Look, you have that stew, I can have some more later.'

'Are you sure?'

'Yes. Have a seat in the armchair.'

He didn't need asking twice: he sunk in the chair and began to quickly spoon the thick cawl into his mouth. It appeared as though he hadn't eaten for days. She went to the scullery to fetch a hunk of bread for him, which he eagerly accepted, and then he proceeded to mop up the remainder of the cawl with the bread. Finally, he closed his eyes, likely savouring what a fine meal it had been. It was only a lamb stew, basic but nourishing food.

His eyes flicked open. 'I'm sorry,' he said. 'I've been on the road for days.'

'Oh, why is that?'

'I've travelled all the way from Liverpool back home to Merthyr. I was on my way to America and about to board the ship, but there was a turn of events. That's why I realised I needed to remain behind and get back home as quickly as possible. The trouble was I ran out of money towards the end of the journey, so I've been walking for the past few days.' He lifted his leg to show her the sole had detached from his shoe and had been secured with a piece of string.

Mari was about to say something when she heard the front door open and close.

'Mam!' Mari blinked several times. For some reason she'd assumed that her brother would return home first.

Her mother stared at the man in the fireside chair like she'd seen a ghost. 'Frank? What are you doing here?'

The man stood and, holding his cap in his hand, said, 'Hello, Mavis. It's been a long time...'

'It sure has. Can I get you anything?'

He nodded his head and sat himself back down. 'Thank you, a glass of water or a cup of tea would be most welcome. Your daughter kindly shared some of that delicious stew with me.' He pointed to the empty bowl on the fireside table.

Mam nodded and then left the room to fetch a glass of water for her surprise visitor, which she then placed on the small table beside him. 'But to what do we owe the pleasure of this visit?'

'You'd better take a seat, as it's not pleasure I've brought to your door, I'm afraid.'

At the man's words, a cold shiver coursed down Mari's spine. It was the same sort of sensation she'd felt that day her brother had been injured in the pit accident – something was badly wrong.

She guided her mother over to the fireside and sat her in the armchair opposite where Frank was seated. Then, squeezing his cap between his hands as though his life depended on it, he said in a quiet tone of voice, 'It was when we arrived in Liverpool, you see.'

'We?' Mam arched an eyebrow as though flummoxed by this situation presenting itself.

'Aye, me and your husband.'

'I... I didn't realise you were the man who went with him.'

'Yes, it was me. But what I didn't know was that he'd not told you he'd even left the village. I thought he was free to go. We both had enough money in our pockets for our passage to America. We intended going to work in the coal pits of Pennsylvania. Welsh labour is highly sought after there.'

'I did hear a whisper of the sort,' said Mam, sitting up poker-straight now.

'Well anyway, we spent a few nights at a hostelry quite close to the docks. We had to sort things out with an agent first, see. And even then, get inspected by a medical officer before we'd be allowed to board the ship. It was all sorted, we had our tickets ready to go but the night before we were due to set sail, Gwynfor seemed to be experiencing a change of heart. He kept telling me repeatedly that he must return home to his family. I think his intention of leaving in the first place was to earn good money and set up home in America and then send for you all. But I know he'd got himself in a right mess by...' He glanced at Mari as though maybe he shouldn't say any more, but then Mam nodded her permission at him.

'It's all right, Mari knows everything,' she said curtly.

'Well... impregnating that young woman like that, though I don't think he'd have shirked his duties. He wanted to make amends there also.'

Frank paused for a spell for her mother to digest the information; it was a lot to take in.

Mam opened her mouth to say something, but no words emerged. Instead, she bit her bottom lip and brought her closed fist to her mouth. It was almost as though she was silencing herself, forcing herself to not say something she shouldn't.

Mari fixed her gaze on the man. 'So, what happened the next day?'

Frank shook his head as a sad expression came over his face. 'Your husband downed so much ale in the pub that he got drunk and in an argumentative mood with folk. I tried to stop him, to get him to return to the hostelry with me, but he wouldn't. He was outside on the dock and threatened a passing sailor, who landed a punch that knocked him from the dock into the sea. The sailor and his mates, when they realised what was happening, wised up and tried to save your father. A couple of them dived in, even went under the water, but he'd disappeared from view. It was hard to see as it was pitch-black that night. Apart from the light from a nearby pub and a couple of vessels, visibility was poor. One moment he was bobbing around in the water, the next...' He swallowed hard. 'The next he had gone. No one could find him to save him. I jumped in too and called out his name. A policeman took down details of the event afterwards which he put down to being a "provoked accident". There was no doubt about it, Mrs Evans,' he said, looking directly at Mari's mother, 'your husband was asking for it. It was almost as though he wanted someone to punish him, like he was looking for a fight with someone. Sadly, he drowned.'

Mam's shoulders began to tremble. 'M... my dream!' she yelled. 'When did all this happen, Frank? What date was it?'

'Christmas Eve, early in the morning, just before daybreak, as it was still dark. Might have been easier if it had been daylight.'

Mari remembered her mother's nightmare where she'd said she'd felt like she'd been unable to breathe, and her head was slipping under water. Somehow, she'd experienced what had happened to Dad.

A cold shiver coursed down Mari's spine.

* * *

It seemed an age before any of them uttered a word, the shock of what had happened taking time to sink in. Finally, Mam composed herself and in a business-like tone of voice she thanked Frank for calling to the house to relay the news to them. She'd wanted to know if he had somewhere to stay and he told her he'd return to his family in Troedyrhiw, explaining after Gwynfor had died like that he hadn't the heart to go to America after all. If only Dad hadn't decided to leave, and what was worse was that in the end he'd decided to stay and return home to his family. But consuming alcohol had made him aggressive and provocative towards that group of sailors, which in the end had caused his death.

A sudden thought occurred to Mari as her mother saw Frank to the door: Bryn would need to be informed – and Nerys and Tommy too – that they'd never, ever see their father again, and at that thought, she began to weep profusely.

* * *

Bryn, once over the initial shock of his father's death, insisted that Mari should not begin work at the pit that day. Instead, Al Probert offered to see the foreman to explain the situation and to instruct him to pass on the news to the other men at the pit as they'd been very fond of Gwynfor Evans. He'd been a hard worker and a firm friend to most of them over the years. Mam realised in her grief that Blodwyn and her mother would need to be given the news before it spread all over the village and everyone else found out before they did. So, Al offered to do that too before calling to the pit itself. The baby the young woman

was carrying would never have a father now, and it was more
likely than ever the Parrys would end up in the workhouse soon.

## 21

There would be no funeral as such for Gwynfor Evans as his body was never recovered from the dockside. Bryn had told Mari when she'd enquired about it that no doubt their father's body had been washed out to sea. For weeks their mother had seemed numbed by the tragic news, and Mari wondered whether Mam was still angry with him for what he'd done to them all. There'd been a hearing held which Frank, along with the sailors and policeman from that night, had to attend. A verdict of 'Death by Misadventure' was recorded by the coroner so that her father could be legally pronounced dead, even though no body was ever recovered. Her mother was now officially classed as a widow.

It became apparent with time, following an examination by Doctor Pritchard, that Bryn would be left with a slight limp for life. Although his body had healed well, the doctor said it was the crush injury that had caused the impediment.

When Mari finally returned to work at the pit, the first thing she noticed was the noise of the tip girls working on the top, occasionally shouting across the filled drams with the odd curse word that was enough to turn the air blue. Down beneath ground, it was a different matter because some of the men could be working miles apart from one another. Still, it was good to be back at work and the women and girls were welcoming enough. She guessed they'd instantly warmed towards her presence as they already knew her father and brother, and many would feel sympathetic knowing what had recently happened to Dad.

It was a few days later when the foreman approached her. She was sorting coal from one dram to another and, initially, she wondered if she was in trouble for not being quick enough, as some of the girls seemed to work at lightning speed, but then she reminded herself, they were most used to this sorting job and had become fit and muscular as a result. But she, herself, had only done this for a few days.

'If you can ask your Bryn to call to the pit office to see me tomorrow afternoon, if he's up to it...' he was saying.

She narrowed her gaze. Why did Mr Roberts want to see Bryn? Mystified, she forced a smile at the man. 'Yes, I will, Mr Roberts.'

'Tell him to get here for two o'clock sharp. I'll see him then.' He nodded at her and, turning, walked away. Mari remained incredulous that Mr Roberts hadn't realised she had previously worked at the pit disguised as a young lad.

The foreman was a busy fellow though – if he wasn't in the pit office organising things, then he was underground checking on conditions for the men or sorting out a complaint. At the back of Mari's mind was a concern that maybe the man would tell Bryn not to return at all as he'd been off from work for longer than was expected, and that limp of his didn't help. She hoped he wouldn't lose his job because of it.

* * *

The following afternoon, Mam ensured that Bryn spruced himself up for his meeting with the foreman. 'You best make a good impression,' she advised as she brushed the shoulders of Bryn's Sunday best jacket with a clothes brush. Mari didn't notice anything on the jacket, but her mother still insisted on brushing away some imaginary piece of fluff or strand of hair. 'Clothes might not maketh the man,' she said, handing the jacket to him, 'but they'll certainly help.'

Bryn just nodded at her, realising that there was no use arguing with their mother when she had her mind set on something. 'Thanks, Mam,' he said, slipping the jacket on and smiling. He'd even slicked his hair down with some of that pomade stuff he often laughed at others for wearing, referring to them as 'right Jessies' for using it. But then again, Mari guessed it might have been Glenda's influence on her brother that had smartened up his appearance – any suggestion the young woman made he took very seriously indeed.

So, setting out to leave the house, Mam called after him, 'And make sure you hold your shoulders back; don't slump, whatever you do!'

Mari smiled as Bryn rolled his eyes yet again.

'Good luck!' she called after him, and then he was gone.

The time when he was away seemed to drag. Mari wasn't working at the pit today; she had a rare day off from everything. Tomorrow she'd return to working at the shop for a couple of days. Meanwhile, Mam busied herself tidying the scullery, putting pots and pans away and sweeping the floor, but Mari found herself unable to settle as her mind wandered with concerns about her brother. So she was relieved an hour and a half later, when Bryn stepped back through the door, bringing their mother rushing from the scullery.

'Well?' she said, blinking as she wiped her hands on her pinafore.

Mari couldn't tell from her brother's expression whether he was happy or not. Then he began to lower his head.

'Oh no. They've sacked you!' A feeling of dread washed over her. What would her brother do now?

Bryn lifted his head to make eye contact and he smiled broadly; then his eyes lit up. 'No. Quite the reverse, in fact!'

'So, your job at the pit is still safe?' Mam asked, eyes wide.

'It's better than that.'

'How can it be better than that, Bryn?' Mam's forehead creased into a soft frown.

'Because they've allocated me a new position and I'll not be working underground any longer. I'll be working on top of it!'

'Huh?' Mari was puzzled by this. 'You'll be helping us tip girls?'

'No. You're both looking at the new wages clerk!'

Mam's face lit up as she beamed. 'Oh, my goodness! This is such good news. But tell us all about it. I don't understand.'

'It's quite simple really. Mr Thomas is retiring from his position at the office, and I was offered his job.'

'But you're not a scholar though, Bryn?' Mam said.

'No, Mr Roberts is aware of that. But he knew from Dad that I'm good with figures, working out sums and such, and that I read a lot too. He reckons that's good enough for him as he's had to step in a time or two to do the same job himself when Mr Thomas hasn't been available or was unwell. He did set me a little test though to ensure I'm capable of doing the job.'

'What did you have to do?' Mari asked, curious now.

'Just calculate a few sums on paper for him, addition and subtraction, that sort of thing. He also asked me what I'd do if certain situations arose.'

'Such as what?' Mari folded her arms as she listened intently.

'Well, one thing he wanted to know was what I'd do if someone requested their wages a week early.'

'And how did you answer that one?'

'I said I'd check if there were any special circumstances in the first place and if there wasn't then I'd refuse their request, but if there was a special reason for it, I'd call to see him – Mr Roberts, I mean – to request his permission to issue those wages a week early.'

'Sounds like you gave the correct answer there!' Mari said, beaming at her brother. Things were looking up at last.

Bryn gazed at his sister intently. 'You know what this means now though, our Mari?'

She shook her head.

'When I begin work next month as a wages clerk, you won't have to work as a tip girl any longer!'

That honestly hadn't occurred to her and, although she didn't mind working to help her family, it would be a relief to just work at the shop for Mrs Jones as she'd previously done and to help Mam around the home.

* * *

Mam might have chosen to turn her back on the Parry women, but Mari was not surprised that she didn't. She visited them both at the workhouse on a regular basis.

'There's no way I'm ever going to ignore them!' she'd said to Mari one day. 'That baby will be your brother or sister. So, we'll not lose touch with them.'

Mrs Parry had been restored to full health and was helping in the workhouse sewing room; and although Blodwyn had to attend to daily chores at the place, she was permitted periods of rest due to her advancing pregnancy. The young woman had been devastated of course to hear of Gwynfor's death, but there was nothing she could do about the predicament she found herself in. Help came from an unexpected source though, in the form of Mrs Jones, who came to the women's aid, offering them a room at her house in exchange for help around the home and occasionally at the shop. Blodwyn's baby would not need to be born in the workhouse after all and both women, along with the baby, would be company for the elderly woman, in some ways a replacement of the family she'd lost many years ago.

Bryn was now making something of himself working as a wages clerk at the pit. He'd always been clever with figures and Glenda's father finally relented after hearing about his new position, allowing him to meet regularly with his daughter providing they were chaperoned. It seemed the man now had a better opinion of Bryn due to his new status at the pit. This suited Bryn very well, as he told Mari he intended asking for Glenda's hand in marriage someday and his intention was to secure her father's blessing.

Mari wondered if there'd be another wedding before that though, as her mother and Al Probert were seeing one another regularly. They weren't being overt about it, oh no. Mam realised full well what the gossips were like in the village. This was a closeted romance where two people who had lost a lot in life found comfort in one another. All the stars had seemed to line up for them both as a couple.

Mari was able to see Bobby, her best friend, more now that she wasn't working at the pit. The lad would often call to the shop to see her and walk her back home after a day's work, and they'd chuckle together thinking back to the time when she'd had the audacity to disguise herself as a boy to work underground.

Today was a beautiful spring day with a clear blue sky and the sun was high above as Mari climbed the mountain with a mission ahead of her. She'd have to pass the pit with its big black ever-turning wheel to reach her destination where she could feel close to her father once again. She'd stroll through the woods and jump over the brook, but this time without her father's strong hand to guide her, until she reached the spot she was looking for where all those glorious daffodils lay blowing and bowing their heads in the gentle breeze. Here, she'd remember how life had once been for her, when her father had been a part of the family. From that spot she'd be able to gaze down on the village below and count her blessings, forever thankful that her family had survived it all.

\* \* \*

## MORE FROM LYNETTE REES

Another book from Lynette Rees, *The Coal Miner's Wife*, is available to order now here:

https://mybook.to/CoalMinersWifeBackAd

# ABOUT THE AUTHOR

**Lynette Rees** lives in Wales and has been writing since she was a child. She enjoys the freedom of writing in a variety of genres including: crime fiction and contemporary romance, though her first love is historical fiction. When she's not writing, or even when she is writing, Lynette enjoys a glass of wine and the odd piece of chocolate as she creates stories where the characters guide her hand. She honestly has no idea how a story will turn out until the characters tell their own tales in their own unique ways.

Sign up to Lynette Rees' mailing list here for news, competitions and updates on future books.

Visit Lynette's website: www.lynetterees.wordpress.com

Follow Lynette on social media:

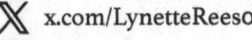 facebook.com/authorlynetterees

X x.com/LynetteRees0

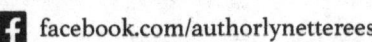 instagram.com/booksbylynetterees7

BB bookbub.com/authors/lynette-rees

# ALSO BY LYNETTE REES

The Winter Waif

The Workhouse Girl

The Cobbler's Apprentice

The Pit Girl

The Coal Miner's Wife